WE KEPT
HER IN THE
CELLAR

WE KEPT HER IN THE CELLAR

A NOVEL

W. R. GORMAN

CROOKED
LANE

NEW YORK

Published in the United States by Crooked Lane Books, an imprint of The Quick Brown Fox & Company LLC.

Crooked Lane Books and its logo are trademarks of The Quick Brown Fox & Company LLC.

Library of Congress Catalog-in-Publication data available upon request.

ISBN (hardcover): 978-1-63910-914-2
ISBN (ebook): 978-1-63910-915-9

Cover design by Amanda Shaffer

Printed in the United States.

www.crookedlanebooks.com

Crooked Lane Books
34 West 27th St., 10th Floor
New York, NY 10001

First Edition: November 2024

10 9 8 7 6 5 4 3 2 1

To Tom, who looked into our future
and saw this. I love you.

Part 1

First Impressions

I FIRST MET CINDERELLA when I was eleven and she was twelve. Hortense was only five and was excited about having another older sister.

"Mother," Hortense would say, eyes shining, "do you think my new sister will read to me like Eunice does?"

Mother would laugh and press a kiss to Hortense's head. "I don't know if she'll read to you like Eunice does, but you'll still have Eunice to read to you! Maybe you'll read to her! Wouldn't that be fun, to teach someone else to read?" She didn't mention that our books were being sold, one by one, to pay off the debts and make sure we could keep the house.

During the lead-up to Cinderella joining our family, I must have heard that question a million times, with the same variation of a non-answer. I realize now Mother thought Cinderella had some sort of unusual way of interacting with the world and wanted Hortense to come around to the idea of a big sister who was different from her. I don't know that this message came through to us, but I know that Hortense's certainty that a new sister would be a boon never once wavered prior to meeting Cinderella.

I was less certain. I was used to being the oldest, and I wasn't sure I wanted someone coming in to lay claim to that role. What if Mother liked Cinderella better than me? What if Hortense didn't want to play with me anymore, faced with a newer sister? Hortense's enthusiasm at the idea of a new big sister only made me nervous. I was certain that I would lose Hortense to Cinderella.

Mother found me sulking in my tree right before we were scheduled to meet with our new stepfather and sister. My tree—or Eunice's tree, as everyone in our household called it—was a huge, sprawling thing, with lots of low branches easy for a child to scramble onto, and branches that went out rather than up, so that a determined child could prop themselves between the trunk and the branch and just kind of dangle there. Mother said it gave her heart palpitations to see me dangling from the branches of the tree like a sloth, so she had Mr. Calton build a platform in the tree, out of shining wood, with a little wooden ladder nailed into the tree trunk. I loved my platform, and took to it at once, but sometimes, when Mother couldn't see me, I still dangled from the branches. That day, however, I was curled up in a ball of misery in the center of my platform, too upset to even think of dangling.

"Eunice, come down from there!" Mother called, exasperated. "They're going to be here any minute now, and you've absolutely ruined your stockings!" I glanced down. She was right. That morning I'd been dressed in neat white stockings with a small frill around the top. Now they were full of jagged runs and rips and had more than one smudge of dirt on them. The shortcut I'd taken through the field before climbing up into my tree had taken its toll. The frills drooped at me in reproach. They were my last pair that fit me. Mother had been carefully darning all the runs and holes that inevitably showed up in my stockings, but even she could not make more material out of nothing.

Mother continued. "What were you thinking, going up into the tree like that? You know it's important to me to make a good impression on your new papa and your new sister!"

I did know it, unfortunately. Mother had spent the past few months floating around the house, sighing over letters and generally being totally unlike my sensible, no-nonsense mother. I knew that she had been sad because of Papa dying, but I didn't know any other way. For me, it was just a fact of life. My name was Eunice, I had a little sister named Hortense, and Mother was sad because our papa had died when I was six and Hortense was a big round ball in Mother's stomach. There was also the unspoken absence of almost all our servants, Mother's dresses vanishing, and the fine silver being sold. I knew that our family needed money and marriage seemed like a good way to get it. I just didn't have to like it.

I refused to get down from the tree, curling more tightly into a lump on the wooden platform.

"I shan't come down," I said. "If I come down, then I'm going to have to go meet my new papa and my new sister, and I don't *want* a new papa and a new sister. I already have a sister, and I had a papa before—why should I have another one now?" I was petulant in the way that only a child can be, but looking back now, I can't help but think that I was justified.

Mother heaved a long sigh, and then hiked up her long skirts and climbed up the wooden slats nailed into the trunk. She managed to do so without mussing her hair or tearing her stockings, unlike me. We sat together there in the tree, and she rubbed soothing circles on my trembling back.

"Darling, I know this is hard," said Mother. "But sometimes families change. You don't have to call him your new papa if you don't want to. You can call him Mr. Fitzwilliam. And it will probably take some time to adjust to having a new sister, it's true, but that doesn't mean it can't be a good thing. Hortense will still be your sister even with Cinderella here."

I uncurled slightly from my tight ball. It sounded pretty good to not have to call anyone Papa.

Mother went on. "I know you're scared, darling, but think of it this way. You only have to adjust to one new sister, but Cinderella has to adjust to two. It's probably very frightening for her too! She doesn't know at all what sweet girls you and Hortense are, and she's had to move all the way from her home to come live with us."

This all made sense to me, and I uncurled further. I couldn't imagine how scared I would be if we had to leave our manor house, with my tree and my bedroom and all the little nooks and crannies that I'd discovered and made my own. A tendril of sympathy started within me for this girl I had never met. I sat up on the platform and looked at Mother's face. She smiled at me, and I gave her a tentative smile back.

"I suppose it would be scary to have to move," I said. "She's probably feeling very lost and alone. She only has a papa, and I have a mother and a sister."

"You're right, darling," said Mother, her hands stroking and smoothing my hair back into place. "She does only have a papa. How lucky for her to be gaining a sister like you! Maybe you can help show her how to be a good big sister? Why don't you take her around the house this afternoon? You can show her where everything is, and your—Mr. Fitzwilliam and I will pretend not to notice if some cookies go missing. Hortense can come too, of course, but it will be you that I'm counting on to make Cinderella feel at home."

I nodded, my heart swelling with pride, fear forgotten. Of course I could show Cinderella how to be a big sister! Even though sometimes Hortense was a nuisance, I loved her very much, and I took great pride in my role as a big sister. I could teach Cinderella to do the same, and maybe it would be like having another Hortense, or maybe I would be the Hortense, and Cinderella could be the me? I puzzled over that for a minute before giving up. It didn't matter if Cinderella was the new Hortense or the new me. Either way, I'd begun to feel the stirrings of excitement at an afternoon spent running around the house and eating cookies. My anxiety began to dissipate.

Mother and I climbed down from the tree and headed to the front of the manor, where we would wait for our new family members to arrive. Hortense was already there, looking much put upon in her brand-new yellow dress, kicking at a clump of dirt while Mr. Calton, our last servant that we hadn't let go, scolded her, to no apparent effect. I can't imagine Mother could afford to pay him what he was worth to stay with our family and cook and clean and tend to the house, but he was fond of me and of Hortense. And whenever we had a part-time governess, Mother let Mr. Calton's son, Leo, sit in on our lessons. Mr. Calton was a soft touch with us, however, and Hortense knew it.

"Hortense," Mother called out. "Please don't get your nice shoes dirty. We want to make a good impression, don't we?"

Hortense brightened and squirmed out of Mr. Calton's grasp to run into Mother's arms.

"Mother, is our new sister here yet?" she asked.

Mother laughed. "You're looking at the same view I am, sweetheart! Do you see a new sister yet?" she teased.

Hortense giggled, and then went back to searching the road. We were all quiet for a moment, the only sound Mr. Calton drawing deeply on his pipe, together in anticipation of the changes to our family that were about to occur. I think of that moment sometimes, as the last time the three of us were a whole unit, before she came into the picture and turned everything upside down.

Hortense was the first one to spot them. She always had a keen eye for observation, even from a young age.

"There!" yelled Hortense, pointing. Mother and I winced. Her young voice was very, very loud in our ears.

A cloud of dust had appeared in the distance, moving directly toward our manor house. Mother made minute adjustments to our clothing, fussing with my hair and despairing of my ruined stockings. Some of my previous dread returned when confronted with the immediacy of my new sister, but I did my best to ignore it, focusing on how sad Cinderella must be to have only a papa and have to leave her home behind.

The cloud of dust materialized into a horse-drawn carriage, but it was of a style that I had never seen before. Mother drew in a sharp breath next to me, and Hortense had a puzzled look on her face.

"Well, now," said Mr. Calton, dark brows furrowed. "That's something, isn't it?"

Instead of the normal carriages that we knew, with windows cut into the sides and a graceful shape for better traversing bumpy roads, often with small ornamentations here and there, this carriage was a solid cube of metal. It had no windows, and the doors were reinforced with extra steel plating. I thought I saw a glimmer of wards of protection, beaten into the edges of the carriage. That was some serious magic, and it would have cost a pretty penny to enchant something so large with protection wards. Only the royal mages, or perhaps a very, very powerful coven, could have done it. The coachmen in the front looked nervous, and the horses were the draft type that were commonly seen in the fields, not the fancy team that one would expect to see pulling a wealthy merchant and his young daughter.

The carriage pulled to a stop in front of us, and the coachman jumped down to open the door, then quickly backed away. I glanced up at Mother, uncertain. This was not how I envisioned meeting my new sister.

An elegant leg emerged from the door onto a small metal step, followed by the well-dressed figure of Adrian Fitzwilliam. He stepped out of the strange carriage, and then paused for a moment, reaching back into the carriage. I held my breath.

Out stepped the most beautiful girl I had ever seen. Her cheeks were rosy and full of health. Her eyes were a clear spring green and sparkled in the light, giving her a sweet but mischievous air. Her hair hung in blonde ringlets, corkscrewing gently out from under a perfectly tied travel bonnet. Her stockings were pristine and white, and she looked as if she'd never so much as thought of climbing a tree when she ought to have been keeping her nice clothes clean. She looked at me, and smiled, a sweet upturn of her lips that made me think that I'd been panicking over our upcoming sisterhood for nothing.

Mr. Fitzwilliam cleared his throat.

"Bettina, Eunice, Hortense, may I present to you my daughter, Cinderella. Cinderella, these are your soon-to-be new family members, your new stepmother, Bettina, her eldest daughter, Eunice, who is just about your age, and Hortense, who is five. Cinderella, please greet them." His tone was level and even, but he was gripping Cinderella's hand very tightly in his own. He must be nervous about all of us getting along.

Cinderella dipped into a flawless curtsy, her skirts parting in just the right way, her balance perfect. I saw her hair bounce, and as I fumbled through my own curtsy in return, I felt impossibly drab and plain. My own curtsy was nothing special, and I was aware of my thin, limp hair that would not hold a curl no matter what Mother did. I found myself in awe that a human being such as Cinderella could exist. She was like a porcelain doll come to life.

Hortense was immediately enchanted by this beautiful young girl. Before Mother had even managed to greet Adrian, Hortense had once more squirmed out of Mother's grasp, and run up to our new sister, eager to meet her new playmate.

It's one of those memories that has crystallized itself in my brain as a series of fragments. I remember Hortense's delighted giggle as she threw herself at Cinderella. I remember Mr. Fitzwilliam's eyes growing wide and round with horror. I remember Cinderella's smile expanding over her face, exposing white and even teeth, and the mischievous glint I'd seen earlier turn into something sharper, more focused. Mostly though, I remember the cry of my little sister as she jerked back from making contact with Cinderella, cradling her hand in front of her.

Fat drops of blood slid down Hortense's hand to her wrist. I saw the crescent shaped impression of teeth marks on the side of her hand, just below her pinky finger.

We all stood there in shock, watching the blood trickle down her wrist. None of us moved. I think it was just too much for us to process.

The shock was broken when Hortense began to sob, and Mother rushed to her side, already whipping a handkerchief out of her pocket to wrap around the wound.

What was wrong with Hortense? I remember being confused as to what had happened, even though I had just seen Cinderella reach out and bite my sister. But my brain refused to entertain the idea that the girl I was now supposed to call sister had reached out and bitten Hortense. Then I saw Cinderella's face. Her eyes held the same focused sharpness as before, and below that was her mouth, smeared with blood from my little sister's hand. Cinderella saw me looking, and she winked at me, sucking the blood from her lips before it could roll down and mar her starched white dress.

Mr. Fitzwilliam stepped in front of me, breaking Cinderella's eye contact with me and blocking my view of her entirely. Before I could fully process what I had seen, he had bundled Cinderella back into the strange carriage they'd come in and was snapping at his footmen to draw them up to the back of the house. I watched them go with a feeling of shock. In all of the worst-case scenarios that I'd imagined for this moment, never had I imagined a scenario involving blood.

Mr. Calton scooped up Hortense, who was sobbing, huge, fat tears rolling down her face, and hurried toward the house, Mother following close behind. Hortense was a small, limp figure in Mr. Calton's arms, and the sight of her scared me.

I stood in the dust in front of my house, alone, staring at the spot on the ground where a few drops of Hortense's blood had mixed with the brown dirt. I couldn't stay there, with the blood so near and so fresh, the metallic scent of it still clinging to my nostrils. I gathered up my skirts and headed right back to my tree. I wanted the solitude and the solidity that came from being up in the crook of my tree, high above everyone else. At least, it had seemed high above everyone else when I was eleven. Besides, I had already ruined my stockings. What further damage could I do? I climbed up the solid trunk, my feet sure on the worn ladder, and curled into the same ball that Mother had found me in earlier.

2

The Rules

THINGS DID NOT improve from that first meeting. I eventually came down from my tree and made my way inside, through the entrance hall and into my second-favorite drawing room, where my mother and Mr. Fitzwilliam were having a conversation they certainly did not intend for my ears. I ducked behind a couch, not wishing to be seen, and began to eavesdrop shamelessly.

"She's just like this?" said my mother. I'd never heard her sound like that before, angry and hard. "Adrian, she bit Hortense! With her teeth! You told me she was a bit unusual, and that she'd had some problems—I thought you meant she was skipping lessons, or was impudent with you, or was climbing up into trees like my Eunice! She *bit* my daughter! And not just a little nip—you could see down to the bone in that wound, Adrian! The bone!"

I peeked around the edge of the couch. They were on the opposite side of the room from me, and neither had noticed my presence. I could see my mother's back, hunched over, her head in her hands. I wondered if she was crying. Mr. Fitzwilliam hovered behind her, his hand uncertain over her back, like he wanted to reach out and touch her but was unsure of his welcome.

"My dove, what would you have me do?" he asked, his voice broken and low. "If people knew of my daughter's peculiarities, I would be ruined. A merchant is nothing without his reputation. She is my daughter, just as Eunice and Hortense are yours. I cannot turn my back on her. She *is* unusual, and she *does* have problems, but she is my responsibility, and I hoped . . ." he trailed off.

"You hoped she wouldn't enact violence upon her new family?" said my mother bitterly.

"Yes, I did. Naively, I assumed we could get through the introductions, and then we could go back to our routines. I suppose I was not used to the enthusiasm of small girls—in your last letter, you'd written how nervous Eunice was to meet her new sister, and I thought it was true of both of them. Please, I beg of you. I never intended any harm to your daughters. At home, no one touches Cinderella. I'm the only one who even gets near her. I wasn't expecting Hortense to be so enthusiastic in her greeting. If I had known, I would have warned you," he said.

"Of course you should have warned me!" spat my mother. "Hortense is *five*. To risk her like that—" She broke off, too overcome to speak.

"Darling, please," begged Mr. Fitzwilliam. "The only five-year-old I have ever known has been Cinderella herself, and I am given to understand she is not typical. I never believed this would happen, you must believe me."

My mother made no response. I held my breath, not wanting to give away my position behind the couch.

Mr. Fitzwilliam broke the silence again, his voice low and quiet, barely above a whisper. I strained to hear him over the crackling of the fire.

"I suppose too, if I am being perfectly honest with you, that I did not want to disclose the severity of Cinderella's troubles for fear that it would impact your good opinion of me. It has always been my wish to be joined together with you in matrimony, since almost the instant we met, and I feared that if you knew of my daughter's problems, you would reject me. But now you know the truth of it, before we are to be wed. And if you so desire, I will break it off, in such a way that will not impugn your dignity or your social position. I will spread a rumor that I have had an affair and that you quite rightfully broke our engagement. Bettina, I would if I could spare you this pain, and if I had to do it all over again, I would set up this day differently, even if it means losing you. Your happiness—" He faltered, choked with emotion. "Your happiness is my primary concern. Please allow me to know in what way I may further that happiness, even if it means the absence of myself and my daughter."

Another silence met this declaration. I wanted to know what was happening, so I risked another peek around the couch. What I saw was quite disgusting. My mother and Mr. Fitzwilliam were kissing passionately, and I could see in the firelight that both of them had tears running down their faces, even as they pressed their bodies and mouths against each other. I pulled back, appalled at having seen such a display, made worse by the fact that one of the participants was my own mother.

After another moment of kissing, my mother spoke again.

"I don't want you to leave, Adrian. I just want you to tell me about the important things in your life. I don't like to be kept in the dark. Tell me what the dangers are, what her routines are, and we'll figure out a way to keep everyone safe and happy. Including Cinderella."

The quality of the silence that followed this statement told me that they were probably embracing again, so I took advantage of their distraction to sneak out of the room. I crept up the stairs to my bedchamber, next to Hortense's room. No one had noticed me missing, what with the commotion of dealing with both Hortense and Cinderella. As I opened the door to my room, I was seized with a sudden, sharp panic. What if they had put Cinderella in my room? What if she was there, lying in wait, to do to me what she had done to Hortense, or worse? My mind filled with terrible visions, so vivid and sharp that I was sure they must be real, of Cinderella sinking her teeth into my own flesh, ripping a piece of it off. In my mind, she did not bite my hand, but ripped off the skin of my cheek, a horrible wet piece that tore off like a flap of leather. She held the flap of flesh with her long, spindly fingers, and then, while making eye contact with me, lifted the piece of bloody tissue to her mouth, and tore off a large bite, chewing with absolute relish. Her eyes were no longer the clear green of spring that I had thought them to be when we'd met previously that day; they were the green of mold, of decay, of the sludge at the bottom of a river where all the plants and animals have died and turned into a slimy muck that sticks to your feet no matter how much you wish it wouldn't. Those eyes trapped me, and I felt like I was falling into them, and I would be lost forever.

I woke up gasping. I was alone in my bed, although I had no memory of getting into it, nor of falling asleep the night before. The sheets were soaked with my sweat, and tears rushed down my face. I lifted a trembling hand to my cheek, half expecting to feel the jagged ends of a wound, but I felt only smooth flesh. I let out a sigh of relief. Just a nightmare. Cinderella had not been in my room. I was uninjured.

That was the first of the night terrors that I would experience daily for the next seven years. That morning, I merely cursed my imagination, and tried to shake it off. I would soon come to learn that ignoring things with Cinderella was never the best course of action.

After this frightening awakening, I did what was natural to any eleven-year-old who had experienced a shock. I went to look for my mother. I found her in the dining room, seated at the head of the table, going over some papers. Her long, dark hair was bound up in the same elaborate knot it had been in last night, and wisps of hair made their escape whenever possible. She looked sad and drawn. This was how she normally looked, and yet it still filled me with a sense of wrongness. This was not how things were supposed to be. Mr. Fitzwilliam was supposed to bring the happiness back to her countenance and the light back into her eyes. Instead, she was carrying around the same grief she always had, compounded by the events of yesterday.

She looked up from the papers when I came in and opened her arms to me. Wordlessly, I ran to her, burying my head in her chest, taking comfort in the warm press of her arms and the light, floral smell of her perfume.

We held our embrace for a long moment, and then broke apart. I took my customary seat next to Mother and found that I had slept later than I'd thought. Breakfast was already on the table. Mr. Calton had been doing the cooking for the last several months, after Mother had to let go of our last cook, but he mostly just did porridge. This was a proper spread, with eggs and bread and hot tea. Mr. Fitzwilliam must have brought more servants than I'd realized, for them to already be making breakfast. I helped myself to a hard-boiled egg and peeled it. The act of cracking it and fiddling little parts of the shell away soothed something in me. The strangeness of my dreams lessened and dimmed while sitting in that room, with my mother, doing something as mundane as peeling a hard-boiled egg.

Mother took a sip of her tea and cleared her throat. I looked up from my growing pile of jagged shell bits.

"Hortense is resting today and won't be able to come out and play. The doctors have been in to see her, and so we just need to keep her wound clean and hope for the best. I'm having Mr. Calton stay with her today, along with Leo, so she won't be too lonely, and someone will be able to keep an eye on her."

I nodded. I didn't know what to say. What was there to say? I had been nervous about acquiring a new sister, but yesterday had surpassed all of my worst fears. Normally I might have been excited about a surprise day off from lessons, but it was not worth the cost of seeing Hortense traumatized by being bitten by the newest member of our family.

Mother took another sip of her tea, then drew a deep breath, steeling herself to tell me something. I watched with interest. Mother was always very open with me. I hadn't seen this side of her before.

"We need to talk about Cinderella, you and I. I will also be talking with Hortense, but you are older and more capable, and I'm going to rely on you to help me keep Hortense safe. I've been talking with Adrian, and we think we have a plan to keep everyone safe and happy." She paused, and the dining room was silent except for the gentle ticking of a large grandfather clock in the corner.

I looked down at my own breakfast. The eggs seemed to lose their luster, and even the hot tea didn't tempt me the way it had just before.

"I don't want a new sister," I whispered, not making eye contact.

Mother's hand was warm on mine, brief and comforting, before she pulled back and sipped gently at her tea.

"We're out of options, Eunice," she said calmly, but I saw in her expression how true it was. "There is no other way forward. Without this alliance, Hortense will continue to sicken. And the house . . ." She trailed off. I nodded. Marrying Mr. Fitzwilliam meant we got to keep our house. Mother didn't like to talk about it, but there was a reason she'd set her sights on Mr. Fitzwilliam in the first place. She'd grown to truly love him, but his wealth was also sorely needed by our family. She fixed her calm, practical gaze on me once more, and returned to our conversation.

"There are some things we are going to need to do, Eunice, that aren't what we're used to doing. You and I, we are going to need to adjust to this new addition, even though some parts may be hard or frightening. Do you remember when Hortense was born, and I taught you how to hold her?"

I nodded, confused as to where this was going.

"Well, you were afraid to hurt her, because she was so little, and it was scary to hold her. You told me you never would, because you were too afraid of dropping her or hurting her. But I taught you how to support her neck, and how to have gentle hands so she would be safe, and you promised to only hold Hortense when I was around. And did you drop Hortense, or forget to hold her neck?"

I shook my head. I had been terrified of hurting her, but at the same time I had loved holding her when she'd been so tiny. I'd followed all of Mother's rules, and it had been fine.

"Well, these are the sorts of rules we're going to have to follow at home now, for everyone to be happy. Cinderella is not like other children, and so it's going to be important that we follow these rules to make sure everyone is safe—you, me, Hortense, Mr. Fitzwilliam, and even Cinderella herself, all right? Adrian has been explaining to me how this all works, and I do believe we can make it work. Cinderella has her own set of rules that she has to follow, and we can use those rules to help us coexist with her."

I nodded. I could follow the rules. I didn't know if I cared about keeping Cinderella safe, but protecting Hortense had long been in my purview. I was willing to do whatever it took to make sure that she was taken care of.

Mother gave me another strained smile and got up from the table. She then led me by the hand to the cellar, where I began to learn about the conditions under which Cinderella operated, and the ways to use those to our advantage as best we could.

CHAPTER

3

She Will Obey Her Family

"THE FIRST THING to remember," said Mr. Fitzwilliam in a tone of false cheer, "is that Cinderella will do anything that is commanded of her by a family member. Right now, that means she will only listen to me, but once Bettina and I are legally wed, that will extend to you, and your mother, and also to Hortense, although that one's a little tricky, for reasons we will get into later."

It was just after breakfast. Mother had led me down to the cellar and helped me into one of her old coats, a long-sleeved garment that went down to my ankles. She then covered my head with a lumpy woolen hat and wrapped a scarf over my face so that only my eyes peeked out. Then she fit my hands into a pair of stout gloves.

"It's hot," I complained. "It's not winter. Why are you dressing me for snow?"

"Hush, darling," said Mother. "Remember, I said that we would have to do things that weren't much fun to keep everyone safe. This is one of those things.

Mr. Fitzwilliam is going to explain—for now, I just want
you to focus on not exposing any of your skin to Cinderella, understood? We just want her to see clothes."

"So, as I was saying," continued Mr. Fitzwilliam, as
if I hadn't spoken, "she will only obey the commands of
family members. This means it is of the utmost impor-
tance that Cinderella consider you family. It is equally
important that you consider her to be family as well."

I made my most skeptical face at him. I may even
have stuck my tongue out. I was not thrilled to discover
that the success of keeping everyone safe meant I had to
believe this girl was my sister.

"Most of that will get taken care of by the marriage,"
said Mr. Fitzwilliam, seeing my distress. "The rest of it
will be language. Call her your sister, or stepsister, at the
very least, if anyone asks. That should be enough to
make sure that she knows she is part of our clan, and she
should follow your commands."

I nodded.

"All right," I said. "I can call her my sister. Or stepsister, if I'm feeling cross, so that she'll listen to me."

Mother tucked a stray piece of hair into my hat and
gave me a quick kiss on the forehead before pulling the
hat down over my eyebrows.

"That will do nicely, dearest," she murmured.

"However," continued Mr. Fitzwilliam, his round
face growing shiny with sweat as he continued his explanation, "it's very important to remember that the way
you intend a command and the way she interprets it are
not always the same. You must be extremely careful and
specific. Please, watch, but stay back, and keep your hat
low over your eyes."

He slid back a heavy metal door to one of our cellars.
Previously, it had held bottles of wine, but it had slowly

emptied as Mother sold them off one by one. The door was new. I recognized it as one of the doors from the odd carriage he'd arrived in the day before. Sometime in the night, our cellar had been transformed into a jail cell. Behind the metal door lay another door, this one made of heavy iron bars.

Inside the cell was Cinderella. She sat upon a small bed, fitted with drab sheets and blankets. A small table sat next to her bed, and there was a chair on the opposite side of the cell from her bed. Despite her dingy surroundings, she looked as pristine and fresh as she had when I saw her yesterday. Her dress was pure and white, her ringlets blonde and sleek, and her cheeks were flushed with youth and health.

She cocked her head as the door opened, and for the first time, I heard her speak.

"Father, is this to be my new home?" she asked. Her voice was as lovely as the rest of her. Her accent was clear and sharp, and her voice suggested both wealth and intelligence.

"This is to be your new home," affirmed Mr. Fitzwilliam. "I brought you a present. Here, take it." He held out in his hand a shiny red apple that looked as if it had been freshly plucked from our orchards that morning.

Cinderella stood up from the bed, and then she was at the door. I didn't see her move, but I convinced myself that she had just moved very quickly, and I must have blinked. Or maybe the hat that I had pulled down low over my eyes was interfering with my vision. It only looked like she was on the bed one moment and at the bars the next.

Her pale, thin arm reached out between the bars, palm up, looking for all the world like a little girl asking for a treat from her indulgent father.

"Here," said Mr. Fitzwilliam, standing several feet back from the door, without handing her the apple. "Eat it."

What happened next was my first true glimpse of Cinderella's power—the first thing I saw that could not be explained away.

Her lips pulled back from her teeth, which were not the white, even teeth I recalled her having earlier. Her mouth was revealed to be filled with concentric circles of dentition, each row spinning and churning like a meat grinder. As I watched with mounting horror, she ejected her mouth across the space between her cell and her father's hand. The concentric circles of teeth shot out of her body, trailed by the long fleshy tube of her throat.

The rotating circles of teeth latched on to the apple in her father's hands, and they began to pulverize the flesh into a goopy mess. A long, thin tongue snaked out from between the rows of teeth, and with a terrible shlorping sound, it began to suck the pulverized apple into the gaping maw of her mouth. The lump of apple purée was visible in her throat as it traveled back along to her body. After a few seconds of this, there was nothing left on Mr. Fitzwilliam's gloved hand, and Cinderella was still behind her bars, looking for all the world like an innocent little girl.

"Well, that was dramatic," said Mr. Fitzwilliam, no more perturbed than if he were commenting on the weather. "I haven't seen that configuration of you before. Are you trying to impress your new sister? She's certainly never seen anything like that before either."

I was trembling, half hidden behind my mother, clinging to her waist with my gloved hands. I was horrified to see that Cinderella was staring right at me, still with her head cocked to one side, an inquisitive and yet somehow mean-spirited look on her face.

"I just wanted to see her reaction," she said, in the same conversational tone as her father. "But she didn't even scream. I think I like her."

"Good! That's wonderful," said Mr. Fitzwilliam, like he really did think it was wonderful that this abomination liked me. "Because as we talked about, she's going to be your sister. That means you'll have a similar relationship to her that you do to me, with all that entails."

"Oh, I know," said Cinderella, not looking away from me. "I tasted her dreams last night. She's got a delicious imagination. I think I will be quite happy here." With that last cryptic statement, she turned and went back to her bed, lying down on it with her back to us.

Mr. Fitzwilliam heaved the second metal door shut, obscuring our view of Cinderella.

"Adrian," said my mother, her voice trembling.

"Not now," said Mr. Fitzwilliam, curt and low. "Let's get a little farther away. We can take this discussion to the drawing room." He ushered us upstairs, throwing an uneasy glance over his shoulder at the shut and locked door behind which lurked Cinderella, a gesture with which I would become very familiar as time went on.

Only when we were all situated in the drawing room, which was not only a flight of stairs up from Cinderella but also on the opposite side of the house, did Mr. Fitzwilliam relax.

"Adrian," repeated my mother, more impatient than scared, "what was that? That *thing* was not human!"

Mr. Fitzwilliam took off his glasses and polished them on a handkerchief he pulled from his breast pocket.

"Well, perhaps not entirely," he admitted. "I didn't know her mother very well. It was a union arranged by our parents, and she was quiet, reserved. She died giving birth to Cinderella, and I don't have much information beyond that. For all I know, she may have been one of the Fae, the Cold Ones, or she may have just been a human woman who got unlucky and fell afoul of some monstrous curse. But that's neither here nor there. Cinderella is most assuredly my daughter, and I am responsible for her. As you can see, she followed the letter of my command and did eat the apple. As you also saw, since I did not give her any further directions, or make it easy for her to do so, she chose to do it in a fairly singular way. I will admit, even I was unsettled by the form she took. I had anticipated that she'd just float it into her hand, or elongate her arm, or something of the sort, but, well . . ." he said, with a guilty glance in my direction. "She was determined to make an impression on young Eunice there, so we got one of her more fanciful iterations."

"So she's . . . what . . . a shapeshifter?" asked my mother.

"In part, yes. She can change form to a limited degree. Most of the time she's a girl, like you saw just now. She likes many of the same things I'm sure your girls do—hair ribbons, and new dresses, and dolls. She takes very good care of all of her possessions; it's definitely one of her defining traits." Mr. Fitzwilliam sounded like an indulgent father as he spoke, proud of his little girl.

Mother snorted and shot me an incredulous glance. I had to agree with her. I couldn't recall the last time I'd worn hair ribbons voluntarily. I didn't hate them, and I would submit to having them put into my hair for formal occasions, but no one had ever before accused me of liking hair ribbons or new dresses. I did quite like dolls though.

"What did she mean," I piped up, giving voice to the thought that had been nagging at me since the cellar, "what did she mean when she said she'd tasted my dreams? And that I had a delicious imagination?"

Mr. Fitzwilliam looked distinctly uncomfortable. "I don't know."

"What?" snapped my mother. "What do you mean, you don't know?"

He shrugged helplessly, his palms upturned in a gesture of supplication. "I don't know. She's never said that before. Darling, please, I'm trying my best here. It has not been easy to raise this child, not knowing what can happen or what she is capable of. I swear, I will teach you everything I know so we can best live as a family. There are certain rules she seems to be bound by, but I have had to discover those through painstaking trial and error. She did not come with a guidebook, and I am but a fallible human, as are we all."

Well, all of us except Cinderella, I thought but did not say. I could tell that it would not be well received.

"So, anyway," said Mr. Fitzwilliam, trying to hurry past this terrible moment between the three of us. "Rule number one: She must obey her family. Although, as you saw, specificity is important. She will try to manipulate anything you say, so be careful. Try not to leave her any loopholes, because she will take advantage of them in a heartbeat."

"Why bother with the rules?" asked Mother. "Why not just lock her up? We could provide a room, and all the luxuries and comforts she could want—"

"No," said Mr. Fitzwilliam. "No, it cannot be borne."

"Adrian, I know she's your daughter, but this just seems so incredibly risky. If we could just—"

Mr. Fitzwilliam let out a harsh bark of laughter, entirely devoid of any humor.

"No, no, it's not that I won't lock her up for sentimental reasons. It's that she *can't* just be locked up and forgotten about. She's one of those things that festers in the dark. If she is not taken out and directed into some sort of task, she will sit and brood and grow in power, until no amount of rules or luck can save us. I have tried to lock her up, my dear," he said, turning to Mother with a broken look on his face. "And believe me when I say that the price is one that I would not willingly pay again. No, she must come out, and perform tasks, every day, or she will become untenable."

"But you just said that we had to be very careful giving her commands," I said. "And yet we must give them?"

"Exactly, my child. Exactly. You must choose wisely what you tell Cinderella to do, and you must tell her what to do. Be careful as well with asking questions— you never know what she might do to acquire the answer."

Mother put her hand on my shoulder.

"We will practice," she said. "After the wedding, when we are part of her family and bound to her in the same way that Adrian is, we will practice together, and Adrian and I will be there to help you, and make sure nothing goes wrong."

I looked at them anxiously.

"But what if it does go wrong? She bit Hortense!"

"It won't," said Mr. Fitzwilliam, firm and convinced. "We are better prepared now. We will not let it."

* * *

My first chance to practice came rather more quickly than I might have liked and was particularly memorable. Mother was tending to Hortense, who was still doing poorly, and Mr. Fitzwilliam and I were going to practice with Cinderella while she was still in her cell.

"It will be better this way," he said. "I want to make sure you have an idea of the scope of things, and the way she works, before you have to give commands that we can depend on. Now, your control over her may be somewhat less right now, since you've no legal relation to her just yet. I know you've been calling her sister, and that will help, but just to be safe, this is what we'll do. You'll give a command, we'll see how Cinderella responds, and if she doesn't listen to you, I'll just repeat what you've said. Does that sound all right, Eunice? That way you can see the effect your commands will have on her, once your mother and I are wed."

I nodded, tamping down my nervousness. Mother had bundled me up again in a series of scarves, mittens, and my heaviest coats, and I was sweating and cranky, but trying not to let it show. I already wanted to make sure things went right for Mother, and that meant making a good impression on Mr. Fitzwilliam. And with Mr. Fitzwilliam came Cinderella.

"I'm ready," I said. I wasn't doing as good a job of masking my nervousness as I thought—my voice came out croaky and hoarse, as if my throat was made of sand. I swallowed to try and accumulate more moisture in my mouth and hide my nervousness from Mr. Fitzwilliam. He just nodded back at me, and we descended the stairs to the cellar. Over his back he carried a large sack bulging with unknown items, and I had the rather hysterical thought that he looked like Saint Nicholas descending to give presents. If there was ever a child who did not deserve presents, it was Cinderella, but the thought, ridiculous as it was, cheered me enough that I waddled my way down the stairs, encumbered as I was by my many layers of clothing.

We reached the bottom of the stairs, and the heavy metal door stared back at me. Mr. Fitzwilliam laid out his sack, which turned out to be full of lengths of wood, a pile of broken china, tiny slivers of soap too small to be used, brushes, a pair of dirty shoes, several small jars full of thick, viscous substances, and a basket of unshelled peas. I stared at him, uncomprehending. He shrugged and then looked back at his pile.

"I asked the staff what tasks needed to be done that I could take with me. Said it was character building for my girls. I don't know if they believed me, but this way we can practice and contribute to the household." I would come to learn that Mr. Fitzwilliam was a great believer in trying to teach Cinderella about productivity and contributing to the household, although I am not sure if any of his lessons ever took.

"Right, shall we get on with it?" He rolled up his sleeves and heaved back the door. Mr. Fitzwilliam was, and is, a well-muscled man, and I believe that the amount of time he spent hauling open the cellar door definitely contributed to his strength.

The first door was opened and I saw Cinderella sitting on her bed, head cocked at us, looking beautiful and pristine. At that time, I had not yet come to hate her beauty, and I was still a little awed by such a picturesque young girl. Even the earlier experience with the apple had not entirely deterred me from thinking of her as something to aspire to. Her beauty was like that even as a child—she drew me in, made me want to get closer to her. I would be thoroughly cured of that desire over a grueling process of years.

"Hello, Cinderella. How are you today?" asked Mr. Fitzwilliam. He was always polite and kind when he entered Cinderella's space, although I knew he could be stern as well. Cinderella didn't respond, staring at him with her murky green eyes, but he didn't seem to mind, carrying on as if that were normal. I would come to learn that it was, for her. She vacillated between verbose and near mute.

"We're going to do some chores today, all right? Except instead of just you and me, we're going to have Eunice help us. You remember Eunice is your new sister, yes?"

Cinderella inclined her head at him, and her unsettling gaze switched over to me. I focused my own gaze on her left ear, so that I wouldn't fall prey to her stare once more. It was an effective strategy when dealing with Cinderella, one that I would continue to use over the years.

Mr. Fitzwilliam unlocked a smaller door set within the wrought iron door and slid through the bowl of unshelled peas. He nodded at me. I took a deep breath and gave Cinderella an order.

"Cinderella, shell those peas and put the shelled peas into the bowl. Please," I added belatedly because I thought Mr. Fitzwilliam would like it, and trying to be specific so she would have no cause to turn into a horrible monster in front of me. This was before I understood that she needed no cause to turn into a horrible monster and was largely doing it to get a rise out of me. At the time, however, I was still learning, so I looked at Mr. Fitzwilliam, anxious for his approval of my command, and he gave me an encouraging smile. I took it to mean I had done well.

Cinderella continued to stare at me with her too intent green eyes, and I thought that Mr. Fitzwilliam was going to have to repeat my order, but just as he opened his mouth to command her, Cinderella held out her hand to the bowl of peas. The green pods split open, and the fat little peas inside tumbled out of their casings, all without her laying a finger on the bowl or the peas.

Cinderella smirked at me. She'd left the shells a jumbled mess inside the bowl with the peas, so the task wasn't yet complete, and she knew it. I looked at Mr. Fitzwilliam, and he nodded encouragingly. I gave her another command.

"Cinderella, please remove only the pods of the peas from the bowl. Put them in this bowl." I found another bowl in the pile of things that Mr. Fitzwilliam had brought down, and he took it from me and slid it into her cell.

Cinderella smirked at me again, and I knew she'd found a loophole, but I wasn't sure what it was until she acted. She reached into the bowl and scooped up a huge handful of peas and pods alike, which she then crushed in her hand, pulverizing the taut little peas into a green mush. She scraped the mush back into the bowl before depositing the pods into the second bowl.

I interrupted her. "Do not damage the peas when you do it. Don't hurt them or mess them up, leave them whole so that the cook can use them!" Frustration had entered my voice, but I feel I can be forgiven. I was only eleven, and Cinderella was a particularly vexing child.

Cinderella glared at me, and I felt a little thrill of triumph. She shook her hand again, and the pods floated up out of the first bowl and into the second, leaving the peas in the first unharmed.

"Lovely job, Cinderella, and you too, Eunice. Cinderella, thank you for shelling the peas and for listening to your sister. Eunice, thank you for helping Cinderella figure out how to best help the family with the peas, which is of course what we are in pursuit of here." Mr. Fitzwilliam was careful to be fair with Cinderella and me as we both completed tasks. That most of my tasks were caused by the difficulties Cinderella presented didn't seem to trouble him unduly.

"Let's try another chore, shall we? Eunice, the stable boys were going to make new torches for the barn today, so I thought we'd take that task for them, with Cinderella's help, of course! Let's see here . . ." He took up the lengths of wood, and I saw that one of little jars was full of black pine pitch. He slid the torch materials into the cell through the little door, reserving one stick and a small chunk of pitch from the jar, which he held out to me expectantly. "Cinderella, Eunice will make one first so she gets a feel for it, and you can watch her, but then she'll also give you instructions."

"Um, I am not certain how to make a torch," I admitted. I knew that the pitch had to be affixed to the wood, but I wasn't sure how it all went together.

Mr. Fitzwilliam smiled at me, and clapped his hands, genuinely delighted.

"Well, then, we can all learn together! You'll notice, girls, that these sticks are split at one end several times, so that there are smaller sections of the stick split off from each other." We looked at the sticks, and I saw that it was so. It reminded me of a rope unraveling, except the rope was made of wood, and the strings were just smaller pieces of the stick.

"Now, there are chunks of pitch in that jar. The way to make these torches is to take a chunk of pitch and wedge it down into the cut end of the stick, so that it can be lit, but it won't fall out, and the fire will stay at the top of the stick where the pitch is." He wedged the pitch into the split end of the wood, and I saw that it did look like the unlit torches I occasionally saw outdoors late at night.

It seemed simple enough, so I thought it would be a good time to practice my commands to Cinderella, since the actual task didn't seem to have very many steps. I cleared my throat, feeling more confident after my—eventual—success with the peas.

"Cinderella, using your hands, please open the jar of pitch, take out an appropriately sized chunk, and insert it into the end of the stick—without breaking the stick or the pitch—so it can be used as a torch." I was quite proud of that command, and I looked at Mr. Fitzwilliam once more for his approval. He nodded at me, and we both turned to look at Cinderella, who just sat there and did nothing. He frowned at her, and repeated my command, word for word. I looked up at him seeking reassurance that I hadn't done the command wrong, that this was merely a problem of us not being legally family yet.

His attention was not on me but rather fixed on Cinderella, his face with a peculiar expression that I had not seen before. I looked at Cinderella, trying to see what was so interesting about her making torches, and my jaw dropped.

Cinderella had a stick with a split end in one hand, and next to her lay the jar full of chunks of pine pitch. She was reaching out toward the jar with her hand but cowering away from it with the rest of her body. Her lips were pulled back from her teeth in a soundless snarl, and as I watched, her body seized before me. Her skin rippled across her body, the same way a pond ripples when it meets a wind, but it was rippling away from the jar of pitch. Her beautiful hair all stood up from her head, so she was surrounded by a corona of waving tendrils. She looked like a wild animal, with her great mane and her snarl. Mr. Fitzwilliam and I watched in horror as she sprouted another hand on a long, spindly arm directly from her neck, this one also reaching out toward the pitch. Cinderella began to vibrate and twitch, her skin rippling faster and faster, hands shooting out from all parts of her body, grasping and clawing at the jar of pitch without actually touching it, the hands supported by weak, stretchy limbs. Her lips pulled back even farther from her teeth, until I could see all of her gums, and then her mouth was just an open, sucking hole, and Cinderella began to scream.

That scream jolted Mr. Fitzwilliam from his stupor, and he shouted over her screaming to make himself heard.

"Cinderella, ignore that last command!"

The shrieking stopped, and Cinderella gradually retracted her many, many limbs, and her lips grew back in over the gaping expanse of her mouth and exposed teeth, and her hair settled down into its customary ringlets around her face, but even as she returned to normal her eyes were huge and green, with the pupil so small that they looked to be made entirely of murky, churning green, and I was not sure that the pupil had not vanished entirely from her eyes.

"I think we're done with chores for the day. Eunice, go upstairs, I'll meet you there. Cinderella, do you want me to take those things out of your room?" said

Mr. Fitzwilliam. Cinderella nodded, but before her father went in to collect the wood, he shooed me upstairs, not wanting me to be in a room with Cinderella unseparated by bars before he and Mother were legally wed.

I went up the stairs dutifully, but lay in wait for him at the top, just beyond the wooden door that led down to our cellar.

He emerged a few moments after I did, looking weary and drawn.

"What was that?" I asked.

He shook his head and glanced meaningfully at the door. I remembered that we never had conversations about Cinderella near the door. I trailed along behind him to the drawing room on the opposite side of the house, and we sank into comfortable chairs. I could hear Mother and Hortense laughing from upstairs, and the clink of dishes in the kitchen as the cook washed up from breakfast.

We sat in silence. Mr. Fitzwilliam stared into space, and I stared at him. I grew bored with this fairly quickly, and so I asked my question again.

"What was that?"

He shook his head at me again, but not to tell me to stop talking. Instead, it seemed its own answer. He spoke, but his voice was slow and weary, and his countenance drawn.

"I don't know," he said, still staring off into space. "She has balked at commands a time or two in the past, but nothing to this degree. I'm not sure why she acted the way she did, and why it seemed like she couldn't do the task. I have no answers for you."

We sat in silence a while longer, contemplating Cinderella and life and who knows what else, before

Mr. Calton came down and dragged us back into conscious states.

"Where's the new little thing's bedroom going to be, then?" he asked. He was fresh down from Hortense's room. Mother must have gone up to relieve him. "Did you bring her own furnishings, or will you be wanting me to build something or order something special from the market?" Mr. Calton was a fair carpenter, although he was right to ask if Mr. Fitzwilliam would want to order things—he had very fine tastes.

"No, she doesn't need anything. I brought everything she needs," said Mr. Fitzwilliam absently. He didn't always consider servants as real people, it seemed. Or maybe it was just that he was so used to being secretive and he didn't know Mr. Calton.

"So should I set her up next to Eunice, then?" Mr. Calton asked.

There was an empty bedroom next to my own. I'd used it as a playroom when I was younger, but it had mostly just been empty for the past few years. I jerked my head up to stare at Mr. Calton in horror as he suggested that Cinderella move in next to me. But he wasn't paying me any attention. His gaze was fixed on Mr. Fitzwilliam, who had a similarly strong reaction.

"Absolutely not," Mr. Fitzwilliam said firmly. "We've spruced up the cellar. Cinderella has health issues that make it important for her to stay underground. I assure you, her every need is being met."

"You're keeping that girl *underground*?" asked Mr. Calton, his brow furrowing. "In a dusty old cellar?"

"Not so dusty anymore," said Mr. Fitzwilliam. "I am looking to acquire some new dresses for her, however. Can you take a message to the dressmaker in town for me? I have her measurements here." Mr. Fitzwilliam fumbled in his pockets, pulling out some scraps of parchment, which Mr. Calton took, frowning the whole time. "And is there some sort of animal trader? If I wanted to get an unusual pet, where would I go?"

Mr. Calton was now drawn into the conversation, distracted from his concerns about the girl in the cellar. I used the opportunity to slip off before I had to wash up for supper. I should have paid more attention to Mr. Calton, but I was only eleven at the time.

Away from the adults, I headed for my tree, climbing up into the secure branches and taking a deep breath. I was trembling, nervous at both the strength of Cinderella and the thought of having to become better at giving her directions. I closed my eyes and let the sunlight bleed into my skin, hoping it would erase all thoughts of her. I didn't realize that Mr. Calton had followed me until he spoke.

"Little Miss Eunice, how are you today?" he asked, standing directly beneath me. He smelled of horses and fresh hay and I breathed in deeply. Cinderella's cellar smelled of rot, and I was worried I was starting to as well.

He pulled a brightly striped peppermint out of his pocket, proffering it to me through a gap in the platform boards. I accepted eagerly and the taste of sweet, clean mint in my mouth washed away the last memories of Cinderella writhing. I smiled down at him with genuine happiness.

"Better now," I said truthfully, my words a bit garbled by the candy. He smiled up at me, popping a peppermint into his own mouth and sucking with enjoyment. He sat down on the ground next to my tree and stretched out his booted feet in front of him.

"Lot of changes for a family," he said, looking out toward the stables. "How are you holding up? You look tired." He still held the piece of parchment from Mr. Fitzwilliam in his hand. I wondered how Mr. Fitzwilliam got Cinderella's sizes. Maybe he ordered her to stay still and took a string to her, the way Mother did to me. I shuddered at the thought, my trembling increasing.

Mr. Calton jerked me back to reality by saying, "It's not healthy for a girl your age to be so tired. Aren't you sleeping?"

I knew he was right—I did look tired—but it stung a little to hear it from someone else. I turned my face from him, allowing my hair to fall down and cover it. If I moved a bit more, he wouldn't be able to see me through the slats in the platform of my tree.

"Hey now, I don't mean anything unkind," he said, his voice gentle. "I just know that you've been spending a lot of time with your new stepsister, and it seems like maybe it's got you down a bit. If you want to talk, I'm here. I can even peel a carrot if it makes you feel more comfortable."

I smiled a little at him through the curtain of my hair, liking that he remembered our time in the kitchens together. He winked at me and pulled out a carrot intended for the horses, scraping the rough exterior away with a small pocketknife.

"It's just hard," I said. "I want Hortense and Mother to be happy, but it's hard. I hate seeing Cinderella!"

Mr. Calton's knife froze on the carrot, and I realized belatedly that I'd said too much. I stood up, brushing off my skirts, wanting to be anywhere but here.

"I have to go," I said. "I just—I just have to go." I shimmied down the tree, past Mr. Calton, and darted back along the way I'd come.

I cursed myself with words that I'd only learned recently as I hurried back into the house. I knew that I wasn't supposed to say anything, and yet there I was, blathering on about my feelings. Even if it was only to Mr. Calton.

I could still feel his eyes on me as I walked back into the house, but I didn't stop to look back. I was too ashamed that I'd slipped up so fast.

What I should have done was go to Mr. Fitzwilliam then, or to Mother if he'd seemed too intimidating. But I left it alone, not wanting to expose my own failings. I know now that this was a mistake, although it would not be my last. I reasoned that there was no need to bother them, not with the wedding so soon. Mother and Mr. Fitzwilliam had more important things to focus on and didn't need to know about my very minor outburst.

4

She Draws Her Power From Living Things

THE SECOND RULE came several days after I learned the first. Mr. Fitzwilliam said he'd given a list of them to Mother, but he didn't want to overwhelm me, so we'd take the rules slowly. I grumbled, but Mother sided with him, and they stood firm. I was still only a child, and although they needed me to be informed about Cinderella, I would find things out on their schedule, not mine.

For the next several days, everything was extremely dull. Lessons were still canceled, since Hortense was ill and Leo was enlisted to help watch her, and Mother didn't have time to teach me herself or hire a new governess just for me. The wound on Hortense's finger was not healing well, and the doctors had been in and out of the house. I'd come around several corners and surprised Mother and Mr. Fitzwilliam having deep conversations about it, but they always stopped when they saw I was near, and I was unable to eavesdrop on them like I had earlier in the week.

My tree was my solace. I would sneak books out of the library, climb up into the tree's branches, and read for hours, sprawled on the small deck Mother insisted I use. If I was bored, and unwilling to read anything more, I would eschew Mother's rules about staying on the platform and climb up high into the branches, trying to see how high I could get before I grew too scared to continue. If Mother was available to have lunch with me, I'd beg and plead and she'd acquiesce, and we'd lunch under the sprawling branches of my tree, shaded from the summer sun.

In the evenings I was permitted to sit with Hortense, provided we did quiet activities. Leo joined us more often than not, for he was a quiet boy, though of course he went home when Mr. Calton did, so he wasn't always available. Hortense's room was an odd place, even then. She was an avid bug collector, of both living and dead specimens. Someone had given her the unusual gift of a butterfly pinned under glass when she was three, and it had sparked something deep within her, making her passionate about bugs and creepy crawlies of all types. Her room was full of glass jars containing sticks and leaves and pieces of dirt to make little habitats for her many bugs. I thought they were awful, but whenever I voiced such an opinion, Hortense would look at me with reproach and tell me all about how fascinating bugs were, and show me all the drawings she'd done of them, and then beg me to read to her from the various books on insects we had in our library. Leo was a soft touch and would have read to her whatever she desired. But she only wanted me to read to her, since I was her big sister.

During her forced convalescence, I read more about bugs than I'd ever wanted to. Normally I'd put up a fight about what sorts of books we'd read together, always championing some fantastic tale, or maybe something with a little bit of romance, but while she was ill we read exclusively about bugs. I could deny her weak little face nothing. I'd offered to try and catch some new bugs for her, so she'd have something new to look at while she was sick, but she was having none of that.

"You don't know what they like," she said. "You'll probably try to give leaves to a bee to eat or put a spider in a jar with a flower. No, I don't need any new bugs. I'll catch my own when I'm better." Hortense was like that. She wanted to know how things worked, and she didn't trust other people to figure it out. I certainly knew that a bee couldn't eat a leaf, but to my sister it didn't matter. She didn't trust anyone else with her bugs.

The whole time she was sick she lay in bed, clammy and flushed, her temperature running high from the bite on her hand. I stroked her uninjured hand with mine and felt cold chills down my spine. She needed to get well. Any other outcome was unacceptable. I'd put up with mountains of bugs in the house if only my baby sister would pull through.

Mr. Calton was also unavailable to spend time with me. Mr. Fitzwilliam had indeed brought a whole host of servants with him, including cooks and lady's maids and all sorts of people we hadn't had in the house for ages. Mr. Fitzwilliam was very careful to make sure that none of them spent the night, furnishing accommodations in the long-abandoned servants' quarters separate from the house or finding them rooms in town. All of the servants he brought with him were serious, no-nonsense folk. I supposed they had to be in order to share a house with Cinderella. Mr. Fitzwilliam paid them handsomely, and it was their job not to ask too many questions or think too hard about the fact that he kept his daughter locked up in the cellar. This meant that Mr. Calton was relieved of many of his responsibilities and went back to his original role, which was stablemaster. Mr. Fitzwilliam had brought four gorgeous horses with him, and he promised to buy me a pony. But so far the pony had not appeared, and Mr. Calton spent his time in the stables instead of in the house with me.

I continued my routine of flopping around the house and visiting Hortense whenever I could for several days, scarcely able to believe how having a monstrous stepsister locked in the cellar could be so boring. I missed Hortense and our games and lessons. I missed Mother and her company. I missed spending time with Mr. Calton in the kitchen. I would even have taken the chance to spend time with boring Mr. Fitzwilliam, who had no sense of proper mealtime conversation and liked to talk about things like the economy, or the price of a pound of tea, or the gold standard.

So when I was woken up early by Mother shaking me gently, Mr. Fitzwilliam lurking in my doorway behind her, I was not exactly displeased. I had been plagued by nightmares and had not slept well. This was becoming my new normal. Vague, amorphous dreams that I could scarcely remember upon awakening, but that left me sweat-stained and gasping every night.

"Eunice, we need you to come with us," said Mother quietly. "And please be quiet; we need to finish up while Hortense is still asleep."

I stumbled out of bed, and Mother held out to me the same clothes that I'd worn the last time we visited Cinderella down in the cellar. She herself was similarly garbed, complete with gloves covering her long, delicate hands, and a hat pulled down low over her face, although Mr. Fitzwilliam just wore one of his regular elegant suits, hands and face bare to the world.

I became more alert at once.

"Are we going to see Cinderella?" I asked, moving quickly to put on the garments that Mother held.

"Yes," said Mother, helping me pull the hat down low over my eyes, "It's time. But we need to be quick and quiet, remember?"

I nodded and followed after them through the house, down the stairs to the first floor, and then to the cellar stairs. We walked all in a row, with Mr. Fitzwilliam first, and then my mother, and then me trailing after like a little duckling. Mr. Fitzwilliam carried a small box with a cloth over it, and Mother carried a tray of breakfast. I carried nothing, merely sweated my way through the many layers I was swaddled in.

At the top of the stairs to the cellar, before opening the door, Mr. Fitzwilliam stopped.

"Under ordinary circumstances, I would not do such a thing intentionally," he said, his voice low and serious. "But I think it is best that you know the consequences. We need to be prepared for mistakes. It is one thing to tell you this rule and quite another for you to see it and internalize it. Bettina and I agree that it's best for you to see this, although I am sorry there is no other way." With that cryptic statement, he opened the door and disappeared down the wooden steps.

I looked up at my mother, hoping for guidance, but she merely shook her head and followed Mr. Fitzwilliam downstairs, motioning for me to join them.

We arrived in front of the now familiar large iron door. Mr. Fitzwilliam set down his cloth-covered package a good two yards back from the door and heaved it open once more.

The scene was almost unchanged from the last time I had been there. Cinderella sat on her bed, looking beautiful and pristine, head cocked to the side in an inquisitive manner. Someone had added a large ward-robe and a set of small shelves since I had last seen her room. The shelves held a number of pretty porcelain dolls, their faces blank and smiling. Once more, I was struck by the similarity between Cinderella and a doll, and I shivered. I was unsure how I had ever thought it was a compliment to compare a girl to a doll—the simi-larities rendered that which should be beautiful into an uncanny mockery.

Cinderella arose from the bed and walked over to the bars. Her eyes were locked on me again. Memories of the previous night's terrors swam up in front of my eyes unbidden. For a moment, I felt myself begin to sink into the same fears that plagued me at night, only this time Cinderella's face was real.

Before I could truly begin to panic, Mr. Fitzwilliam stepped between us, much as he had on the first day that I met Cinderella.

"Good morning, dear," he said. "How are you liking your new wardrobe?"

"It's very nice, Papa," she said. "It has all my dresses and hats and things. And I have three new dresses; they're very nice. Why have you hidden my new sister from me?"

"She's not your sister yet, dearest. I'm afraid you'll overwhelm her. Once Bettina and I are married, you can spend more time with her, all right?" He stepped back so I could see Cinderella again but watched her carefully, ready to spring back in and disrupt her if I seemed to be falling under her thrall.

Cinderella pouted but took no other action. Mr. Fitz-william backed up, keeping his eyes on Cinderella, and picked up the small box he'd been carrying from the floor. He pulled the cloth covering off, revealing a small cage containing a sweet little white rat, the kind they sold in shops in town. It had tiny whiskers and clean, soft fur, with a lavender ribbon tied around its neck. It stood on its hind legs and sniffed the edges of the cage, curious about its new environment. Hortense had been begging for one for ages. She'd made many impassioned pleas to Mother, citing her care of her bug collection as proof that she was responsible enough for a pet rat. I felt some level of childish indignation rise up in me. Why was Cinderella getting a pet when she'd only just arrived and bitten Hortense besides? Surely Hortense should get one first?

Mr. Fitzwilliam opened the small door cut into the larger to pass the rat in to her. The cage was a tight squeeze, but it made it through.

Cinderella was delighted.

"For me? Papa, you shouldn't have!" she exclaimed. Mr. Fitzwilliam looked like he quite agreed with her and was having regrets about the whole experience.

She reached the tip of one delicate finger between the bars of the cage. The rat obligingly scampered over and sniffed curiously at the new item in his cage. The moment his little snout made contact with Cinderella's finger, a shock went through the rat. He collapsed to the floor of the cage, twitching and shaking, caught in the throes of a spectacular fit.

I jerked forward, unsure what I was going to do but wanting to make it stop. Mother's arm shot out in front of me, blocking me from advancing any further toward the cage.

The rat's convulsions ceased, and it lay there without moving. His pink eyes were flat and lifeless, and I knew that the rat was dead.

I turned to Mr. Fitzwilliam, assuming that we were done and that this was what he had wanted me to witness, but he was still staring intently at Cinderella, expectant and waiting, so I turned back to look as well.

Cinderella's eyes were blown huge and dark. The muddy green of her eyes had spread and obliterated the white of her eye, as well as her pupil. There was only the putrid green, green the color of an apple forgotten and left to mold. For a moment, I could almost smell the scent of decay and rot. She was totally fixated on the dead rat, her mouth curving upward into a wicked grin. She took in a deep breath through her nostrils and let it out with a heavy sigh. This time, I was sure that the scent of death and decay permeated the room. I tugged my scarf further up over my nose, and out of the corner of my eye, I saw my mother do the same. Mr. Fitzwilliam's nostrils flared, but he stayed motionless, his eyes intent on his daughter.

As Cinderella breathed out the scent of rot and decay, a tendril of steam bled from her mouth down to the rat, still lying lifeless in the bottom of the cage. As the steam made contact with the rat, it gave a mighty jerk. I watched in horror as the rat suddenly lurched to its feet and staggered to the door of the cage. Cinderella undid the latch, her eyes still huge and green, the stench heavy in the air, and the rat tumbled out of the cage onto the dirt floor of her cell. It then continued its stagger over to the door, where it slipped through the bars and then began to laboriously climb the thick metal of the door, headed for the lock. The rat was sticking its dead paw into the lock when Mr. Fitzwilliam plucked it off of the door and crushed it beneath his heel. The corpse of the rat gave a horrible crunch and a squelch. I closed my eyes, swallowing the bile that rose in my throat. Mr. Fitzwilliam lifted his elegant boot, and the mangled corpse of the rat twitched feebly, although with its body so mutilated it could not go far.

"Thank you, Papa," said Cinderella. I startled. The voice did not match what I expected to hear from her. Normally she sounded like a regular girl, albeit a fairly flat one. The sound that emerged from her now was gravely and had a strange vibration to it, as if two people were talking at once, one very high-pitched and one low and deep. It made my head hurt.

Mr. Fitzwilliam used the cloth that had been covering the rat's cage to scoop up the body, and nodded to my mother, who handed him the tray of porridge and apples with trembling hands. He slid the tray into Cinderella's cell, and then closed everything up tight, keeping the cloth holding the rat tight in one hand all the while.

The three of us then began the trek back upstairs. This time, Mother and I knew better than to ask questions before we reached the drawing room. Mr. Fitzwilliam immediately lit the fire, and we observed in silence as he deposited the rat into the fireplace, watching it carefully to make sure that every last part of it burned. My rational brain tried to insist that the rat couldn't possibly still be moving, but at this point, rationality did not seem to be my guiding star when it came to Cinderella.

We sat in silence until Mr. Fitzwilliam was satisfied that the rat was entirely burnt, and then he turned to us.

"I do apologize for that. I wish it had not been necessary. You needed to know. Cinderella is not to be trusted around rats or mice. They respond to her, somehow, and she's able to absorb them into her and then reanimate them."

I had nothing to say to this. Mother too was at a loss for words. Mr. Fitzwilliam sighed.

"And, to a lesser extent, she can do this with other living beings. That's why we've been bundling you up, Eunice. She can't drain you if she can't touch you. Once you're family, it should be easier. Something in her recognizes what family is, and she doesn't drain from it. That doesn't mean she can't harm you, but it does mean that she can't affect you to the degree she can others."

"Does that mean she's draining Hortense's energy right now?" I asked with a rising sense of panic.

Mother and Mr. Fitzwilliam exchanged a meaningful glance. I could tell they were trying to decide how much they should tell me.

In the end, it was Mother who answered me.

"We think so, darling. We weren't sure at first, because even normal human bites can be very dangerous. But with Hortense not recovering . . . We're moving up the wedding, in the hopes that the traditional family bonds will help speed up her healing, and that Cinderella will stop draining her once she realizes they are sisters. But since she bit her when they didn't mean anything to each other, officially or emotionally, we're not sure how much we can do. Hopefully being stepsisters in a legal sense will be enough to bring her out of it, but we just don't know. We're guessing at this point. It would help us greatly if you were to get Hortense used to Cinderella being her sister. Once she's well, of course. You know how much she looks up to you. She's more likely to go along with being Cinderella's sister if you lead by example."

I stared at her incredulously. "Hortense was so ready to be Cinderella's sister. I was the one who didn't want a new sister! But now that Cinderella's bitten Hortense and is draining her, we have to both believe she's our sister?"

"Er, yes," said Mr. Fitzwilliam. He had not expected resistance. It was becoming more and more obvious that he didn't spend any time around children except for Cinderella, who was not a good example.

I sighed.

"Well, I suppose I can do my best. It's not like we have other options, is it?"

Mother hugged me tightly. I think she was impressed by my attitude and maturity. Really, it was just naivete. My eleven-year-old self had no concept of what living with Cinderella would be like.

After that conversation, there was no way I was going to be kept from visiting Hortense. But I knew Mother still worried it would upset me to see her while she was still sickly. I snuck upstairs when Mother normally took tea with Mr. Fitzwilliam, hoping she'd be too distracted to notice the sound of the slightly creaky steps.

Once I was upstairs, I went directly to my room, then doubled back. It was maybe unnecessary, given that I didn't think they'd heard me, but I wanted to make sure I got to actually see Hortense. I padded gently down the hall in stocking feet and eased open the door to her room.

Hortense lay in bed amongst her many jars and bottles and strange oddments. She was asleep but did not look peaceful. Her face was tense and her hair fell lank and sweaty over her cheeks. Her cheeks were flushed with fever.

"Hortense," I called softly, walking over to her.

"She won't wake," said a voice from the corner of the room and I jumped, startled.

Sitting in a rocking chair in the corner of the room, a heavy book laid on his lap, sat Leo. I relaxed. I knew Leo had been watching over Hortense and I was pretty sure he wouldn't give me away.

Leo continued. "She's been like that since last night. I wanted to stay the night with her, sleep on the floor or something, just in case she needed me, but Papa said no. He said your new papa—excuse me, Mr. Fitzwilliam— said we weren't allowed. I hated to think of her alone like this, not able to wake up, and worried she'd think I abandoned her." His dark eyes, so like Mr. Calton's, were soft and sad. Leo was a very sensitive boy, good with both Hortense and the horses that we used to own. I'd known him since he was five and came to live with us when his father started working for Mother.

Mr. Fitzwilliam had said Mr. Calton and Leo couldn't live in the house anymore, though, so they'd recently moved to the quarters over the stables. Mr. Calton thought this was a slight, that Mr. Fitzwilliam didn't trust him in the house with "the girls," as he called Hortense, Mother, and I. But I knew it was because of Cinderella. Looking at Leo's sad eyes, it was clear that he too thought they had been banished from the house as a punishment, one that he did not understand.

I squirmed, wanting to reveal everything to Leo, but Mr. Fitzwilliam and Mother both had been quite clear on the fact that Cinderella needed to remain a secret. I knew that it was dangerous for Leo to be in the house at night, although I wasn't entirely sure why. I wanted to reassure him, to wipe the sad look off of his face, but even then I couldn't risk sharing Cinderella's true nature.

"Well, we're with her now," I said decisively, looking away from Leo to stare at Hortense. "Shall we read to her? I know she wants more articles about bugs from the encyclopedia."

A shadow passed over Leo's face, but he nodded. He moved close to the bed next to me, bringing the heavy book he'd been reading.

"'We continue with the life cycle of the moth,'" I read from the heavy tome that he held out for me, "'For it begins as an egg before passing on to the stage of a caterpillar.'"

After reading aloud several articles, I left, creeping away only once I'd extracted a promise from Leo that he wouldn't tell anyone I'd been there. My resolve to learn how to control Cinderella had been strengthened. Hortense needed my help, and if making Cinderella obey me was the price then I would gladly pay it.

5

Cinderella Cannot Hide What She Is Between Twelve and Three

I SAT UPRIGHT IN my bed, covered in my own sweat. I had soaked through the sheets once more. Visions of Cinderella's face, distorted and elongated, always with her swampy green eyes boring into me, danced in my head. I shivered, a combination of fear and cold, for my sweat was cooling rapidly. The nightmare that had awakened me was particularly bad. I had dreamed that Cinderella stood over me, leaning over my bed, her mouth beginning to open, exposing long, sharp teeth that alternated between churning in concentric circles and gnashing like the fangs of a wolf. Everything had felt so real. I couldn't shake the sense that she was lurking somewhere in my bedroom, waiting to pounce or sweep me into her clutches.

I lay awake in the wet bedclothes for a moment longer, my imagination providing me with increasingly more vivid ways that Cinderella could appear in my room and do me harm. I got out of bed, slipped on my dressing gown, pulled a hat over my eyes, dug up a pair of satin gloves from somewhere, and bundled my feet into thick stockings. I would go visit Cinderella and see for myself that she was safely locked away. Then maybe I could go back to sleep. I justified it to myself in that Mother and Mr. Fitzwilliam had never explicitly said I shouldn't visit Cinderella alone. And besides, I was taking all the precautions that they normally insisted on when we made our trips down to the cellar. I wouldn't open both doors; I wasn't a fool. I'd just crack open the big metal door, see that she was there, then leave. Somehow, late that night, their insistence on going with me, on making sure I was always supervised, vanished from my brain, and I was left only with that uniquely childish logic of "well, they never said I *couldn't* do it."

The grandfather clock in the small drawing room at the base of the stairs chimed softly, calling out two AM. Rather than frightening me, it encouraged me that I might yet be able to go back to sleep after completing my errand, instead of tossing, turning, and stressing all night long. I crept toward the cellar, not wanting to disturb anyone. I'd seen the same bags under Mother's eyes that greeted me every morning in the mirror. Neither of us were sleeping well with Cinderella in the house.

I made it to the cellar door, and I can now only thank luck and timing that I had this monumental moment of idiocy when I did. If I'd gotten it into my head to visit Cinderella alone at night a week later, I think that would have been it for me, and my story would have turned out very differently.

I opened the cellar door, the one leading to the steps going down to where Cinderella was kept. It opened with a loud creak, but at this point I was not as concerned with being overheard. All of the bedrooms were upstairs, and the only one on this side of the house was mine, which was directly above. The implications of that would only occur to me later.

I had scarcely had time to put my stocking-covered foot onto the first step when a strong hand yanked me back and slammed the door. Mr. Fitzwilliam was standing beside me in a pair of silk striped nightclothes, his hair rumpled with sleep, his eyes wild and panicked. I had forgotten that he was staying in the spare room down on the garden level until the wedding. I wonder now if he hadn't insisted on that room directly next to the stairs leading to his daughter's cell precisely to prevent this sort of occurrence, as a self-appointed guardian. After the wedding he would move up into Mother's room, but that was still two days away.

We both stood there, in our nightclothes, the slam of the door echoing in our ears, waiting to see if anyone else had heard.

After several tense moments, with no one coming in to see what was wrong or Mother coming down from upstairs, Mr. Fitzwilliam let out a heavy sigh, and some of the tension broke. Without speaking, he gestured to me, and I followed him to the little drawing room on the other side of the house from Cinderella's cellar.

He moved heavily and with an air of great tiredness to a cabinet tucked into the corner of the room that I had very rarely seen open. He pulled out a heavy cut-glass bottle partially filled with an amber liquid and two matching tumblers. He motioned me to sit opposite him on a low velvet couch, and I did, perching nervously on the edge. He still had not said a word since he discovered me at the top of the stairs. I watched him pour a measure of liquid into one of the glasses and a much smaller measure into the second glass, which he handed to me. I accepted it with some surprise. The fumes from the alcohol hit my nose, stronger than I expected. Mother never let me have alcohol at any of the parties or feasts we attended. I watched Mr. Fitzwilliam, unsure if this was some sort of test that I was supposed to pass by not drinking.

Throughout all this time, without either of us speaking, the severity of my actions had nevertheless started to bleed through to me. The reasons I had had for visiting Cinderella alone in the middle of the night, which had seemed so reasonable and strong as I was preparing my trip down the stairs, now seemed weak and foolish. What did I hope to achieve? Did I really think that I was capable of facing her alone, when Hortense lay upstairs, weak and unable to play or join me in my lessons during the day?

Mr. Fitzwilliam took a long sip from his glass and spoke for the first time since he'd found me.

"Drink," he said. His tone left no room for argument. I took a sip. It burned my mouth, and I coughed a little as it went down.

He downed the rest of his glass. I took another hesitant sip when he gestured for me to do so. It was sweet and sharp and unpleasant all at once. I drank only enough to let it touch my tongue and still my eyes watered.

He heaved a sigh and poured another measure into his now empty glass.

"I have done you a disservice," he said. I did not speak; I didn't know if it was allowed. "I have brought this thing into your home, and I have claimed that I will teach you, but I have let you wander around unprepared, liable to fall into the simplest of her machinations. For this, I am sorry. I love your mother very much, and I hope with time that you and I will come to know and care for one another as well. But I sometimes wonder if I can truly love this family, when what I bring with me will wreak such havoc and sorrow upon it. I told myself that you would know what it meant, why I did not let the servants stay the night, that I barred her door, allowed you no access without supervision. But I kept from you the barest facts. I did not account for your age, or your curiosity. For that, I have no one to blame but myself."

He tossed back the remainder of his drink but did not refill it, merely stared into the depths of the glass, as if the last dregs of alcohol carried within it the secrets of the universe. I had nothing to say to this unexpected confession. Adults did not talk like this to children, and I was out of my depth.

"The thing you must know about Cinderella is that what you see is not always the truth. You had some small taste of this, when I asked her to eat the apple in front of you, but it goes much deeper. She looks like a young girl about your age, with my features. She is not. I know she must be part human, because much as I might like to, there is no denying that I am her father. But Eunice, she is not a human girl. She passes remarkably well, but there are times when her power is too great, and she cannot keep it contained in the human shell that she normally puts on for the rest of us. Now is one of those times. Between the hours of midnight and three, her power is at its zenith. All the things I have taught you, all the rules that we have gone over . . . I do not know how well they will hold during these hours. Cinderella cannot hide what she is while her power is at its peak and you must never go to her during that time. To see her, as she truly is—it would undo you."

At that, I found my voice.

"You mean it would kill me? To look at her during this time?"

Mr. Fitzwilliam shook his head.

"No, Eunice. If it were to merely kill you, that would be a great tragedy, and we would mourn you, but your death would be the end of it. If you look upon Cinderella during those hours, encountered the truth of her—and the truth of her is not to be borne lightly—it would not end there. Our brains cannot comprehend what it is to look upon her, and as such, we are driven out of ourselves, an experience from which there is no coming back. If you looked upon her, you would not die, but everything you are, every spark of personality, every like, desire, and dislike, would all be warped, twisted, until you were a mockery of your former self, drawn only toward Cinderella, and serving her darkest desires.

"You would not rest until she was free to walk among the rest of us, and I pray you understand at this point why that is an unacceptable outcome. You would lose yourself in service to her, and either fulfill her whims or die trying. Her whims are not kind, and believe me when I say they are outstandingly painful. Your life would be reduced to a torment of fear and pain. At some point, we, your mother and I, or perhaps even Hortense, would have no choice but to put you down ourselves, unable to bear to see you so pained and tortured."

My stomach heaved and roiled, whether from the alcohol or the picture he painted, I had no idea. I waited until I was sure nothing would come up when I opened my mouth, and I asked the burning question that had filled me during his speech. "How do you know? Have you looked upon her? Wouldn't that have driven you to madness, like you say it would do to me if I had successfully opened the door tonight?"

His voice was a picture of sorrow, and I regretted asking even as I was filled with the burning desire to know.

"You are correct," he said. "I have not looked upon her during these times myself. When she was a babe in arms, there were signs. I knew something was not right, and through painstaking trial and error, I figured out these rules. I trained my staff, and we adhered to them. I don't know why she follows the rules she does, but certain things matter to her—the bonds of family, the legalities of our world. Both are constraints we can use to direct her. Still, those early days, when everything was still new, and we were still discovering the rules and the extent of her obedience, were extremely difficult. My whole household lived in fear of her, with one exception."

He paused for so long that I felt compelled to prompt him to continue, for he seemed liable to be lost in his thoughts for an eternity without help.

"Who?" I asked.

"My father," he said, and a leaden weight settled in my stomach. I could guess where this was going, and it was nowhere good. "My father always loved her. He never believed that there was anything wrong with her that the love of a good family and a solid upbringing couldn't cure. He was so, so devoted to her, so patient with her." His eyes were far away, lost in memories.

"He traveled often, back in those days, so he did not see what the servants and I saw. He did not believe me when I told him of the dangers. Although I begged and pleaded with him to listen to me, in his mind Cinderella was his only grandchild and a precious gift. One night, when Cinderella was six, he returned a day early from a business trip. He got back at two AM, right around the time that you awoke tonight. We know this because the stable boy who helped him with his horse heard the clock chime, clear as day. Father came home, and I don't know if she called out to him or if he just wanted to check on his granddaughter. What I do know is that we found him the next morning in her room, and by then it was too late. He was a gibbering pile on the floor, unable to string together a sentence, covered in his own sweat and piss. Cinderella was in the corner, neat and pristine as always. She had but to smile before he'd start ripping out chunks of his own hair and presenting them to her as an offering. He'd break into her room and she'd drain him, much like she's draining Hortense right now, but worse than that, because she had unlimited access to his power. Her powers grew, his dwindled, but he did not die."

He paused again, and this time, I could not have dreamed of interrupting. I waited for him to go on, certain that there was more to the story. He did not disappoint.

"He was my father, and I loved him. But he wouldn't stay away from Cinderella, no matter what we tried. He figured out how to pick the lock to his room, and he was possessed with a determination and a strength that meant he just shoved away whatever heavy objects we placed in front of his door. So we tied him up so that he couldn't get out—I bound his wrists to the bed myself. All the while I was frantically searching for a cure. When he found that he could not undo the bindings with which I had secured him, he turned his own teeth upon his wrists, and gnawed through the skin, flesh, and bone to release himself. We found him with his hands gone, in a pool of blood, outside Cinderella's door later that day. Somehow, even with his mutilation and his strength faded, he managed to knock the guard at his door unconscious and make it to her room. Without his hands, he was unable to open her door, but even then he pawed at it, leaving great tracks of blood down the door. It was then that I understood in my heart that my father was gone and was not coming back."

"What . . . what did you do?" I whispered. I had to ask, even if I already knew the answer.

"I killed him myself," said Mr. Fitzwilliam. "I couldn't bear to see him like that. I took a knife from the kitchen, and I slit his throat. As he was dying, he used his last gasp of air to try and break down her door with his bloody stumps. Even in death, Cinderella's control over him was complete."

This time, there was no restraining the bile that rose in my mouth, and I found myself vomiting directly into my heavy glass tumbler, still with an inch or so of fine whiskey left in the bottom of it.

I was sure that Mr. Fitzwilliam was going to be angry, but he got up from his chair and knelt down in front of me. He took the vomit-covered tumbler from my trembling hand and pulled one of his ever-present handkerchiefs from the pocket of his dressing gown, which he used to gently clean my mouth. He used a different handkerchief, also from his dressing gown, to dab at my cheeks, and it was only then that I realized I was crying.

"Why do you tell me this?" I whispered.

"Your mother thinks I should not. But I believe that we do better as humans with more information rather than less. I need you to know the extent of the stakes, and, my dear, the stakes are very, very high. You need to know what we are dealing with."

I stared at him, my breath sour, his earnest face close to mine. Looking back on this moment, I do believe it was then that he became my father, not later, with the wedding and the adoption and when everything became legal and official, but that night, at three in the morning, when he bared his soul and his trauma to me, and then knelt down and wiped the tears and the vomit from my cheeks.

I threw myself at him, startling him, and I sobbed openly into his shoulder. He was stiff with surprise at first, but then he began to pat my back soothingly, murmuring calming nonsense into my ear.

My mother found us like this sometime later. She helped me back to bed, and I could hear them whispering furiously behind me as I slid under my covers.

"Goodnight, Mother," I said drowsily. "Goodnight, Mr. Father."

Mother let out a gentle sigh, and I could almost swear that I heard Mr. Fitzwilliam curse softly in surprise. But at that point I lost consciousness and I remembered nothing further.

The three rules, and the ways that we were to act in response to them, would guide my life for the next seven years. Cinderella was bound to us by the rules of what she was, and we were able to rein in her power to some extent. But we were just as firmly bound to her, my new older sister.

CHAPTER

6

The Routine

T HE MORNING AFTER I learned of the last rule,
Mother was furious with Mr. Fitzwilliam. From
what I could understand, she was not happy that he had
chosen to tell me all that he had in such bluntness the
night before. Mother and Mr. Fitzwilliam were always
having long, fretful conversations between the two of
them, and as soon as they saw me Mother would clam
up and maintain a stubborn silence whenever she spotted me hiding in corners or around the other side of
doorways. Or she would start a bright, false conversation
about something totally banal. At the time, I felt it was
a betrayal. How could my own mother be less honest
with me than a man I had only known for precious few
days? With more time and perspective, I can see that she
was scared, and I do not blame her. There is no guidebook for integrating an eldritch abomination of a stepdaughter into your home, and I know that Mother was
doing the best she knew how.

I took to hiding under open windows outside, hoping to catch a snippet of conversation without Mother

noticing me. This strategy paid off when I was lurking under the open window outside the entrance hall, and they walked into the house mid-conversation. Mr. Fitzwilliam saw me out the open window, but I ducked down. He said nothing to Mother, so she was none the wiser as to my presence as he continued what was clearly a well-worn argument between the two of them.

"—it's part of the strategy that no one knows something is wrong. If we rush things, they'll think we've been improper, and that you are in the family way," said Mr. Fitzwilliam.

I regretted my actions already. Even with my newfound rapport with Mr. Fitzwilliam, I did not want to hear about anything to do with my mother and any sort of sexual situation. Nevertheless, I continued listening, figuring that this was the best chance I was going to get to actually hear what was going on in the house.

"Adrian, we need to do something! It's clear that Hortense is being drained. The doctors said she should have made a full recovery by now, and they can't understand why she's still so weak," said Mother.

I held my breath. Finally, what I'd been hoping to hear.

"Darling, if people realize that you're not with child, they will start to wonder why we rushed the wedding, and they may look more closely at our family. We've already moved it to next week; we can't afford to move it any closer. I agree that Hortense is being drained but she's not being depleted. She's weaker than she should be, but she's maintaining that weakness, not getting worse. She will make it to next week, and in the meantime we can keep working with Eunice to get her to accept Cinderella as part of the family. The stronger that connection is when we are wed, the better it will be for

Hortense." Mr. Fitzwilliam sounded like he hadn't slept well. I could relate, for I was still having night terrors. I trembled just thinking about them, the way I felt so impossibly cold and so impossibly alone when I woke up.

"She needs to start on the routine," continued Mr. Fitzwilliam, and I realized that I had missed part of their conversation. "We agreed that it was important, Bettina! And not for Cinderella's sake—for hers!"

I was confused. Why would Hortense need to start on a routine?

"She's just a child still," protested Mother, and I found myself nodding along. I wanted to protect Hortense from Cinderella as much as possible.

"She's the same age as Cinderella, and we agreed before that we would have her help," argued Mr. Fitzwilliam. I sucked in a sharp breath, and then clapped my hand over my mouth, trying to remain as silent as possible. They weren't talking about Hortense any longer— they were talking about me.

My shock had given me away. Mother recognized the sound of my breath and stuck her head outside the window, where I was lying out of sight. She sighed and pulled me in through the window, brushing dirt and leaves off of my shoulders.

"Well, I suppose you now know that we want you to build some routines with Cinderella," she said with a wry twist of her mouth. "How much else did you hear?"

"It doesn't matter," Mr. Fitzwilliam said. "It's time now. We needed you to come to your own opinions about your new sister, without being influenced by Hortense." He seemed to have decided that our heart-to-heart the night before meant that he was going to just speak to me as another rational adult, which I found very refreshing.

In turn, our newfound closeness had given me the free-dom to react to him more as I would to Mother, and less as I would to a guest.

I stared at him, nonplussed.

"Of course I'm going to be influenced by Hortense," I said. "She's my only—I mean, she's my sister."

Mr. Fitzwilliam nodded approvingly.

"Excellent, excellent. Let's keep that up, I think it's having an effect already on the familial bonds that Cin-derella feels, insofar as she is able to feel such things. Yes, Hortense is your sister, and of course she will have an influence on you, but it is easier to come to terms with something if you are not watching that something drain the life out of your beloved younger sister. Some space to come to your own conclusions was necessary. If it helps any, Bettina didn't want to keep this from you, but I convinced her of the merits of the idea."

I shot a betrayed look at Mother. It was proof that things were no longer just the three of us—Mr. Fitzwil-liam and Cinderella were embedded as part of our lives.

I opened my mouth to complain. What had hap-pened to all his talk last night of humans doing better with more information rather than less? He held up a hand to forestall me.

"Yes, I have since come around on that particular point. We need your help, and we can't get that if you don't know what's going on. Cinderella is certainly draining Hortense, but we still need Hortense to accept Cinderella as her sister. For that to happen, I am con-vinced that we need you."

Before I could respond to him, Mother jumped in as well.

"Eunice, we really do need your help," said Mother. "In order for us to be a family. It's all I've ever wanted, really." I saw in her face the same sadness that I'd seen for years, that had really only lifted when she looked at Mr. Fitzwilliam, or read his letters, or thought of him. I saw her fine clothes, new for the first time in years, as she'd sold off dress after dress in an attempt to keep the house. Eleven is not the most extrospective age—I was more focused on my own issues, and what Cinderella and Mr. Fitzwilliam meant for me and my life. But I loved my mother fiercely, and I still do. I wanted her happiness. Mr. Fitzwilliam was what made her happy and paid for the new dresses, despite the baggage he brought with him.

"Of course I'll help," I said. "Just let me know what I need to do."

Mother beamed and hugged me tight against her. Mr. Fitzwilliam gave me a small smile over her shoulder, which I returned. It was a good moment, a happy moment, to have them proud of me.

"And you must remember, Eunice dear," Mother whispered into my ear. "Tell no one of Cinderella. If asked, just say that her health is delicate and she needs specialized care. It's even true, in a way. She does need special care, and we, her family, are going to provide it."

I nodded solemnly. Unbidden, my conversation with Mr. Calton, when I'd been perched in the tree and revealed more than I thought I should have, came into my mind. I pushed that thought away hurriedly. Mr. Fitzwilliam nodded in the background, clearly having heard Mother's whisper.

"I don't know exactly what would happen if knowledge of her were to become common," he said, "But I think treating her like a human girl, as much as we can, is another layer of defense. By acting as though she *is* a girl, some of her assumes the form of a girl and is less powerful as a result." I nodded, although I was wracked with guilt. Still, it was not enough for me to say anything. I rationalized away that I hadn't said anything specific to Mr. Calton and that he might have thought I was just jealous. I simply nodded and said I would do my best.

Although I'd agreed to help, neither Mother nor Mr. Fitzwilliam wanted me to do anything with Cinderella unsupervised. Mr. Fitzwilliam still insisted on shouldering the bulk of her care. I visited her once a day and Mr. Fitzwilliam had me practice giving her commands and anticipating the way she'd twist them to suit her own needs. These sessions left me drained and it made me feel a little better to go outside when they were done.

It was after a particularly grueling session, during which Cinderella had not listened to a word I'd said and had transformed into a gruesome-looking tentacled monster, that I next saw Leo. I was sitting on a hay bale near the stable, letting the sun soak into my skin, trying to banish the vision of Cinderella writhing and screaming and reaching for me from behind my eyelids.

"Hi," said Leo, plopping down on the hay bale next to me. I was startled, as I hadn't heard him approach. He cocked his head at me and I shuddered, as for a second I was reminded powerfully of Cinderella doing the same motion. But Leo smiled and the thought was banished, gone in a moment. Cinderella would never smile like Leo—slightly shy, very sweet. Still, he must have seen my shudder and misinterpreted it.

"The new quarters above the stable aren't so bad," he said tentatively. I could tell he was trying to cheer me up, but how could he succeed when all I could think of was her? "I was going to ask—do you want to see the new kittens? They're up in the barn. Papa says they'll keep the mice down and when your—when Mr. Fitzwilliam heard, he said we should keep them and raise them up. They're really soft, and I thought—I thought we might bring one to Hortense? Just to see if maybe she'd like to touch it."

"Hortense still isn't awake," I replied. I was interested in the kittens, but my mood had collapsed at the mention of my sister. Mother assured me that the wedding would solve things and help Hortense get better, but she was still trapped in a strange, feverish sleep. I was sure it couldn't be good for her to be stuck like that, but I didn't know what else to do.

"Yes, but Papa says sometimes people who don't respond well to humans can respond to animals. And maybe even if Hortense can't show it, she'll know we're visiting her and bringing her something nice."

I was tempted. I wanted to see the kittens, wanted to believe that bringing one to Hortense would show her that I still cared. I was on the verge of going with Leo when he opened his mouth again and ruined it all.

"Or maybe we could take a kitten down to see Cinderella," he said, too casually, his eyes darting to mine in a quick, nervous glance. "Maybe she'd like to see a kitten."

"Absolutely not," I said, getting to my feet in a huff. "I don't ever want to hear you say her name again, do you understand me, Leo?"

Rather than backing away as I expected, Leo set his jaw and stared up at me, determined.

"But Papa says—"

"I don't care what your papa says," I interrupted, trying to mimic Mother's frosty tone, the one that brooked no arguments. She'd used it for the debt collectors before. "I won't be going to visit her, and I won't have you doing so either. See that you mind me." With that, I turned on my heel and I was gone, although I glanced over my shoulder to give Leo a quelling glare. He didn't notice, slumped down in disappointment on the hay bale as he was.

I once again failed to bring this conversation to Mr. Fitzwilliam or Mother's attention. They were in a flurry of preparations for the wedding, trying to get everything ready as fast as possible without it looking like it was done as fast as possible. Mother had been contemplating hiring one of the court mages to cast glamours for the decorations instead of doing them herself, but in the end it was too expensive, even with Mr. Fitzwilliam's money. So she was doing everything herself. The thought of new servants, who weren't trusted by the family, coming into the home and decorating so close to the cellar made Mother very nervous, so she was working nonstop to have everything perfect, with only Mr. Fitzwilliam's regular household for help. The only time I saw Mother was when we had Cinderella lessons together. She'd received word from a third cousin of hers that he'd be attending the reception, which had her and Mr. Fitzwilliam in a tizzy, since he was a current favorite of King Reymond's. The rumor was that this relative would soon be made an earl. Therefore I didn't think they needed to hear that Leo and Mr. Calton had clearly been talking about Cinderella. That was my second mistake.

That night, I went to bed as normal. Mother insisted on a nine o'clock bedtime for me, even on nights when I didn't have anything to do the next morning. She said a disciplined and growing young mind needed sleep. But that night I couldn't sleep. I stayed awake, tossing and turning for hours. As it grew later and later, my general feelings of discontent coalesced into something stronger. I was certain that the source of my discomfort was Cinderella.

Having learned my lesson earlier, I wasn't so foolish as to go down to see her alone. First, I checked the time: just past eleven-thirty. Very near her time of transformation, but there were a few minutes left yet. I tried to squeeze my eyes shut, but once I started thinking about Cinderella approaching the zenith of her power, I couldn't stop. I slipped out of bed, and without even bothering to put on my slippers, hurried downstairs to Mr. Fitzwilliam.

He was still sleeping in the room on the ground floor, but this time he didn't awaken when I hurried down the stairs. The wedding preparations had taken a toll on him too, although he still looked in slightly better shape than Mother. He was more used to juggling his normal day-to-day stress and responsibilities with Cinderella, I think.

I hesitated at Mr. Fitzwilliam's door, and almost didn't knock, but I screwed up my courage and tapped on the wooden door. I heard a faint rustling and then he appeared in the door, his striped nightclothes rumpled, his hair askew.

"Eunice? What is it? What time is it?"

The sleep fell from him quickly, and he looked around intently, as though he thought Cinderella might be beside me. He had correctly jumped to the conclusion that there was something going on with Cinderella.

"It's almost midnight," I replied. "And I don't know, there's just—I couldn't sleep. There's something. It's just—I'm sorry. I shouldn't be here. I'll go." I turned to leave, feeling foolish at showing up at his door without even my slippers on.

"No," he said, putting an arresting hand on my shoulder. "No, it's good that you came to me. Let me just—Wait here. I'll be right back." He took off toward the cellar at once, leaving his bedchamber door standing wide open.

Despite my intense fear of Cinderella at midnight, a quick glance at the grandfather clock in the hall showed that we still had a good ten minutes. I crept along behind Mr. Fitzwilliam, hoping I could see what was going on yet still escape if need be.

I heard a great scuttle and a clatter ahead of me, and then a great shout. I peeked around the corner of the door leading to the long set of stairs down to the cellar and, to my surprise, Mr. Fitzwilliam was tussling with Mr. Calton.

"She's your *daughter*," yelled Mr. Calton, struggling in Mr. Fitzwilliam's grasp. "She deserves better than to be locked up like this! When I think of doing that to my Leo—"

"You utter *fool*," hissed Mr. Fitzwilliam. "She is not like Leo! Have you not been paying attention? I told Bettina—"

"You've warped her! The Bettina I know would never agree to locking up a sweet innocent girl in the cellar—"

I realized that this whole time Mr. Calton had been struggling to open the outer cell door, and with a well-placed elbow to Mr. Fitzwilliam's chest, he broke free of him long enough to finish hauling open the huge metal door.

A low groaning sound filled the air, and a thick white mist spilled out of Cinderella's cell. I faintly heard the sound of a young girl sobbing. Mr. Calton's whole body took on a sorrowful mien, and he surged toward the door.

"Don't worry, sweetheart, I'll save y—"

Before he'd even gotten to the doorframe, a long, powerful tentacle shot out, tipped with a hundred tiny teeth, gnashing and wailing and going directly for

Mr. Calton's face. From my hiding spot I saw his eyes widen with horror and I trembled, certain I was about to see him eaten alive by Cinderella's tentacle.

But just as the tentacle reached Mr. Calton's face, Mr. Fitzwilliam heaved the door closed, the heavy metal shutting with a *thunk*, slicing the tentacle clean in two. Thick, black blood seeped from the cut end of the tentacle, and it still writhed a little.

Even from behind the door, which normally muffled such sounds, the wail that started up could be heard. It was a terrible, awful sound that contained the screaming of stars and every painful thing. I clapped my hands over my ears but to no avail. The shriek was short-lived, thankfully, followed by a deep groaning. Just as the sounds died down, I heard the grandfather clock begin to chime softly in the hall. Midnight. It had been even closer than I'd thought.

"What . . . How . . . I didn't . . ." Mr. Calton stammered. I saw that he wasn't entirely unscathed—a small ring of bite marks marred his cheek and blood flowed freely from the open wounds.

"Get out," said Mr. Fitzwilliam from between clenched teeth.

"I swear I didn't know! I just thought—"

"Get *out*!" roared Mr. Fitzwilliam, angrier than I'd ever seen him before. "You just thought . . . what? You just thought you'd take things into your own hands? You just thought you'd jeopardize everyone in this household? You just thought you'd be able to get away with *hurting my child* and I'd just wave my hands and all would be forgiven? You are to leave this place at once and I never want to see your face again. If you tell *anyone* what you have seen, I promise, I will ruin you."

"But— the girls— Eunice, Hortense—"

"They certainly don't need *you* to protect them," sneered Mr. Fitzwilliam. "You should thank your lucky stars that Eunice is as perceptive a girl as she is. Without her, you'd be nothing more than a pile of pulp right now and the rest of us would be dead or worse. Now get out of my sight."

I ducked back around the door just in time, as Mr. Calton came thundering up the stairs. I caught a brief glance of his white, terrified face and then he was gone, scurrying out of the house without a word.

I peeked my head around the door again, hoping to see Mr. Fitzwilliam, and almost smacked my head on his knee. He too had come up the stairs, wasting no time in following Mr. Calton.

When he saw me he said not a word, merely shut the door at the top of the stairs and threw the bolt. We both breathed a sigh of relief when it slid home, although we could still hear a keening from down below.

"Is she . . . is she badly hurt?" I asked. I didn't know what else to say.

Mr. Fitzwilliam shook his head.

"I doubt it. She'll be in pain for tonight though, and that means she'll be in an awful mood tomorrow. Run along to bed, Eunice. There's nothing more you can do for now."

He slumped down, his back against the cellar door, and closed his eyes. "Forgive me," he said, and I thought this time he was not speaking to me, but he didn't clarify. "Forgive me."

I scampered off to bed, but it was not until the clock struck three and I felt some of the tension in the house lessen that I was able to drift off to sleep.

The next morning, Mr. Calton's departure was common news. Mother must have heard everything from

Mr. Fitzwilliam, but the rumors were flying thick and fast among the servants. I heard several outlandish tales before I even made it to breakfast.

"Eunice, you won't be taking Cinderella breakfast today," said Mother when I joined her at the table. I'd been piling up a second plate, as I'd begun taking her breakfast while Mr. Fitzwilliam opened the doors for me. "Mr. Fitzwilliam is going to do the feedings today. Cinderella is still a little out of sorts, and besides, I need you to sit with Hortense."

"Why do I need to sit with Hortense?" I asked. I quite liked to sit with my sister, but normally Mother thought it upset me too much, so she preferred to have me train with Mr. Fitzwilliam on how to control Cinderella.

"I don't want her to be alone. And now that Leo's gone . . ." she trailed off, and my heart sank. Of course. Mr. Calton would hardly leave Leo behind. If he was leaving, so was his son. Tears welled in my eyes. I hadn't even gotten to say goodbye. I threw myself into my mother's arms, burying my face in the fabric of her dress.

"I know, sweetheart, I know," she whispered, petting my hair and rocking me as she had when I was a small child. "It's not what we imagined. But we just have to make it through the wedding. We just have to make it through the wedding. We're almost there." I wasn't sure if she was trying to convince me or herself, but we sat there for another few minutes until I slipped away and went to keep my vigil over Hortense. I dabbed at her skin with cool cloths to keep her from overheating and wiped the sweat from her brow while praying for the wedding day to arrive.

7

The Wedding

THE CEREMONY WAS beautiful, small and intimate, with only the four of us and some very close friends. Hortense was still too ill to attend. We'd solved the problem of what to do with Cinderella by making her a flower girl, positioned up front close to her father. Mr. Fitzwilliam had primed her for the occasion with some very specific instructions, which he thought would at least hold for the ceremony. He'd thought she might enjoy the chance to wear a beautiful new dress and shiny new hair ribbons, and he was right. If the flowers strewn about the aisle had the slightest whiff of rot to them, who could blame Cinderella? Surely she was given faulty flowers. Things went off without a hitch. If her smile was too fierce, her eyes too intent, the ceremony was short enough that few witnessed it, and most importantly, no one questioned it. I officially had two new family members.

Immediately after the ceremony, Mr. Fitzwilliam bundled Cinderella away, and Mother and I went to Hortense. We found her awake and demanding food,

which Mother promptly ordered, before sinking onto
Hortense's bed and holding her close, murmuring into
her hair. Hortense complained that she wasn't a baby
and please couldn't Mother let her go so she could go
take a bath. Mother laughed and then called for hot
water to be drawn. So far, the day was going according
to plan, although we still had to survive the reception.

The reception, in contrast to the ceremony, was a
lavish affair. Mother had decided that they simply must
have a reception, or people would talk. Mr. Fitzwilliam
agreed, and due to their positions, nothing less than an
extravagant feast would suffice. Mr. Fitzwilliam had
made his fortune through trade and was not of noble
blood, but Mother had connections to the crown on
both sides. Neither of her branches of our family tree led
to King Reymond, but there were more than a few dukes
and counts and earls floating around in her extended
family. It would have looked suspicious not to have some
sort of celebration.

The guests were all milling about at the reception,
eating delicious treats, making small talk with each
other, and drinking glass after glass of wine, rendering
their tongues looser than they might otherwise have
been. I'd overheard more than one of them complaining
that it was such a waste that Mother was marrying Mr.
Fitzwilliam.

"Such a shame," one guest murmured, voice full of
false sympathy. "She's so beautiful, and from such a good
family, and he no more than a merchant! Ah, well, I suppose there are other . . . advantages . . . to this match."

At the time, I wasn't sure exactly what they were referring to. What advantage could they be speaking of? Looking back, I understand that it was because Mr. Fitzwilliam
was a startlingly attractive man. Even now, many years

hence, aged and going gray at the temples, he maintains a handsome and striking visage. But at the age of eleven I was oblivious to such things. Also, Mother had done a careful job of hiding our dwindling finances from the world, so while I knew she needed Mr. Fitzwilliam's money, many of those in our social circles did not. Of course, no one knew about Hortense's illness and that this wedding had become necessary to revive her.

Still, I was indignant on Mr. Fitzwilliam's behalf. Our newly formed understanding left me in the position of wanting to defend him. How dare they say he wasn't good enough for Mother! And what did it say about Mother that these people thought she was incapable of choosing her own companion? Mostly, though, I did not understand at the time that in our social circles and situation marriages were made for lots of reasons, very few of them for love. What was so obvious to me was that Mother and Mr. Fitzwilliam loved each other deeply and terribly, so much so that they were willing to risk it all rather than be apart. If Mother also needed to marry again so that she could support her children, who were any of these people to judge her? Mr. Fitzwilliam brought her both companionship and wealth, both of which she desperately needed. Naively, I assumed that all of this must be obvious to everyone. How could anyone look at our family and think that anything other than love would make all of this worthwhile? It did not occur to me then that not everyone had the same view I did, and that my view was somewhat simplistic. The guests at the wedding were not privy to the many changes we'd been forced to make due to Cinderella, nor should they be. That had been impressed upon me most firmly the day before.

"And remember," Mr. Fitzwilliam had finished after giving me an exhaustive list of tasks that I could confidently command Cinderella to perform during the reception, when it would look odd and suspicious for the new groom to have abandoned his bride to spend time with his daughter, "Tell no one. Cinderella is our secret. Part of this is personal interest on my part—it is hard to be a respected merchant when your daughter is known as some sort of monster. But in a much more practical sense, the more people who know about Cinderella, the more risks we take. The more people who fear her, the more opportunities she has to grow. Do you understand me?"

I said I did, and then we'd gone over the rules again. It was the first time I was in charge of Cinderella when other people were around, and Mr. Fitzwilliam was understandably nervous and wanted to make sure everything went according to plan. After all, the last time he'd introduced Cinderella to new people, she'd bitten Hortense and we were still dealing with the consequences. With Cinderella, it didn't do to take chances.

So at the reception I was the Cinderella-minder. Hortense was having the time of her life, flitting from guest to guest and smiling her large, gap-toothed smile, beaming at everyone around her. For the first time since Cinderella had bitten her, Hortense had an appetite, and she was making the most of the little hors d'oeuvres scattered around the room. She'd grab a tiny pastry, stuff it into her mouth, and then run off to tell some indulgent guest how she was getting a new papa *and* a new sister.

My experience of the wedding was somewhat less charming. I stayed within arm's reach of Cinderella at all times. I was still leery of making direct contact with her skin, although Mr. Fitzwilliam assured me that once he and my mother were wed, the danger was over. I wore long silk gloves, which probably looked ridiculous on a girl of eleven years. At the time, I thought I looked very elegant and dashing.

My job was largely to keep Cinderella focused on various menial tasks and allow her to be seen by our guests without touching or directly interacting with them in any way. Cinderella was also wearing long gloves, in an effort on our part to keep everyone safe. But that was just a precaution. The real first line of defense was me.

Cinderella was enjoying the opportunity to wear a fancy new dress, with her hair done up in beautiful silk ribbons that Mr. Fitzwilliam had given her the night before. I think she liked the way people looked at her, admiring her, cooing over her appearance. She looked as enchanting as ever, with her ringlets and her delicately blushing cheeks and her large eyes. I could see she was beautiful but in an abstract way. Her beauty no longer spoke to me as something lovely and desirable. I'd seen those green, rotting eyes too many times in my dreams to fall for that trick. Just because they were a normal clear green today didn't mean they couldn't become a mucky, rotten mess at a moment's notice.

The plan was to have us children present and seen by all of the guests for a short time and then sent off to bed. It might be seen as unusually strict, given that it was a party, but it was the sort of strictness that no one would question. If it was odd, it was odd in the usual human way, and not in the way of something eldritch in nature that needed to be hidden from the world. With this plan I just had to survive with Cinderella for an hour at the party, and then we could take our leave. Cinderella had already been instructed not to harm any guests, in the most specific and wide-ranging set of commands possible, so my job was to protect our secret and keep

Cinderella from doing anything obviously strange that might attract the attention of the guests.

We stood near the largest table, which was weighed down with elaborate foodstuffs. No expense had been spared. There were dozens of delicacies: tiny fried tidbits, teensy hard-boiled quail eggs, succulent pieces of crystalized fruit, along with a sea of sauces to dip these dainty morsels into. There were also larger treats, such as a beautifully glazed ham cut into wafer-thin sheets with apple slices arranged like petals on the surface, and loaves of bread decorated with elaborate patterns etched into their thick crusts. The crowning glory of it all was a towering jelly, which wobbled gently every time someone grabbed another bite from the table. It was truly a masterpiece, the body formed by a clear, red-tinted jelly in which a myriad of individual fruit pieces were suspended. The edges were decorated with delicate crystalized mint leaves and cherry blossoms, which looked almost like gemstones with the way their layers of sugar caught and sparkled in the light. At the top, an exuberant display of candied citrus peels made for a festive hat. The whole thing was at least three feet tall, and that plus the additional height of the table meant that it was taller than I. The guests were appropriately in awe of this spread, although many of them took this as an excuse to gossip about money and speculate as to which newlywed was really marrying up.

Mother and Mr. Fitzwilliam were off mingling with the guests, although more than once I caught them shooting nervous glances at us. Mr. Fitzwilliam gestured at me to get on with it. Time to begin my new role as Cinderella's minder.

"Cinderella," I said, capturing her attention from where she'd been staring, head cocked, at a group of women wearing extremely frilly dresses. "Using your hands and your human mouth, eat one of the olive canapés on that table. Please." I didn't know if politeness helped, but I figured it couldn't hurt anything.

Cinderella cocked her head at me but reached out toward the table. I'd positioned us near a doorway, close enough that if she started to do anything too odd I could yank her out of sight. She grabbed a fat green olive, stuffed with some sort of stinky cheese, and put it into her mouth. Everything about her movements was too slow and slightly too practiced. Again I was reminded of a doll that someone else was making mimic eating but that had no desire to eat on its own.

Despite her awkwardness, Cinderella ate the olive without incident. I watched her chew for what felt like an impossibly long time and then swallow. Her throat bobbed, and the olive made it down. She turned to me with a wicked gleam in her eyes, and I watched as her stomach and throat rippled, just a little. It hit me what she was trying to do.

"Cinderella," I said sharply, "do not throw up that olive."

She glared at me and turned her head away, sullen. I was beginning to understand that she didn't talk very often. I wasn't sure if it was because she couldn't always form words in the various permutations of her body or because she chose not to. I still don't know. I would become very familiar with all of Cinderella's silences over the coming years, but I did not need extensive experience to know that she was mad at me for spoiling her fun. I took that moment as a win. Her spitting up an olive wouldn't have been the end of the world, since children spit things up out of distaste all the time, but it still felt good to have seen through her tricks and prevented an issue.

We worked our way through the rest of the canapés. After the stuffed olives, I successfully commanded Cinderella to consume a meat pie (which she tried to swallow whole, until I instructed her to chew), a quail egg (she tried to eat it with the shell on, but I anticipated this fairly easily), and a piece of candied ginger. She did not try to circumvent me with the candied ginger; I think she must have enjoyed it.

Due to her strange and precise way of eating, and the time it took for me to issue commands, eating four tiny canapés had taken us half an hour. I allowed myself to relax a little. We only had to survive for thirty more minutes, and then Mother would usher us off to bed. I still had to undergo the ordeal of locking Cinderella up myself, something I wasn't looking forward to, but Mr. Fitzwilliam and I had been practicing. I knew I could do it, but I still carried some anxiety.

It turns out I was worrying about entirely the wrong thing. As soon as I began to think that my evening would not be so terrible, I felt Cinderella stiffen with excitement next to me. She reminded me of a hunting dog locked onto her prey. I followed her gaze, and my heart leapt into my throat.

Sitting on the floor, sniffing the air with an acute interest, separated from us only by the length of the buffet table, sat a small, plump brown mouse. This mouse was unfazed by all of the well-polished shoes that were passing it by on all sides, and the cacophony of noise that is only truly producible by a wedding party full of slightly drunk guests. Truly, the bravery of this mouse cannot be overstated.

For a moment, I panicked, my eyes darting between Cinderella and the hapless mouse. Cinderella's gaze never wavered, her horrible green eyes intent on the mouse's every movement.

To this day, I do not know how we avoided detection. We were not exactly subtle in our actions for the next few minutes.

What happened was this: Cinderella, having locked in with single-minded focus on the mouse, pounced. I watched in horror as her teeth elongated, her eyes turned the color of mold and sludge, and her limbs took on a liquid quality that no human body could ever hope to emulate. Desperate to keep her from exposing us all, I did the only thing that my eleven-year-old brain could think of. I tackled her into the buffet table.

Cinderella shrieked, a high-pitched, terrible sound. I prayed fervently that it would be mistaken for the normal sound of a girl in distress, and that the guests would not take it as the inhuman sound that it was.

It was just my luck that due to the angle and force of my tackle, I knocked her directly into that masterful centerpiece, that mountain of culinary achievement—the glorious jelly. In some ways we were lucky; the jelly broke our fall in a way that the tureens of sauces and soups would not have. There were no dangerous knives sticking out of the jelly, ready to stab into us at a moment's notice. Instead there was just an unholy mess.

No part of us remained unscathed. Red globs of gelatin and fruit dripped from Cinderella's hair, her perfect ringlets weighed down and flattened by the sheer preponderance of jelly stuck in her hair. Her beautiful dress, once a lovely yellow color, had huge red stains smeared across it, which even my unpracticed eye could tell were going to be nigh impossible to get out of the delicate fabric.

I myself had not fared much better. My face had landed squarely in the midst of the jelly, and I swallowed a mouthful of the concoction. It was absolutely as delicious as it looked. I had the stray thought that I would be the only one to taste it now, since no one else would want to eat it after Cinderella and I had fallen into it. My own hair was soaked in jelly as well, and I could feel the contents of a bowl of sauce dripping down the back of my neck. I reached my hand up and gave in to the inane urge to taste the sauce. It was mint.

Even now, I do not know what stayed Cinderella's hand. I had given no orders. I had left myself open to retaliation. Yet she did not lash out at me, as I would have expected. Nor did she reveal herself to all those around us. Instead, she just wailed her frustration and rage to the sky. Perhaps she was just surprised. Being tackled into a buffet table is not on anyone's list of expected consequences, not even such a dark being as Cinderella. Or perhaps it was merely that she did not have time to enact her great and terrible revenge before Mr. Fitzwilliam was at our side, almost as quickly as if he had flown there.

At this point I noticed that all the guests were staring at us in a shocked silence, waiting to see what would happen next. Mr. Fitzwilliam reached out to both of us and, taking a wrist in each of his strong hands, he hauled us up from the jelly into a standing position.

Once removed from the dessert I could see the extent of the havoc we had wreaked on the table. I had been so focused on the destruction of the many-layered jelly that I had not noticed the rest. Quail eggs lay smashed on the ground, and every single sauce had managed to spill. The stuffed olives that I'd coaxed Cinderella into eating earlier rolled disconsolately on the ground, wondering what they had done to deserve such a fate. Loaves of bread lay crushed, candied fruit shattered, and the glorious ham, while not directly impacted by our fall, was spattered with the remains of every other dish on the table. It was a disaster, but as I frantically looked over the tableau, I relaxed. The mouse was nowhere in sight.

Mr. Fitzwilliam must have seen something in my gaze, but at this point it was out of our hands. We each had a part to play in order to keep people's suspicions from turning to Cinderella, and his was the role of the angry parent.

"What is the meaning of this!" he roared. I hung my head, shamming repentance. He gave me no chance to respond before he began yelling again.

"You should be ashamed of yourself! The wedding is no time for your sibling rivalry! I think it is well past time we put an end to this. Cinderella, come with me. I'll help you get cleaned up and I'll fetch you a snack before bed. Eunice—go to your room! I will deal with you later."

I hoped the guests were fooled by our charade. Somehow I knew what he was really saying: he would put Cinderella back in her cellar and I could flee upstairs to clean off, where he'd come talk to me after the wedding. I indeed fled, feeling a strange joy at having thwarted Cinderella, but as I left the room the shame grew in me as I heard the whispers and comments of the invited guests.

"Such a shame . . . Clearly not as well-bred as Cinderella . . . Does she have no manners? Such a plain little child . . . What can you expect? Such ugly behavior . . . Her poor mother . . ."

Their comments were too much for me, and even though I still believed in my heart that what I'd done was the correct course of action given the circumstances, I felt hot tears prick at my eyes. But I dared not dash them away. This was the beginning of my reputation as an unpleasant, uncooperative girl. Back then, however, I was not thinking of such things. I was just an eleven-year-old girl with too much responsibility thrust upon her. I hung my head and tried to hide that I was crying until I made it up to my room and threw myself, food-covered clothes and all, into my bed, where I sobbed myself to sleep.

Several hours later, I was awakened by a gentle rap at my door. I grunted some sort of response and the door swung open. On the other side stood Mother, looking beautiful but tired in her wedding clothes, and Mr. Fitzwilliam behind her. They came into the room and sat down on my bed, one on either side of me. I pressed myself into Mother's lap, feeling like a much younger child. She stroked my hair and Mr. Fitzwilliam rubbed gently at my shoulder.

Haltingly, with not a few tears, I told them everything. I told them about my early experimentation commanding Cinderella to eat the olive. I told them about the mouse. I told them about my fear and how my mind went blank when I didn't know what to do. I sobbed into my mother's lap, sure that I had ruined us all, for now people were going to talk, and that was what we had been trying to avoid.

"You've done very well, child," said Mr. Fitzwilliam, his voice gruff. He cleared his throat a few times, and I realized that he too had been crying. "You kept Cinderella from exposing herself to the world."

"But I ruined the buffet!" I cried. "Everyone was talking about how terrible I was! I drew so much attention to the family."

Mother smoothed back my hair and spoke in low, soothing tones.

"Darling, they do that because they don't know. You know these people. They wish to gossip about any old thing. I'm sure you heard them say worse about me tonight."

I kept silent, because I had but didn't want to admit it. What child wants to tell her own mother that she's heard the terrible things people say about her?

Mr. Fitzwilliam cut in again.

"Also, while you did draw attention, and people will be talking, this is not the worst situation possible. People look at today's wedding and see ill manners, and jealousy, and a scandal . . . but that's it. They have a perfectly mundane explanation for what happened, and they will not bother to look further. I assure you, whatever things they have to say about us cannot possibly be as damaging as what would have happened had she been allowed to ingest that mouse. I commend you, Eunice, and I thank you. Your quick thinking prevented a good deal of problems, and quite possibly prevented an outbreak of violence as well. You have behaved admirably, and you have surpassed my wildest expectations when I put you in charge of Cinderella's care for the evening."

His words bolstered me and I felt a surge of hope, like maybe with enough effort on my part I could forcibly make this family work.

It was not enough. My parents, as well-prepared as they thought they were, had made one enormous miscalculation when they planned out the lives of our strange little family. That miscalculation was Hortense.

8

A Problem of Attitude

Hortense's glee from the wedding did not last long. After receiving a more age-appropriate explanation of how things in the house were going to work with Cinderella around, Hortense let her true feelings be known. She was not happy about having Cinderella as a sister. I suppose that's understandable, seeing as she was only five at the time and had been expecting a new playmate and confidant. She'd been expecting another me, I think. I wish even now that there was any way I could have given it to her. Mother and I had the conversation with her together, in her room. It was midday, when the sun was strongest. Mr. Fitzwilliam wasn't sure if the power of the sun had any restraining effect on Cinderella, but we thought it wise to give ourselves any possible advantage.

"So she can't play with me?" Hortense asked, lip trembling. I saw her fidgeting at the scar on her finger with her thumb. The scar was white and eerily cold to the touch. It looked almost like a ring made of ivory or bone. She would have it for the rest of her life.

"No, my sweet," said Mother. "It's too dangerous to play with Cinderella. Remember, we have to be careful around her."

"Well, what if I want her to go bug collecting with me?" asked Hortense. "Bug collecting isn't playing. Maybe we could do that together instead?"

Mother shook her head. "I'm afraid bug collecting is also too dangerous. Cinderella needs to stay in her room, and she can't do much bug collecting from there."

Hortense considered this, her pudgy face solemn.

"But Eunice can still play with me?" she asked. "And collect bugs with me? And read to me?"

"Of course she can," said Mother. "Unless she's taking care of Cinderella, Eunice will be free to play with you like always."

Hortense pouted.

"I want Eunice and Leo," she said, in her determined little way.

Mother and I exchanged a glance.

"Leo's gone away, darling. He couldn't stay here." We'd made the decision to leave out Cinderella's role in Leo's departure. Hortense was struggling enough with the new status quo.

That was not what Hortense wanted to hear, although thankfully she didn't question us further about Leo's absence. Her little frown grew thunderous.

"So Cinderella can't play, can't collect bugs, I can't have a pet rat, and Eunice will spend less time with me?" Hortense asked. Mother nodded, and Hortense exploded.

"I don't want a new Cinderella sister!" she cried. "I don't need one! What good is she? Eunice is my *real* sister. Cinderella is not my sister!"

At those words, the scent of rot and decay filled the room. Mother and I watched in horror as Hortense's wound from Cinderella's bite mark, long since healed up, split open before our very eyes. Instead of blood, a thick, foul-smelling green sludge gushed from the wound, dripping over Hortense's hand. It was the exact color of Cinderella's eyes.

"Adrian!" screamed Mother. We'd elected to have this conversation without him, just the three of us, in the hopes that it would go over better coming from Hortense's mother and sister. That was clearly an error.

Hortense screamed, and Mr. Fitzwilliam burst into the room. The blood drained from his face and he fell to his knees in front of her, one of his ever-present handkerchiefs already out. With a haste that I only saw him exhibit in matters related to Cinderella, he wiped the sludge from her hand, attempting to keep it off of the rest of her skin. It didn't matter, because as he touched her skin, Hortense heaved, a horrible, wrenching sound that started deep in her stomach and traveled up through her torso and into her neck. Mr. Fitzwilliam looked up in alarm, but it was too late. Hortense regurgitated a deluge of thick, swampy green liquid all over his face. It stuck in his hair, got in his eyes, and stained his neatly pressed white shirt a horrid swamp green color. The stench filled the room, causing all of us to cough and gag. I narrowly avoided imitating Hortense by spewing the contents of my own stomach onto the floor to mingle with whatever foul excrement was coming from her mouth.

With one last spout of vomit, Hortense's eyes rolled back into her head, and she collapsed to the floor. Mother and Mr. Fitzwilliam were on their knees, carefully cleaning up the green sludge. Wherever it touched Hortense, it sizzled slightly, leaving a slowly worsening burn on her skin. Mother and Mr. Fitzwilliam frantically wiped away the sludge, which left them unharmed, despite the damage it was doing to Hortense. The price of her repudiation. I stood paralyzed, uncertain how best I could help.

Mr. Fitzwilliam caught my eye, and without ceasing in his ministrations to Hortense, he spoke. "Eunice, please go down and see if you can do something with Cinderella. Reinforce your ties with her. She's sensed the weakening of the familial bond, and combined with her previous experience with Hortense, I'm afraid she's very much taken advantage. Go see what you can do to remind her that she is part of this family, and that Hortense is too."

I nodded, although my heart was in my throat. It was my first solo visit to Cinderella. Since Mr. Fitzwilliam had managed to bundle Cinderella off in the aftermath of the jelly debacle at the wedding, my previously scheduled first solo visit had been canceled. I had never gone without Mr. Fitzwilliam before, and all of his many warnings and the things I'd seen in the cellar before swam in front of my eyes. Nevertheless, I picked up my skirts and made my way to the cellar.

At the top of the stairs I paused, my earlier, ill-conceived late-night journey to visit Cinderella weighing heavily on my mind. Mr. Fitzwilliam had stopped me then, but now, in the light of day, he trusted me enough to go alone. I squared my shoulders and descended into the cellar.

Once in the cellar, I ran into the first problem of my solitary visit. The iron door, which Mr. Fitzwilliam swung open with ease, was impossibly heavy for a young girl. Still, I was determined. I ran back up the stairs and grabbed a thick stick of wood from next to one of the fireplaces. I used it as a lever to pry the door away, and although I was panting and red-faced with exertion, I was also flush with success. The first door was pulled back, and I was face to face with Cinderella, all on my own.

My exultation faded as I faced the reality of being alone in the cellar with the same creature that was currently causing Hortense to purge a river of green sludge from her mouth upstairs. Thankfully, we still had metal bars between us, but at that moment they felt very flimsy. I steeled myself and peered into the gloom.

Cinderella was sitting on her bed, head cocked in her customary fashion. She said nothing when I entered. But I didn't let that discourage me, choosing instead to make assertive eye contact, unconsciously mirroring what I had seen Mr. Fitzwilliam do.

"Hello, Cinderella," I said. "How are you today?" Again, I copied Mr. Fitzwilliam, trying to embody his confidence and nonchalant manner.

"Hello, Eunice," she said, voice clear and sweet like a ringing bell. "I am doing well. How are you?"

I decided that this was my opening.

"Well, Cinderella, I'm actually not doing very well, to be honest," I admitted. I had to play this carefully. It needed to be believable.

She cocked her head in the other direction, her perfect features unconcerned, but I saw a glint of her true nature in her eyes. I had to be so, so careful. That was the look of an apex predator looking for weakness, and I had just admitted to one.

"You see," I continued, "Recently, it has come to my attention that my two sisters haven't been getting along, and that makes me sad. I don't like it when family fights."

Cinderella recoiled from my words, pushing herself further into the gloom.

"She repudiated me," Cinderella growled. I heard the strange harmonics in her voice that I'd heard before, the rasp and hiss of a voice not meant for human ears. "She repudiated me, and I cannot be bound to those not of my kin."

My heart was pounding in my throat, but I forged ahead.

"That's just part of how being sisters works," I said. "Families fight, and then they make up and move on. We need to be able to get past this. It's part of what being a good sister means—letting things like this go. Besides, if you're my sister, and she's my sister, how could the two of you possibly be anything other than sisters as well?"

Cinderella hissed at me then, a sound that spoke of stars from another time and place, opening her mouth wide and revealing a long, writhing tentacle in the place where her tongue should be. It lashed out across the room toward me, but I did not flinch. It was not out of bravery or anything like that. I was frozen with fear, unable to move as the thing whipped across the cellar and stopped just inside the door of iron bars. I felt something hot run down my leg, and I thought I would die of shame for the second time this week. My bladder had released, and hot piss was soaking into my underwear and stockings.

"So," I said, eager to finish this confrontation, deciding that I had done what I could, "Hortense is still your sister. She is family. You must leave her alone."

Ignoring the pulsing and lashing tentacle, I heaved the outer door closed with a strength I didn't know I had, and then turned and bolted up the stairs. I had no concern for my dignity or saving face—I just needed to be gone from that cellar. I did not stop until I was back upstairs, in Hortense's room with my family once more.

The scene was much how I left it. Green sludge spilled down Hortense's front, and Mr. Fitzwilliam and Mother were also covered in the stuff. Mr. Fitzwilliam had somehow managed to get his hair drenched in the goo, and it made him look like he'd dyed his hair green. Mother's hands were covered, and I could tell she'd been holding Hortense up by the particular spray pattern on her hands and dress. The key difference between how I left them and when I came back was that Hortense was no longer actively vomiting. She was weak, and pale, but she had ceased to spew noxious sludge into the room. The stench of what remained was still horrible, still the smell of rot and decay and dying things, but in that moment I was almost glad of it, because it meant no one would pick up the acrid scent of urine and know that I had been such an utter coward in the face of Cinderella.

Looking back, I have no judgment in my heart for my eleven-year-old self. I wish I could tell her that braver folk than her had faced down Cinderella and done much worse than a bit of piss. But at the time it was shameful, and I felt certain that I was too old for these things. So I was humiliated but also glad that Hortense was improving, that my efforts with Cinderella seemed to have worked, and that no one would know of my cowardice.

Hortense was pale and weak for a few days, but then she bounced back to her normal, lively self. Until the next time she repudiated Cinderella. And the next. And the next.

By the time I was eighteen and Hortense was twelve, she had been drained by Cinderella many, many times, and yet she refused to stop rejecting Cinderella as her sister. The reasons varied. Once, Cinderella broke one of her bug jars. Another time, Cinderella was fractious at her breakfast, refusing to eat unless I carefully instructed her on how to consume each bite of food, causing me to be late to a meeting with Hortense to take her to the river and sketch turtles. Another time, it was because Mr. Fitzwilliam accidentally fed a page of Hortense's notes on the robins that lived outside of her windows to Cinderella, which I found particularly unfair, because that was Mr. Fitzwilliam's fault.

For the next seven years, I would be Cinderella's caretaker. I fed her, I cleaned up after her, and gave her commands that were harmless and time consuming to keep her well exercised. I told no one of my struggles, having learned my lesson with Leo and Mr. Calton. As a result, I had few friends. I called her sister, even when I was alone, even in the dark of night when I awoke from my nightly terrors, covered in sweat. I was a devoted daughter to my parents and a model sister to both Hortense and Cinderella.

Hortense, on the other hand, kept rejecting Cinderella at the slightest provocation. Hortense spent weeks of her life in bed, pale and clammy, driving the rest of us sick with worry. And yet no matter what Cinderella threw at her, Hortense maintained that stubborn, fiery core of defiance. In the end, it would cost her everything.

Part 2

Seven Years Later

9

Visiting the Marketplace

"HORTENSE!" I YELLED, pounding on her door. "Hurry up, you're going to be late to breakfast! I need to feed Cinderella before breakfast, and I'm not skipping again, so if you want help with your hair, you better get up now!"

A muffled thump came from inside the bedroom, and a sleepy-eyed Hortense opened the door.

At twelve, she was a very different child than she'd been at five. Gone was the happy, carefree girl of my youth. In her place was a nervous, suspicious adolescent, who was at times listless and weak, unwilling or unable to do what was asked of her. The jars of bugs in her rooms remained, but they had been joined by birds with broken wings, tubs full of frog spawn, and snakes that she'd captured in the garden. Hortense's love for all things creepy and crawly had only grown with time. I'd once joked that she should get along better with Cinder-ella, since she liked creepy things so much, and Hortense hadn't spoken to me for a week, then repudiated Cinder-ella at the end of it. I was sure it was out of spite for me.

Mother assured me that this was usual in children of Hortense's age, and that she would grow out of it, but that did not sit well with me. I had been her age—nay, a little younger—when Cinderella first came to live with us, and I had not once rejected Cinderella or had even a tenth of Hortense's bad attitude.

Hortense peered at me from the door of her room, and I saw that she'd added another bookshelf to her collection of many creatures. It was full of her journals, where she'd take notes and draw pictures of the various animals she collected and observed. On Hortense's face I saw the same bags under her eyes that were under mine. She saw me looking and self-consciously reached up to touch her face. I grimaced in sympathy. The night terrors were never kind to either of us.

"Come back later," she said. "You can do my hair after breakfast. I have important things to do. The snake eggs are about to hatch, and I want to document it. Besides, it won't be fun if you have to run off to take care of that—"

I interrupted her before she could get any further.

"Can we please not do this today?" I begged. "We did this just last week, and I hoped to go to the market today. If you're sick all day, I'll have to cancel my trip. Also, I'm going to pretend I didn't hear you say that you have snake eggs in your room."

Hortense rolled her eyes, but thankfully she acquiesced.

"Fine. It won't be as much fun if you have to run off to take care of our darling and beloved sister, who is of course an integral part of our family." Her words dripped sarcasm, but that was fine. Cinderella didn't have a grasp on sarcasm, so as long as Hortense said the literal words, it was fine.

I sighed with relief, but Hortense was not done.

"Of course, hypothetically . . ." she said, and I tensed up once again. Cinderella also didn't understand hypotheticals, so it was technically safe, but a hypothetical from Hortense usually meant she was going to turn it into reality. "Hypothetically," she continued, "someone could be building up a resistance to their sister slash not sister, if they had repeatedly repudiated her over the years. Like with certain poisons, where repeated small doses build immunity. Hypothetically," she added again. I glared at her, not wanting to deal with this.

"That had better stay a hypothetical, Hortense. I don't understand why you can't just say the words! It doesn't have to mean anything! Quit fighting it, and everything will be better!" It was a familiar argument. I thought she needed to toe the line and do what was necessary for the family. Hortense thought I needed to stop jumping at Mr. Fitzwilliam's every whim. I always responded that I thought she liked Mr. Father, as I'd come to affectionately call him over the years, to which she'd throw up her arms and complain that I was missing the point.

Today, however, it seemed that Hortense wasn't actually looking to pick a fight with me.

"Of course, of course," she agreed readily. "Just a hypothetical. Anyway, I can't reject Cinderella today. I'll miss the snake egg hatching. So you'll come do my hair later? I want it to look nice for Mother's birthday tonight." Technically, Mother's birthday had been last week, but none of us had much felt like celebrating. A rat had gotten into the house, and Cinderella had gotten hold of it before any of us had realized. The aftermath had been unpleasant. Even thinking about it now caused me to shiver. I pulled myself back to my conversation with Hortense and agreed.

"I'll come back later, but it won't be until after I get back from the market. Do you need anything?"

"No," said Hortense. "Well, actually—honeycomb, if you can get it. I want to see if my grubs will eat it." She graced me with a brief smile and then closed the door in my face. I sighed. Despite the relatively peaceful interaction, Hortense was still Hortense: stubborn and sometimes difficult. Also disgusting. I didn't want to think about grubs living in my home. It was bad enough that Cinderella lived with us without having Hortense bring home all manner of horrible creatures. But by god, I loved Hortense fiercely. It occurs to me now that Hortense may have taken my loyal insistence that Cinderella was our sister as a rejection of our own sisterly bond, but nothing could have been further from the truth. Hortense was always my priority, even when making room for Cinderella in our home.

I contemplated my impending visit with Cinderella on my way down to the cellar, the path now well-worn and familiar. Breakfast was my job. Mother was in charge of lunch, and Mr. Father took dinner. Originally there'd been some talk of having Hortense and me take turns with breakfast, but it quickly became clear that was not a good idea.

I grabbed a basket of eggs from the shelf and tossed in a half loaf of stale bread and an apple that was starting to go bad. Cinderella preferred her food slightly past its prime. At first I had been afraid that giving it to her would somehow increase her powers, but mostly it just seemed to make her slightly more tractable, so I fed her scraps and leftovers and things that were not really fit for human consumption.

One of the new cooks gave me a dark look as I collected Cinderella's breakfast, but I ignored him. Many of the servants thought we were absolutely monstrous for the way in which we treated Cinderella, but that was a small price to pay for privacy and safety. Besides, any servants who stuck around long enough usually figured out that there was something not right about Cinderella, and then they'd usually soften toward me, although I don't know how many of them jumped to the conclusion that she was a monster. New staff were always awed by her beauty and couldn't believe that we would treat our own sister in such a way. As I left the kitchen, I heard the new cook say to Mrs. Carnelian, our head chef, "Imagine treating your own sister that way!"

"You hush," said Mrs. Carnelian. "You mind your own business, and don't make things harder for that poor girl than they already are. Eunice has enough on her plate without you butting in about things you don't understand."

"But to keep her locked in the cellar!" exclaimed the new cook, whose name I didn't know. "And have you seen the things they feed her?"

"Listen to Mrs. Carnelian," said another voice. Lilia, a newish maid in the house, must have been in the kitchen as well. I was surprised to hear her speak up. Normally she just gave me wide-eyed looks and then hurried away from me. I thought she was afraid of me. "You'd be wise to respect Miss Eunice. How she goes down there into the cellar to be with that girl every day, I don't know. She's far braver than I! I'd never go down there alone. I hate even having to clean the stairs, and Mr. Fitzwilliam always has me do it at noon, with the door to her room closed, and him watching, and it's still the scariest moment of my week! So you just listen to Mrs. Carnelian and keep your nose out of the family's business. They're doing the best they can."

I was touched by this defense. I hadn't realized that Lilia thought so highly of me, and I tucked that information away. It was nice to know that not everyone thought me a heartless monster who was cruel to her sister, even if perhaps it would have been safer for the family if everyone did.

I descended the stairs and heaved open the door with little effort. Years of moving the solid iron construction had accustomed my muscles to the hard work, and I was now passably strong.

Over the years, Cinderella's cell had become further furnished as we provided her with more and more trinkets and objects. Where once a bare cellar with a few sticks of furniture had been, now there was a lavish bedroom fit for any wealthy young lady. Cinderella had rugs and armoires and mirrors and little tables, just like I had in my own room.

Cinderella sat on her bed, head cocked in her customary greeting. She had grown from a beautiful, doll-like child into an absolutely stunning young woman. Her hair now fell in gorgeous blonde waves, her lips were red and full, her skin unblemished by any of the spots and oiliness that my own was prone to.

"Good morning, Cinderella. I brought you a treat today." I tossed the apple into her cage. We didn't always have rotten fruit, but she loved it when we did.

Before the apple could even hit the ground, one of Cinderella's arms had shot out to grab it. It was not quite a tentacle, since she maintained a vague hand-shaped object at the end of the arm, tipped with wicked, curving talons. But the long, fluid nature of the arms reminded me of past tentacles that she had manifested over the years.

She sucked the apple into her arm by opening up small holes in the tips of her talons and slurping the pieces of rotten apple through them. I raised an eyebrow at her.

"Something got you upset today? It's just breakfast— why are you trying to scare me?"

Cinderella finished absorbing the apple, and her tentacle hand retreated. She picked up an egg when I proffered her the basket and swallowed it whole.

"Eunice, dear sister, I can smell it on you," she said, voice clear and sweet. There was no trace of her spooky harmonics, but the scent that accompanied her words, that of rotten wood and bread mold, left me in no doubt as to her mood.

"Ah, yes, I did get a new cat yesterday," I said. "A big friendly tom cat, only has one ear. I saw him last week when I went to get fresh eggs and told the farmer I'd pay good money for him. He agreed, but I didn't have the coins on me at the time, so I only went back and collected him yesterday. Last night he brought me a nice fat mouse, dropped it right in front of me, and I gave him a little saucer of cream as a thank you. He purred the whole time." Perhaps I shouldn't have rubbed it in, as I was definitely taunting her a little, but the last rodent incident was fresh in my mind. Cinderella had ruined Mother's birthday, and I was still upset with her. And now she was upset with me.

"That makes *six!*" she growled, and this time her voice was no longer sweet and clear, but full of the vibrations of far-off worlds and distant stars, something no human should ever hope to hear. I ignored it. I was used to it.

"Actually, it's ten cats total," I said cheerfully. "Mama M, who lives outside in the stables, just had four little babies yesterday. Two of them are calicos like her, one is all black, and one is a little gray stripey thing. She's an excellent hunter; I'm sure she'll teach her kittens all of her secrets. So that means we've got four adults outside, plus the four kittens, and two inside."

Cinderella's mouth curled into a disdainful sneer. "Two indoors is not enough," she threatened. "I will persevere. They can't catch all the rats and mice in the world."

I nodded, unconcerned. Despite what Cinderella might think, having ten cats around was certainly going to help with any rodents around the house. Our rat incidents had decreased sharply as soon as I started bringing pet cats home.

"I'm sure you will, sister dearest. Now finish your eggs, I want to go to the market today."

Cinderella let out a bloodcurdling shriek, but she was bound to follow my command. Her head unfurled like a flower blooming, and I could see the pieces of blood and flesh and viscera inside. I looked away. Cinderella could transform herself to try and frighten me all she wished, but I didn't have to look. I gave her time, and when I could no longer hear the wet squelching sound of a terrible monster consuming a basketful of eggs, I looked back. Cinderella was back in her human form, perched on the edge of the bed, her dress spotless. It always was. That was the one thing she didn't have in her little room—any sort of laundry hamper. She didn't need one. As she'd grown, we'd given her increasingly beautiful and lavish dresses, mostly as rewards for good behavior. But the dresses never seemed to wear out, or to become dirty, so we never supplied her with any way to clean them. Or worse, an opportunity for her to sneak out while someone was collecting her laundry.

I hurried up the stairs. Cinderella's little tantrum meant that her breakfast had taken more time than I had anticipated, and I really did want to go into town. I dropped off my basket in the kitchen and made my way to the dining room, where Mother and Mr. Father were having breakfast.

I gave them each a quick kiss on the cheek, grabbed a muffin and an apple, and promised to be home in time for dinner. I practically hurled myself out the door and began to walk, whistling to myself as I went.

I escaped the house at any opportunity. Those moments of time when I could leave Cinderella behind were my refuge. I picked up produce for our cook; I'd buy hats for Mother; I'd stock up on cigars for Mr. Father and his business meetings. The errand didn't matter; I would take any pretext to leave the house and spend a few precious minutes by myself.

The day was particularly fine, and I munched on my apple and my muffin as I walked into town. Officially, I was going to pick up a few things that had been forgotten during last week's shopping excursion, but really I was there for the announcement. Everyone in town had been abuzz with the news that the king was going to make an announcement. No one knew what it was, but rumors swirled that it had something to do with his only son, the exceedingly handsome Prince Credence. As the town closest to the royal palace, we were getting the news first.

As much as I tried to tell myself otherwise, I was as susceptible to good gossip as anyone else. I didn't really have anyone to share it with, but it made me feel connected, like I was part of something larger than myself. It was almost like having friends.

Since I didn't get my gossip the traditional way, by having a friend who would pass it along to me, or an acquaintance who knew I hungered for news, I had to resort to more unorthodox methods. To put it bluntly, I eavesdropped. I eavesdropped whenever I got the chance. I loved the tiny, fascinating glimpses into other people's lives—people who were not hiding a monster in their cellar. Or, if they were, they didn't let on in public. I was probably the best-informed person in town, the way I greedily sought out and hoarded the most trivial of information. I'm sure the rest of the townsfolk thought me standoffish and shy, but the truth was I just didn't trust myself. I knew the weight of the secrets I carried would be lessened by sharing—but then what? When someone else knew the secret of Cinderella, the safety of my family was no longer in my control. Better by far to find the joys of secondhand information, the thrill of passing unknown and yet knowing all.

So as I made my way into town, I was in high spirits. The prospect of news, plus some time away from the concerns of my family, was enough to put me in a good mood. I passed through town slowly, nodding at various people whose faces I recognized but speaking to no one. I still wonder how things might have been different if I'd had someone to confide in, or maybe if Hortense had. We were so isolated and alone, and I don't think we realized the toll that took on us both.

My first stop was, as always, the village message board. It was a plain piece of wood hung up at the entrance to the market. People posted little notes and bits of paper, searching for various items or looking to sell their goods. Today the area was brimming with people. Everyone wanted to get a look at the flyer detailing the king's forthcoming announcement. I decided to hang back and wait for the crowd to thin a little. Once everyone else had gotten their fill of the royal flyer, I could peruse the rest of the board at my leisure.

I made my way into the shade of a hat stall, preparing to settle down and observe the people around me, and keep an eye on the board so I could move in as the way became clear. So intent was I on paying attention to the crowd around the message board that I did not notice that there was already someone else hiding under the shade of the hat stand.

I bumped into them, quite hard, my face connecting with a solid shoulder. I hit my tooth in particular very hard—I must have hit a bone—and my nose went mashing into their collarbone.

We both yelped and sprang away from one another. I began stammering apologies even as I reached up to check my nose and my tooth. I prayed that my nose was not bleeding and that I would not lose the tooth. I was already a plain girl, with limp, straight hair, and perpetual bags under my eyes from the lack of sleep caused by night terrors. The loss of a tooth would tip me straight over into ugly.

"I'm so sorry," I stammered, gingerly feeling my nose with my hand. No blood, that was good, although I could tell it was going to be hot and swollen from the force of the blow. I tapped my tongue against my tooth, checking for looseness. It seemed firm enough, so I continued. "I wasn't looking where I was going. Please, if there is anything I can do to make up for it—"

It was then that I looked up and saw who I had run into. There, in front of me, stood none other than Prince Credence himself. His eyes were dark and piercing, his lips full and round, his skin emanated a warm dark glow. He was just as beautiful as everyone had always said. The royal portraiture that I had seen did not do him justice.

"Prince Credence!" I gasped. I shook my head and looked again, worried that I had somehow addled my brain in the collision. What would the prince be doing here?

As I looked, I saw that while my first impressions of the prince were correct, there were some additional details that I had not initially noticed. He wore an orange silk scarf over his wildly curly hair and had it tipped forward so it shadowed his face. He was wearing gloves that covered his hands and arms up to the elbow and a large cloak obscured most of his body.

His eyes widened, and I had a sinking sensation in my stomach. Had I just offended him? Maybe I wasn't supposed to refer to the prince directly. Perhaps I should have called him "Your Highness"? I opened my mouth to apologize, but Prince Credence beat me to it.

"No!" he said, his voice deep and melodious. Despite myself, I swooned a little. "No, you've, ah, mistaken me! I'm not Prince Credence, ha ha! My name is . . . um . . . Colton!"

I looked at him, unconvinced. Mother had a portrait of King Reymond and Prince Credence in our formal parlor. She used it to impress members of her noble family that visited occasionally, but mostly we ignored that room. Still, he was a perfect match for the portrait.

Prince Credence sighed and seemed to give up. I found myself yanked further into the shadows, away from the prying eyes of the townsfolk. My heart did another flip-flop; I was alone with the heir to the throne! It was just like in one of my books!

"Fine—I am Prince Credence. How did you know it was me? I thought my disguise was foolproof! It got me past my royal guards, at least."

I furrowed my brow and gave him a confused look.

"You look exactly like your royal portrait. You just put on some gloves and a scarf. How exactly is that supposed to fool anyone?" I asked. I was genuinely curious. I had no experience with the motives of a prince, and I thought it would make a lovely addition to my collection to have that piece of information tucked away. Not to share, of course. I don't think I've ever shared any of the secrets I've learned, not even the big ones. Certainly not something as trivial as why the prince wanted to go sneaking out.

He sighed and tugged sheepishly at the scarf in question.

"It's actually something I borrowed from one of the palace mages. She comes and goes freely, and she always wears this orange scarf. I think the guards saw the flash of orange and just made their own assumptions."

His casual mention of the mages made me suck in a breath. I'd heard of them before, of course, and like any reasonable citizen, I feared them. Tales of their magics and deeds were widespread in the kingdom, ranging from the benign to the horrific, but it was their capacity for truth divining that I feared most. It was said that they could discern falsehoods based on the beat of a man's heart and know if a letter was true or not by the scent of the lady's perfume on the page. I couldn't afford to come into contact with someone who could so easily expose the truth about my family and Cinderella.

But Prince Credence himself was not a mage, and his explanation as to how he'd escaped made enough sense to me, even if I still thought his disguise was awful. But it didn't answer the most pressing question that I had.

"Why were you sneaking out of the palace?" I asked. "You're the prince. Aren't you in charge?"

He snorted. "You'd think that, wouldn't you? I snuck out because no one would tell me what today's announcement was about! There were all these rumors circulating that the announcement had to do with me, and whenever I asked Father he just told me not to worry about it, that he was taking care of things!" The prince's beautiful features were marred with frustration. I could understand somewhat the idea of not wanting your life controlled for you. God knows Hortense had given me enough lectures on the subject over the years, generally with a disapproving look on her face as I prepared something for Cinderella. Still, this wasn't my little sister—this was the crown prince. A thought occurred to me.

"Should you be telling me all this? You just met me, and you don't even know my name. What if I was trying to get close to you to find out and sell state secrets, or attempt a assassination?" I asked, quite reasonably in my opinion.

At the idea that I might be trying to plumb him for information or make an attempt on his life, Prince Credence looked more interested than anything else.

"Are you?" he asked.

"No!" I said. "But that's not the point! Also, you shouldn't just believe people when they tell you things when the stakes are so high!"

Prince Credence sighed, deflated. "Yes, Father says the same thing," he said gloomily.

"And you *still* don't even know my name."

"I can at least fix one thing. What's your name? I'm Credence."

"Yes, I know," I said. "We've been over this. Extensively. Oh, and my name is Eunice."

"Ah, good victory! Charmed, absolutely charmed." Prince Credence reached out a firm hand, and I shook it, surprised. I had no idea what he was talking about, but I wasn't about to let on to that. He continued.

"Is your family from around here?" he asked. I wasn't surprised. My name often garnered attention for being slightly unusual. Not many people commented on it, with most just assuming that I had an eccentric family. Well, they weren't wrong.

"Papa wasn't," I said, "But he died when I was five. Mother is from around here."

The prince nodded. "I'm sorry for your loss," he said, and his sincerity was apparent. Then again, it would be. Everyone knew that his mother the queen had also died when he was a boy. "Is it just you and your mother now?"

"No," I said reluctantly. I hated talking about my family, but I also needed to take this opportunity to mention Cinderella as my sister, to strengthen the bond. "Mother remarried when I was eleven, so I have a stepfather as well. And then there are my two sisters." I paused, not sure what else to say about my sisters to the future ruler of our kingdom. I couldn't exactly say that Cinderella was a being of unspeakable power and that Hortense derived her thrills from taunting her.

I was spared from answering further by the arrival of a thin, small man on a horse. He was immediately recognizable as the king's herald by his green and gold livery. As he entered the square, a loud murmur went around as everyone told their neighbor that the herald had arrived. Everyone strained eagerly to hear what he had to say, myself and Prince Credence included. Although I noticed that he pulled his scarf down over his eyes a bit in a vain attempt to make himself less noticeable. I had no idea how no one else noticed him. There was something about Prince Credence, besides just his royal status, that ensured that he always stood out in a crowd, and that day was no exception.

We listened with bated breath, waiting to hear what it was that the herald would say. He cleared his throat self-importantly, and then spoke in a loud, booming tone.

"To the royal subjects of His Majesty, King Reymond, I have an announcement on behalf of His Royal Highness. It is with great pride and pleasure that he announces that his only son and heir to the throne, Prince Credence, is now of eligible marrying age."

This announcement was greeted with a roar, as everyone began babbling at once, speculating on who his lucky bride was going to be. I glanced beside me and saw that the prince himself had gone utterly stiff in response to this news. He was clearly as shocked as any of the villagers. I saw dread in his eyes and knew that this was not what he would have chosen, if given even the slightest opportunity to influence his own destiny. I wanted to reach out, to offer comfort, but he was still the crown prince, and I was just me.

The herald harumphed and cleared his throat again, and the crowd fell silent. I was confused as to what else he could possibly have to say. So the prince was of marrying age—what did that have to do with us? He would get married to some princess he'd never met, and we would have a new queen. Still, it was new information, so with an apologetic glance at Credence, whose complexion had taken on a slightly gray tinge, I leaned back in with the rest of the crowd to hear what the herald had to say.

"In the interests of strengthening intra-country relationships, and in a show of good faith to the populace of the kingdom, it has been decided that the palace will host a series of balls, with the intent for the crown prince to choose his queen from among the attendees. All residents of the kingdom who can present a good faith case that their presence would be beneficial to the prince finding love are invited to attend."

The crowd exploded. The herald may well have had other information to impart, but after dropping that bombshell, there was no coming back. People babbled and shouted, and young ladies—and a few enterprising young men—all immediately began planning what they would wear, how they would arrive at the palace, and what they would do to catch the eye of the prince.

Credence and I were the only ones not making some kind of noise, tucked away in the shade of the hat stall.

I do not know what possessed me. It was none of my business; the crown prince was getting married—though he was much sweeter than I'd anticipated. Maybe it was that—the sweetness with which he greeted the world, and his willingness to spill his feelings to the first person who stopped and asked. Maybe he reminded me of Hortense, before she met Cinderella and began to change. Mostly, I think I just felt sorry for him.

I grabbed his hand and pulled him away from the excitable crowd. I threw the shawl I'd been wearing over his ridiculous orange scarf so that we'd attract less attention, and I navigated us away from the town square via back streets and alleyways, discretion being the product of my extensive experience eavesdropping on people.

We made our way to a small orchard at the edge of the city limits. Prince Credence looked awful, shocked and empty, although our brisk walk through the town meant he had lost some of the grayness from earlier.

I realized we were still holding hands, and I quickly released him. I didn't know if I'd overstepped my boundaries, and I didn't know what to say.

"So, you didn't know about this?" I ventured. It was a silly question, but I didn't have anything better. It was obvious that he'd had no idea what his father was planning.

He shook his head, still struck dumb with the weight of the announcement.

"Did you know he wanted you to get married?" I asked, hoping to draw him from his stupor.

Again he shook his head, but he looked up and took in our surroundings for the first time. Now that I know more about our crown prince, I think of that moment of sadness and innocence in the apple orchard and I blame myself for not realizing how easy it would be to deceive poor Credence. I wish that I had done more for him. Despite his naivete, he is as much a victim as the rest of us.

I reached out and touched him gently on the back of his hand, giving in to my desire to comfort him. He just looked so lost. Credence looked at the spot where my pale hand touched his much darker one but said nothing.

"Are you all right?" I asked. "Is there someone who can come get you?" I had nothing else to say, and I didn't know what to do with this man who had just had his autonomy ripped away from him.

He sighed and straightened up.

"I'm sure they'll be here shortly," he said, ignoring the first part of my question. "They always find me. I'm never able to escape for long. Thank you, though. Without your intervention, I'm sure I would have been caught much sooner."

I patted his hand once more, intending to pull away, but was startled when he grasped my hand tightly and pulled me to stand directly in front of him.

We were almost of the same height; I had perhaps an inch on him, but it wasn't very noticeable. It struck me that Credence was not very tall.

"Thank you," he said, in that ridiculously sincere way of his. He stared directly into my eyes. "I mean it. Not everyone would have helped me hide and talked to me, rather than making a scene and showing everyone where I was. I appreciate it." He glanced over my shoulder, and then looked back at me. I was too transfixed by his dark, intense gaze to even check on what he'd been looking at.

"My escorts have found me," he said. "So our acquaintanceship will necessarily have to come to an end—for now. But I hope to see you again soon. If nothing else, it would be nice to . . . to talk to you again, at one of the balls. If I may be so bold, I would welcome the chance to correspond with you. If you show this to the local postmaster, they should know what to do. But for now, I'll just say farewell, my Good Victory."

With those words, he pressed a small piece of paper into my hand. I nodded, struck dumb. He smiled at me once more, then let go of my hand and walked to the edge of the orchard, where two men dressed in the livery of the king stood waiting. They scolded him, but he appeared not to mind, taking it all in stride. As they escorted Prince Credence from the orchard, he looked over his shoulder at me and gave a small, friendly wave. I waved back, then looked at the note he'd shoved into my hand. In a fine, delicate hand, it read:

The bearer of this note has the permission of Prince Credence, heir to the throne, to send letters to the royal palace.

Underneath that note was the royal seal and Prince Credence's signature, all loops and curlicues. I stared at the note, unwilling to believe what I held. At that moment, nothing and no one could have prevented me from going to the balls.

10

In Which I Am Prevented From Going to the Ball

"BUT IT'S NOT *fair*," I screamed, red-faced and angry. "It says *everyone* is invited, and that means me! He specifically asked me to come! Why should I have to stay home?"

Mother and I were facing off in the middle of the dining room over the remains of her birthday dinner. Mr. Father and Hortense watched, wide-eyed and silent. The novelty of the situation had them hesitant to jump in. Generally, it was Hortense and Mother, or Hortense and Mr. Father, or Hortense and a passing breeze who would get into these sorts of screaming matches. I was always silent and supportive, the good daughter. But that day, something in me snapped. I had sacrificed enough. I was going to do something that I wanted, because I wanted it.

"The family has to come first! This business trip of Adrian's has been scheduled for months, with me going along with him, and you've known it! Besides, the prince gave you permission to write to him! You can just do that instead. We can't let you just leave to go to the ball for three nights in a row! What if something were to happen? Cinderella will need care, feeding, instructions, all of her usual routine, and your father and I won't be here to do it! Please, think of the family!" Mother yelled back at me. I couldn't remember the last time she'd yelled, but I think it was sometime shortly after Cinderella came to live with us, before we were used to the extra stress, responsibility, and sleepless nights.

"I'm part of this family!" I yelled back. "I *am* thinking of the family. Do you think it's going to help our family image if some nobody girl gets an invitation from His Royal Highness, Prince Credence himself, strikes up a correspondence with him, and decides to just *not show up at the ball*? How will that look? Don't you think people will question why?" I thought my logic impeccable, but Mother just snorted.

"You think he actually wants to see you again? He was just being polite! It's how they're raised, Eunice! I'm sure he hasn't given you a second thought since the orchard! And here you are, mooning over him like a silly little girl! It's time to grow up, Eunice!"

"You don't know that!" I roared, and then promptly burst into tears.

The effect on the room was like a pin stuck in a balloon. All the anger and tension bled out of the atmosphere, and it was just Mother breathing heavily, cheeks flushed, myself sobbing over my empty plate that the servants were too scared to come collect, and Hortense and Mr. Father still watching silently.

"I'm sorry, Eunice," said Mother at last. "He may well be thinking of you. I shouldn't have said that. But the fact remains that Cinderella needs care, and with your father and I gone, you're the only one who can do it."

Mr. Father nodded with great solemnity from his position at the other end of the table, but his eyes were sympathetic.

"I could do it."

None of us responded for a moment. The simple statement rang out like a glass shattering at a party, in that it sucked all the attention toward the sound as everyone tried to parse what had caused the unexpected noise.

Hortense sat at the table, the weight of our stares upon her. She shrugged.

"I'll do it. You're acting like Eunice is going to be alone with Cinderella in the house, but she's not. I'll be here too. I can help with whatever needs doing, and then Eunice can go to the ball and sweep the handsome prince off his feet." She shot me a wry look, and the small, crooked smile that I loved all the more for its rarity. "I'll even promise to do your hair, even though you weren't back in time to do mine." What with the excitement of meeting the prince, I'd been very late from my trip to the market, and I'd forgotten all about Hortense's hair. The cheek of her statement startled a wet, ugly laugh out of me, and I gave my best effort at continuing to cry while now laughing at the same time.

"Hortense, darling, you know that means, well . . . you'd have to interact with Cinderella. There would be no antagonizing her, no repudiating her, and making sure that you're following all the rules. Respecting her rules. You wouldn't be able to say that you were in the middle of an experiment and forget about her. It's, um . . ." said Mr. Father, as he tried to think of a way to be tactful. "It's not something you've ever showed an interest in before."

Hortense shrugged again.

"Well, she's my sister, isn't she? We make allowances for family. Eunice does it all the time—why shouldn't I?"

Mother beamed at Hortense and her newfound maturity, and Mr. Father clapped her on the back, excited that she was making such progress with her acceptance of Cinderella. I was not so sure. Hortense had looked directly at me as she spoke, leaving me in no doubt of who she meant when she said the word "sister." She was doing this for me, and not out of any familial feeling for Cinderella. Still, I was too giddy with relief to interrogate my feeling of suspicion further.

Just then, I was ecstatic. I leapt up from my chair and threw my arms around Hortense, still crying and laughing and smothering her in my arms.

"Stop, you're getting tears in my hair!" protested Hortense. "If you're going to be throwing your bodily fluids around, you could at least have the decency to put them in a glass jar, so I can look at them more closely later." It was such a Hortense thing to say that we all laughed, relieved. It looked like I would be able to go to the ball after all. My heart swelled and I went to bed floating on air that night.

11

A Letter and a Discovery

THE NEXT TWO weeks were peaceful. Hortense, for once, was agreeable about learning how to care for Cinderella, something she'd been actively sabotaging for years, and the result on the family was palpable. We smiled more, we had more patience and kind words for the servants, and we were in general less miserable. I think it took that misery lifting for us to see how miserable we had truly been. Those two weeks were among the happiest of my life.

The day after our blowup, the invitations arrived for the three Fitzwilliam girls.

"That's not my last name," I informed the royal courier, who had shown up with the mail.

"Ew," said Hortense. "I'm twelve. Am I of marriageable age to the prince? Isn't he thirty?"

"He's nineteen," I informed her. "The same age as Cinderella."

Hortense shot me a betrayed look, and the courier took this opportunity to interject.

"Look, I'm just here to drop off the invitations. Are there three girls who live here, daughters of Mr. Adrian Fitzwilliam and Bettina Constance?"

"Yes," Hortense and I chorused, and then glared at each other for answering in unison. I thought we'd outgrown that long ago.

"Then this is the right place. You can work out the rest of the details on your own." And with that, he was gone.

Hortense and I stared at each other some more, then giggled and went to pore over the invitations.

"I can't believe I'm invited," marveled Hortense. "It's so gross, but also vaguely . . . flattering? Anyway, while I will *not* be accepting this invitation, you will definitely have to memorize everything you see and tell me all about it."

"Of course I will," I said, smiling at her. "You'll be begging me to shut up about it before you know it!"

We both ignored that Cinderella was also technically invited. There was no way that she was going, so why bother discussing it?

I opened my invitation and another sheet of thick, creamy parchment fell out. Puzzled, I grabbed it. When I saw the signature at the bottom my heart soared. It was a letter from Prince Credence!

I couldn't believe he'd sent me something so quickly. I hadn't had a chance to write to him yet, what with the family fight the night before and my duties to Cinderella that morning. He'd beaten me to it.

I treasured every word. It went like this:

Dear Eunice,

Thank you again for rescuing me. I know I gave you a way to contact me before, but I wanted to include this note so you know I meant it! I don't get out much, so I didn't know how bad my disguise was. I asked one of the court magicians when I got back (the same one I borrowed the scarf from) and she said my disguise was terrible, and I should get down on my knees and thank you for saving me from myself by pointing out how terrible my disguise was. Also, she yelled at me for stealing her scarf, but I will say I think I deserved that.

I hope you write me back. Tell me more about yourself. What sort of things do you like to do? You said you have sisters. Do you get along? You mentioned that your father had died, and I really am sorry about that. I suppose you know that my mother is dead. Everyone does.

Before she died, Mother used to say it was rude to demand things of people that you weren't willing to do yourself, and I realized that I've done that to you, asking for more details without providing any myself. Let's see—here are some facts about me, which I hope will amuse you. I am an only child, my favorite color is purple, my favorite hobby is sneaking down to the kitchens and begging people to teach me how to cook things. I'm getting quite good at making orange raisin buns. I don't much like archery or swordplay, but Father says they are essential activities for a prince, so I sometimes am forced to do them anyway.

Hope this letter finds you well! Please write back!

Yours,
Credence

I squealed, clutching the letter to my chest. Hortense grabbed at it, but I pulled it out of her reach. She pouted at me.

"What does it say? Don't keep secrets from me now! Is it extra details about the ball? I should get to know even if I'm not going," she complained, grabbing at the letter again.

"It's . . . it's a letter from the prince," I stammered. "He wants me to write him back. He says he wants to know more about me."

Hortense's eyes widened. "Unbelievable," she said, voice full of awe.

I glared at her. "What's with the surprise?" I asked. "I told you I met Prince Credence in town and that I thought we had a connection!"

"Well, yes," said Hortense, shrugging. "But I assumed it was just you being fanciful. I didn't know you actually meant it. He's a prince! He's probably trained to make everyone think they have a personal connection with him. But if he's writing you and asking you to write him back, then he probably really did feel a connection with you."

"Well, thanks for the vote of confidence," I said with sarcasm, but I was smiling even as I did so. I clutched the letter to my chest, and hurried upstairs, ready to write him back.

Prince Credence and I would go on to write one another every day for the next week. They were missives about nothing and everything that would light up my days. I wrote about everything, that is, except for the truth about Cinderella. I think about that week of letters now and wonder if even then I cemented our fate with each letter that I passed back to Prince Credence. It would have been better for him if he'd forgotten about me.

The morning Hortense and I waved goodbye to our parents was also the day before the first ball. Mother and Mr. Father were clearly worried, but they tried to hide it, waving cheerfully out the window of their carriage as it bore them down the road until they were out of our sight. Hortense had been faithfully helping care for Cinderella for the past two weeks, and even Mr. Father, perpetually anxious, was satisfied with the level she'd achieved in that short time. Hortense took copious notes on all things related to Cinderella and copied everything we did exactly. I even saw her sketching some of Cinderella's more unusual forms and, at the time, it made me smile. I thought it was a sign that she was applying her curious mind to Cinderella and accepting what she found there. She hadn't said anything rude about Cinderella the whole time Mr. Father and I taught her. I was almost bitter at how well Hortense had done. I thought about how much easier our lives could have been if we'd had her competent assistance earlier. But for the most part, I was just relieved that Hortense had volunteered, and that I was to be permitted to attend all three balls.

Our first day without our parents in the house passed as normal. I handled breakfast for Cinderella, because I always handled breakfast, and then lunch. Hortense and I were going to trade off lunches. I didn't mind going first. Hortense was going to feed Cinderella dinner, and the next day I'd do breakfast and then spend the rest of the day being anxious for the ball while getting ready, and Hortense would feed her lunch and dinner. Between feeding Cinderella lunch and eating my own dinner, I wrote and posted a missive to Credence. It was about my cats and the way they kept taking over the farm. I left out the reasons why we needed such vigorous pest control but wrote him little stories of the cats' mannerisms and achievements. All my letters were like that—truths built around the space of Cinderella. The most relevant detail of my life was left out, for I could not conceive of a world where I admitted to Credence any truths about my stepsister. Perhaps that was my mistake.

Hortense and I ate dinner together that night, and although I noticed that Hortense was particularly pensive, I said nothing. She was entitled to her own thoughts, just as I was entitled to mine. I tell myself that now, but the truth is I was thinking about the next night's ball and finally getting to see Credence in person again. I wondered what he'd wear, and if he'd like the dress I'd chosen. I was content to leave Hortense to her thoughts, as long as she left me to my own daydreams.

"Eunice," she finally said, breaking the silence. "Do you remember when I was talking about how someone could—hypothetically, of course—build up an immunity to Cinderella?"

My blood ran cold. My thoughts of music and ballgowns fell and shattered. I stared at Hortense, wishing she'd said nothing.

"Hortense," I warned. "Please don't do this now. You know how much the ball means to me. I'll be seeing Credence tomorrow, and I don't have time for one of your experiments, especially if it causes you to get hurt." My voice was sharper than it usually was when speaking with Hortense, but I was so afraid she was going to try and test some ridiculous theory. I was right to be fearful, but wrong to cut her off. Perhaps if I'd let her go on, treated her with kindness, I could have talked her out of that ridiculous plan of hers.

"Of course," she said. "I'm not going to try anything. It's just, Eunice, I've been keeping notes. I have journals and journals full of notes, documenting everything that's gone on because of *her*, and I really think I might be on to something here."

"You're on to nothing," I said. "Cinderella is not a poisonous plant, she's a monster. And our sister, of course. The rules exist for a reason. The only thing I want you to try tonight is to follow the rules, and make sure everything goes smoothly. Don't stray into unknown territory with Cinderella, Hortense. Please. For me."

Hortense agreed, and then shortly after she excused herself to go up to her room, claiming tiredness. She assured me she would feed Cinderella before she went to bed, no experiments or tricks, and I believed her. It was what I would have done, and I could not imagine Hortense doing something different.

I got my own self ready for bed, lost in a haze of balls and gowns and princes. For once, I went to sleep with a minimum of effort, unconcerned by the terrors I would surely face in my sleep.

I woke that night, as I always did, covered in a fine layer of sweat. I could not define it, but something was off. The dreams were always vivid, but this one felt more so, in a way that I was unable to articulate, even to myself. For reasons I could not explain, I decided to go check on Hortense. I had never checked on her in the middle of the night like this before, but that night I just knew that it was important.

I tiptoed over to her room and peeked in the open door. My stomach plummeted. All of Hortense's jars and terrariums and glass vials lay still and calm. Everything in her bedroom was as it should be, except for one pertinent detail. Her bed was empty.

Frantic, I ran back to my room, praying that I just had the time wrong, that for once I had slept through the night, and it was actually six AM, and my nightmares had just been delayed for some reason. The arms of the small brass clock I kept on my nightstand showed that was a lie. The hands pointed firmly at the one and the twelve. It was one AM, and Hortense was not in her bed.

I tried to take deep breaths. There was no guarantee that Hortense was with Cinderella. She could be anywhere. I decided to go back to her room and see if she'd left any clues as to her whereabouts.

On my way there, something squelched unpleasantly under my foot. Trembling, I reached down to see what I had just stepped on. I scrunched my eyes shut, too scared to look at what I might find.

My hands met fur, and then a wet, sticky fluid that could only be blood. My hands moved onward, desperate to be wrong, but then my fingers hit a silken bow. I'd tied it there just that morning. I had just trod upon the corpse of Miss Whiskers, one of the household cats.

I screamed, but stuffed my clean hand in my mouth, trying to muffle the noise. I needed more information before I truly panicked. Pushing down my revulsion, I scooped up the limp body of Miss Whiskers and brought her with me into my room, where I'd left a candle burning.

Once I could see the body under the orange glow of the candle, my stomach gave out and I heaved. I vomited right there on the floor, with no concern or ability to keep my stomach in check.

The cat had been mutilated. Perfectly circular chunks of flesh were missing from all over her body. One of Cinderella's favorite guises around me included a perfectly circular mouth of churning teeth, and she'd told me how much she hated the cats. This was definitely her work. Which meant . . .

I panicked. I locked the door, barred it shut, and moved my dresser in front of it. Then I grabbed my candle and scoured every corner of my room. It wasn't likely that she was lurking in a corner, but I could take no chances.

My room secured, I almost allowed myself to relax. It was then that a scream rent the air.

My blood ran cold. How could I have forgotten about the reason I had left my room to begin with? Hortense was out there, alone in the house with Cinderella. We never allowed any servants to stay the night, so it was just three of us tonight.

I heaved the dresser away from the door, undid the lock, and slipped the door open just a bit. I peeked through the crack, hoping I could see enough to know whether it was safe, but not enough for me to fall under Cinderella's sway. Emboldened by the nothing I saw out my door, I inched it open until my candle could fit through. If I could just find Hortense . . .

A shadow moved upon the wall, and in my fear, I knew it was Cinderella. I withdrew my arm and candle into my room, slamming the door so quickly that my candle went out. I was alone in the darkness, only the faint light of the moon painting my room with a silvery glow.

I could just barely make out the hands of my clock, which confirmed what I already knew. It was 1:15. If Hortense was out there with Cinderella, it was already too late. There was nothing I could do. If I went out to look for Hortense and encountered Cinderella myself, then I too would be lost, and I would be no good to Hortense or to myself.

Those are the things I still tell myself now, but I am unsure if they are true. What if I had been just a bit braver and gone out that night, confronted Cinderella? Could I have prevented what was to come?

Could I have saved Hortense?

Those were the longest two hours of my life. I stared and shivered, listening intently for any sounds that might indicate to me what was going on outside of the sanctum of my room. After the initial scream, there was nothing. I was cut off from the outside world, my mind allowed to imagine the worst scenarios possible. My imagination did not go far enough.

Finally, *finally*, my tiny brass clock hit three o'clock. I waited, in a herculean act of patience and agony, just to be sure, until 3:05. Cinderella should have passed out of the zenith of her power by then, so I heaved the dresser away from the door to my room and took the familiar path down to the cellar.

Along the way, I discovered the corpse of Lt. Whiskers, Miss Whiskers's brother and an excellent mouser. He was mutilated in the same way his sister had been, and under ordinary circumstances the death of two of my beloved cats would have been enough to cause me to break down. But that night I had no time for cats. I needed to know what had happened to Hortense, and, by extension, to Cinderella.

Although she was no longer at the height of her power, I still had no desire to run into Cinderella unawares. I was alert and cautious as I made my way to the cellar. The wooden stairs stretched before me, mocking me with their familiarity while at the same time inviting me into the unknown. I hesitated, unsure what I would find when I descended into the depths of the cellar. I took a deep breath and stepped down into the darkness.

Cinderella's cell was empty. Both doors hung open. The solid metal one looked to have been opened normally, whereas the iron bars of the second door were mangled, wrenched apart with a strength no human could possess. Most telling of all, a basket with a rotten pumpkin and a stale loaf of bread lay abandoned next to the door.

I cursed Hortense's foolishness even as I was terrified for her fate. The picture formed in my mind's eye as readily as if I had been there myself. Hortense, night owl that she was, had forgotten to feed Cinderella at dinner time and had come down late at night. Maybe she'd just forgotten, maybe she'd fallen asleep; I do not know. Either way, she'd come downstairs without checking the time or without stopping to think about the consequences. She'd come down, opened the first door, beheld Cinderella at the zenith of her power, and then . . . My mind encountered a blank space in the picture I was painting. I would not allow myself to think of what had happened then. I would just keep searching.

I scoured the house. No room escaped me. I grew increasingly frantic as I went, from the cellars all the way to the long-neglected attics, without a single sign of Hortense. I dared not call out for her, in case that drew Cinderella toward Hortense when she was trying to hide, but I left nothing unturned. As dawn's first light began to turn the sky a soft gray, I was forced to conclude that they were no longer in the house. They could have been anywhere.

I pulled on my shoes, and ran outside, intending to search for them in the barns and stables, and perhaps ride one of the horses into town to continue the search if nothing turned up on our property. The servants would start arriving soon, and I didn't want them to accidentally stumble upon a loose Cinderella, so I knew I had to move fast.

In the end, it didn't matter. I didn't have to go far. As soon as I stepped outside, my eyes were drawn to the old tree that I used to play in. Growing up, it had been my refuge, but as I'd gotten older and had to spend more and more time caring for Cinderella, it hadn't been enough. I'd abandoned the tree and couldn't recall the last time I'd visited. Something had been strung throughout the branches, something that all led down to a small, still body.

There, on the small platform where I'd once sat with Mother and confided in her my fears about having a new family, lay Hortense. She was unmoving, and my heart was in my throat as I ran to the tree, intent on reaching her as soon as possible.

As soon as I got closer, I had to stop once more to vomit. My body could not handle the sight of what was before me. What I had taken for strings from the distance of the house were not strings. Hortense's body had been split open, and her entrails had been drawn and strewn about the branches of the tree that had once been my friend, like a grotesque parody of the streamers we used to hang for parties.

I wiped my mouth with the back of my hand, unable to tear my eyes away from the tree. I didn't know whether to advance closer or run away and hide forever. Before my brain could even process fully what I was seeing, I heard a low moan, and my heart lurched. Hortense was still alive.

I clambered up the tree, uncaring about the rotting boards or the nails sticking out from the old ladder. Hortense needed me. I threw myself onto the platform, ignoring the hot, metallic scent of the blood and the stench of viscera and excrement, to behold my sister.

Hortense had been vivisected, but it was no clean cut. Her body had been cut open from just below the hollow of her throat all the way down to where her pubic hair began. The flesh of her chest and abdomen had been peeled back, exposing all of her vital organs. I saw her ribs splayed out into the air, like a grotesque imitation of a butterfly, the faint beat of her heart exposed to the predawn air, and the gentle whoosh of her lungs as they inflated ever so slightly. Other organs, which I could not name, lay wet and inert inside the cavity of her body. I slipped in her blood as I scrambled toward her, repulsed by the carnage, but unable to stay away from my sister. Gently, I lifted her head, the only part of her relatively untouched, into my lap.

Her eyes flew open, and I found myself staring into twin abyssal pools. Gone were Hortense's pleasant brown eyes. The black of the pupil had grown to obscure all other features, and I looked into the void of space. And, once more, I heard the sound of distant stars screaming.

This did not deter me from keeping her head in my lap. I smoothed her hair from her brow and began to whisper to her, knowing there was nothing I could do to help but wanting to reassure her nonetheless.

"Hush, my darling Hortense," I said. My hand was stained red with blood, but I did not care—I just continued petting at her hair, the way I had when she was a child. "It's almost over now. Not much longer. You're so brave, my dove, look at you."

Hortense gurgled, and I could see the insides of her throat as she struggled to make words. I tried to shush her, but she could not be stopped.

"Not . . . over . . ." she croaked. "New . . . beginnings . . . for *her* . . . Long live my queen!" And with that, she reached up and raked her nails across my face, trying to take out an eye.

I cried out, whipping my head back, but she had caught me well and good. Her nails ripped through my skin, peeling up long strips from the bottom of my jaw up over the eye on the opposite side of my face. I managed to close my eyes in time to avoid losing them, but it was close. I pulled back, clutching my bleeding face with one hand as Hortense lay there, cackling to herself at my misfortune.

"Why?" I asked, through the blood and tears. My vision became stained red as my own blood flowed into my eye.

Still cackling, Hortense spoke. "Not yours, Eunice! Oh no! I am for the queen now, the Queen of Darkness, of distant stars, of all things rotting and lovely! Long live the queen!" And with that, Hortense gave a last, rattling gasp, and she died, completely out of her mind, unrecognizable as the girl she'd been just one day earlier.

At this point, kneeling in the tree covered in a mixture of sweat, tears, and a combination of my own and my sister's blood, something in me snapped. My grief was strong, of course, but more than that, I was furious. When senseless tragedy happens, such as when my father died from disease when I was a child, there can be anger, but the truth is that sometimes bad things happen in our wretched world, and we have no one to blame and we must learn to accept it. That was not the case here. I knew exactly who to blame, and I was going to hold her accountable. She couldn't have gone far.

I threw myself down from the tree, ignoring the pain that shot up through my left ankle as I did so. Once on solid ground, I looked up at the last dying stars of night, with the sun's rays brightening the sky, and I screamed, as loud as I knew how.

"Cinderella!" I howled. "You faithless, artful, lowly worm! Betrayer of our family, scourge of my life, come here *now*."

And with a loud, crashing roar, the sound of a ship being wrecked upon the rocks, she did.

CHAPTER

12

Confrontation

WE STOOD, FACE to face, under my childhood tree, with Hortense's intestines strung up in the branches above us. Cinderella was swollen with power from Hortense's death, and she was no longer trying to hide behind the facade of a young woman. Looking upon her was painful, but I could do it if I forced myself to think of anything other than how her eyes swirled with the green of rot and decay, and the way the shadows she cast in the dawn's morning light bled and twisted along their jagged edges, writhing in the new light of our closest star.

"You called, sister dear?" Cinderella said. Her voice rang with screams and resonance not meant for human ears. I realized that even though it was not the time of night when her power was at its peak, this was the strongest I had ever seen her. We'd been starving her of power, kept her weak and biddable, but the sacrifice of Hortense had left her flush and flowing with vibrancy and life.

"You killed Hortense," I said. My tone was matter-of-fact, flat. "You sacrificed your own sister. You broke the rules."

"She broke the rules *first*," screamed Cinderella. She grew and changed before my eyes, her body breaking and elongating, large wings and a multitude of tentacles erupting from her back. "Shouldn't have told me I wasn't her *sister*. Even as I took her mind, broke it down and twisted it and tasted its delights, she fought back, told me I'd never be family. That is, until I had consumed her and left only the desire to serve me in her stead."

"We've talked about this," I said, falling into a well-worn path of conversation with Cinderella. "Being a big sister means you have to be the bigger person too. When she repudiates you, you don't try to consume her, or sacrifice her to the greater good. You keep being her *sister*. And instead, you *killed* her. You killed my Hortense!"

Cinderella laughed, a low, horrible sound that clawed at my ears.

"Wrong, wrong, *wrong*," she cried out, as more tentacles erupted from her back and her legs, writhing in a threatening mass around her. "She killed *herself*. I ate her mind, and she made the decision to slice herself open and string herself up like links of sausage in the tree. And then she died a slow, painful death as I drank her essence, knowing as she did that my power would only grow with every second of pain she endured."

Tears were rolling down my cheeks, and the scratches on my face were bleeding freely. My vision was still painted red. I dared not reach up to wipe the blood out of my eye for fear of aggravating the cuts.

"You killed her," I said again. "As surely as if you'd held a knife to her throat and slid it across, you murdered our sister. Why? Why now?"

She gave me a slow, horrible smile, and I saw that her teeth and her tongue had been replaced by her favorite combination of features: churning circular teeth and a long tentacle for a tongue.

"Because," she said, and I staggered under the onslaught of her great and terrible voice, "because I will be *queen*! Tonight's ball is mine, sister dear, and with the sacrifice of a living human and an invitation addressed specifically to me, not even your petty commands can stop me from going."

This whole thing was about going to the ball? Somehow, Cinderella knew that the king was holding a ball, knew that she was invited, knew that it was tonight. A slow, dawning realization swept over me.

"You've been listening to us," I said. "You heard me fighting with Mother in the dining room."

"How could I not, the way you whined and wailed? Yes, I heard you. I heard you, and I waited for my opportunity. Imagine my surprise when little Hortense volunteered! You should feel lucky, sister," she said, her voice still horrible and powerful. "Originally, my plan was to take the power I needed to free myself from you, but even as ridiculous and addled over that idiot prince as you were, you never slipped up. Bravo for your restraint."

At her words, my rage stoked higher than ever.

"Cinderella, I am your sister still," I insisted. "You will not harm me! I command you to return to your room, and do not leave until you have met all of my instructions!"

She hissed in displeasure, a long, low, tortured sound, and her corona of tentacles roiled and seethed around her.

"You are no sister of mine," she hissed again. "Your blood is not of my blood, just as her blood was not of my blood!"

I stood firm, clinging to what Mr. Father had taught me over the years.

"I am your sister in name, for I have always named you as my sister, since the first day we met. Never once have I said otherwise. I am your sister by legality. We are both listed as the daughters of Adrian Fitzwilliam and Bettina Constance. Your father is my father, my mother is your mother. And," I said, gaining steam, not entirely sure where I was going with this but knowing I needed to establish this now, even as I stood there bleeding and mourning the loss of Hortense, "I am your sister in deed. I have fed you, I have cared for you, I have brought you little treats, I have told you of the world, I have even combed your hair. *You* will not reject *me*, Cinderella. I am the only sister you have left, and by god, you will recognize me! And as your sister, I am telling you now— leave me and go to your room!"

My words rang in the air just as the sun finally crested the horizon, spilling warm, soft yellow light over us both. Cinderella let out a horrid shriek, and for a second, she was a blur of darkness and water, tentacles whipping around her form, unrecognizable from the young woman she'd been before. Then, with a loud squelch, she vanished.

I did not go back to the house to see if she'd done as I asked. I had work to do. Carefully, using a long broom handle and a bucket from the stable, I pulled down every bit of Hortense from the tree that I could find. When I had all of her various pieces assembled in front of me, I cast aside my broom to take up a shovel. There, at the base of my beautiful tree, I dug Hortense's grave and tipped her into it.

By the time I was done, the sun was high and hot in the sky, and many of our servants had arrived at the house to begin the day's work. Some of them must have wondered what I was doing on the lawn so early, but anyone who worked in our household became good at ignoring things that didn't fit. I lay down my shovel, sneaked into my own home, taking routes where no one would see my bloodstained clothes, and returned to my bedroom. A glance at my little brass clock showed me that it was noon. I had been awake for almost twelve hours, after having slept for only four hours the night before. Despite my grief, and my pain, I was helpless in the face of my exertions. I stripped my bloody clothes off, letting them fall to the floor, and collapsed into bed, dropping into a deep, blessedly dreamless sleep.

CHAPTER

13

Transformation

I WOKE WITH A start. Light no longer shone through my windows, and I could not see the face of my clock within the darkness of my room. I had not intended to sleep for so long.

I sprang from my bed, throwing on a robe, and ran down the stairs, past a startled-looking Mrs. Carnelian, who was just leaving for the day.

"I left dinner on the table!" she called out at me as I ran past. "I called for you and Miss Hortense, but no one answered!"

I continued my rush into the cellar, ignoring her audible mutterings about spoiled young women who slept the day away.

I made it to the stairs at the top of the cellar and closed the door tightly behind me. I didn't want any of the servants to witness more than was necessary. I ignored the small voice in my mind that said a closed door would make it harder for me to escape. I ran down the stairs and came to a halt in front of the doors to Cinderella's cell. They were just as I had left them that morning, with the solid metal one laid aside, and the iron bars of the second torn asunder.

Inside her cell was Cinderella, standing upright and serene, back in her flawless human form—without a single stitch of clothing on. Her breasts were full and soft, her hips flared gracefully, and her long legs ended in almost impossibly tiny feet. They probably were impossibly tiny, I thought to myself, considering that she had no need to conform to the actual limits of the human body. She wasn't human, and I needed to stop acting like she was, even when she presented me with this form.

"Well, sister Eunice, dearest," she said in her normal, human voice, "I am ready to go to the ball. As my sister, I feel it is your duty to assist me in my preparations. After all, how am I to catch myself a prince if I don't look my best?"

Cinderella twirled in front of me, showing me her perfect human form. Her intent was to remind me of all the flaws in my own body—my pudgy tummy versus her trim waist, my hair in inconvenient places versus her smooth, hairless skin, my own lackluster tresses versus her luscious blonde waves. Any aspect of my body could be compared and found wanting against her sheer physical perfection. Tonight, however, she had missed the mark with her preening. I did not care about her body, or my own. She had murdered Hortense, and nothing she did to me could possibly hurt as much as that.

As she twirled before me, I felt a wave of regret and sorrow, so acute that it felt like an actual physical wound in my chest and stomach. Hortense was dead, but I did not have time to waste mourning her as she deserved. Instead, as always happened in my life, I had to put away my own desires, my need to grieve my younger sister, and do what was necessary for Cinderella.

"I don't think they'll let you in like that," I said, careful to keep my voice neutral. I didn't yet know what I needed to prevent her from leaving the house, so I kept my cards close to my chest.

"What, you don't think the prince would like it? You think he'd prefer someone like you?" she asked, twirling once more. "My dress didn't survive my transformation, so I'm out of options. I'd ask to borrow something from you, but, well, we're hardly the same size, are we?" Again she missed her mark. Her intent was to be cruel, but how could a dig at my body compare to the loss of my beautiful Hortense? I ignored her and pressed on.

"To clarify—you have no dress, no shoes, and no way to get to the ball. You destroyed your dress when you killed Hortense, you don't want to borrow one from me because I'm too fat, and from what I can see, you're completely out of shoes. What are you planning on doing here, exactly?" I did genuinely want to know. Cinderella was in a chatty mood, and I hoped she'd let something slip.

A smile curled across her lips.

"Eunice dear, I'm so glad you asked. Watch and learn, little sister."

Completely unashamed of her nudity, Cinderella spread her arms and began to chant. It was not a language I recognized, and merely hearing it set all the hair on my body standing on end.

As she chanted, I saw something moving out of the corner of my eye. I turned to face it full on but then recoiled. There were still things that should not be seen by humankind, even after all that I had witnessed that day, and this was one of them.

A cascading wave of rats entered the room, their small, furry bodies scuttling over and under each other as they poured into the cellar. They seemed to just pop out of the walls, aided by some arcane magic of Cinderella's. Seeing rats oozing out of the wall was the stuff of nightmares. I scrambled backward, unable to take my eyes off of the advancing horde even as I was desperate for them not to touch me.

The rats ignored me, swarming into the cell with Cinderella, whose chanting had risen in pitch and strength. The rats ran up and over her body, their tiny feet and claws finding purchase on Cinderella as they engulfed her. I closed my eyes, unwilling to look at the seething pile of rats that covered Cinderella so thickly that I could not see her skin and hair. There were only the rats in a giant roiling mass, the scratching of their feet and the squeaking of their mouths filling the room. After a few minutes, the rats fell silent, and I risked opening my eyes to take a peek at what was happening.

In front of me stood Cinderella, no longer nude. Instead, she was resplendent in one of the most gorgeous ball gowns I had ever seen. It was composed of layers and layers of delicate silver fabric, each layer sheer on its own, but gaining opacity when laid one atop another. The skirt flowed out in a beautiful silver swirl, floating up delicately with every hint of movement. The bodice was made of the same silver fabric, but instead of floating free it was tight and fitted, with delicate boning in a corset shape, with seed pearls acting as pins to anchor the fabric. Her hair was swept up into an elegant knot, another strand of pearls acting as the fastener, the soft, fat, white globes accentuating the delicate honey blonde of her hair. From her ears sprays of tiny pearls cascaded down almost all the way to her shoulders, which were left bare by the dress, with only the vaguest hint of a sleeve in the form of a single translucent layer of fabric around her upper arms. Her face remained unchanged, but that did not matter—she was as heartbreakingly lovely as always.

My heart pounded. This was unlike anything I had seen Cinderella do before. I had never seen her use any of her talents to create anything beautiful; I had only known her to spread rot and decay. I rubbed at my eyes, trying to make sense of what I was witnessing. The cut above my eye from Hortense's nails split open and blood began dripping into my eye once more. I blinked, trying to get it out, but before I could do so I stopped dead, horrified at what I now saw. I looked at Cinderella, and I saw her beautiful silver dress, with pearl accents and a skirt that flared gently at the slightest provocation. My right eye, the one without the blood in it, was unchanged. What I saw with my left eye was far more sinister, the blood that still clouded my vision somehow revealing her true form to me.

The rats had not left. They had subsumed Cinderella, and she had kept them on her. The beautiful silver dress was an illusion. In reality, her ball gown was formed by the putrid, decaying bodies of hundreds and hundreds of rats.

A gentle breeze from nowhere stirred Cinderella's skirts. Out of my right eye, her skirt was just as I had initially perceived it, many layers of delicate, gauzy silver floating and flaring, giving her an enchanting and surreal look. Out of my left eye I saw the truth: the rats wriggling and rotting as a wave of them crested and writhed to give the appearance of movement. The pearls in her hair caught the light, and I saw that they were actually the teeth of what must have been dozens of dead rats, strung together on a chain of disembodied rat tails, naked, pink and wet against her hair.

Even a few hours earlier, this spectacle may have induced me to vomit, but at this point I had nothing left in my stomach. I could only stare in horror at the dual images before me, which swam in front of my face, presenting me with the terrible truth layered under the illusion.

Cinderella smiled at me, somehow sensing that I was able to see her true form.

"Aren't I marvelous?" she said. "Don't you think I look fit to be queen? Just imagine—me as the monarch, with all of my adoring subjects. Why, I think I'd quite like visiting town and blessing babies and such." She batted her eyes at me and lifted the decaying corpse of a rat from her skirt in one hand. Out of one eye, I saw that it was now a tiny purse, beaded all over in seed pearls. My other eye, still filled with blood, could not unsee the rat that wiggled feebly in her grasp, although I could see the rotting skin stretched over bones and a distended, bloating stomach, as if it had been dead for several days.

She cradled the rat in her arms, in a mimicry of someone cradling a small child, and raised the rat to her lips, kissing it gently on the forehead. The rat twitched, and she smiled, stroking a finger down its spine to soothe the beast, before allowing it to dangle from her hand again, simultaneously a purse and a decaying rodent in my double vision once more.

"Just think, Eunice. All those people, able to see me! All of the delicious human minds, just waiting to be tasted. And then once their minds are all but gone, I will do to them as I did to Hortense and fill them with my splendid purpose! All shall do my bidding, and the kingdom shall fall before me and act as a seed buried in this world. From there my newfound thralls and I will burst out, moving in an ever-growing swath as we conquer more and more nations. I shall take over this land as my own, to be ruled over by a dark and terrible queen, the likes of which your planet has never seen."

As she spoke, the rats clinging to her body were shot through by the same tendrils of darkness that I'd seen earlier, erupting out of her body to form a dark corona around her form. I realized that only my left eye saw this, as it was still covered in a film of blood from the seeping wound above my eye. Her true form, which I could only see now, injured as I was and touched by tragedy, was much larger and darker than I could ever have anticipated. How many times had I been alone in the room with this being, assuming that it was a normal girl, if a monstrous one, when really I was trapped in the cellar with an abomination from beyond the stars?

I tried to keep my composure, but I could feel my vision blurring at the edges, as everything swirled and was revealed before me. Cinderella in all of her power was too much for a normal human mind to comprehend. I turned away, trying to focus my brain on anything other than Cinderella.

My eyes lit on the basket that poor Hortense must have left behind before her terrible transformation. The pumpkin lay there, rotting still, and the stale bread offered no inspiration. Below that, however, was a half-full bottle of wine, the green glass dark in the low light of the cellar, which was probably why I had not noticed it earlier. I recognized the bottle as one that had spoiled and then been set aside for Cinderella, much to the disapproving looks of the cook. Hortense must have grabbed it as a treat for Cinderella. This last act of kindness had gotten her nowhere.

I moved as if in a trance. Before I could stop to think about the futility of my actions, I picked up the bottle, the dark wine inside a sloshing black mess through the green glass and hurled it at Cinderella. I hoped to dislodge some of her rats or harm her. To somehow ruin her beautiful gown or puncture the illusion. I'm not sure exactly what I hoped to accomplish; I only knew that I wished her ill, and the bottle was the only weapon available to me in that dark, lonely cellar, where I stood before the monster I had called sister for the last seven years.

I closed my left eye so that I could see only with the eye fooled by her illusions, hoping against hope that I could prevent her from leaving, or buy some time for myself—anything to keep Cinderella here in the cellar with me, rather than unleashing her upon an unsuspecting populace.

Without the benefit of my bloody eye, Cinderella looked heartbreakingly lovely, and even knowing her as I did, I felt something stir within me, so deep and terrible was her beauty. Her dress, her hair, her eyes—she dimmed everything around her, made everything next to her seem less lovely by comparison. It made her seem like she was the only good and beautiful thing in the world, and everything else was just so much waste and ruin. I wanted to drop down on my knees and beg her to let me make her happy, in whatever form that took. I wanted to fight battles for her, kill for her, and I would have happily cut off my own hands for her, had she but asked it of me.

Despite my brain's betrayal, my hand had stayed true, launching the dark green bottle half full of some forgotten vintage turned to vinegar, and it struck, cracking Cinderella on the shoulder. The bottle shattered on impact, sending a deluge of acrid red fluid down her beautiful silver dress. I thought I had won a minor victory. Vain as she was, Cinderella would never leave the house with a horrid splotch of red wine staining her beautiful outfit.

Even as I had that thought, the red wine began to disappear. I opened my other eye, still with a film of blood over it, and looked on in horror.

The rats were licking the wine off where it had spilled, consuming it from their bodies, using their rotting tongues to abrade the wine from the backs of their fellow rats making up the fabric of the dress. One rat, near where the stain had originated, could not get the stain of wine out of its neighbor's fur. It reached over and tore out a hunk of decaying flesh from the neighboring rat, swallowing it and the offending stain as one. I gagged, but even as I saw this horrid pile of rats with my left eye, my right eye saw her dress made shiny and clean and whole once more.

Cinderella picked up the broken end of the wine bottle, and I cursed myself for having given her one more weapon. It did not occur to me that Cinderella did not need weapons, nor that she'd had access to the wine bottle the whole time and could have used it against me whenever she wanted. I only sank into my own despair, hating myself and my actions, convinced that I was to blame for everything. Now, away from it all, I know that she was working upon my psyche, filling in the hole she'd created after years and years of tasting my mind with her own dark thoughts and particular brand of despair.

She looked down at the shattered bottle, then looked at me cowering before her. I was careful to keep both eyes open now. I had no desire to succumb to her beauty the way I had just moments before.

"A last gift from Hortense," she said, turning the broken glass over in her hands. "She listened to you well, Eunice. You always did try to bring me little treats. A bottle of spoiled wine, a rotten pumpkin." She gestured at the basket, sitting forlornly in the corner. "Those are not gifts from Hortense, a girl who hated me. No, Eunice, that has you all over it. You taught her what to bring, and it was for love of you she proffered me these little treats, not out of any desire to make me happy." She said the last word with profound derision, as if being happy were an unforgivable state, all the while stroking the glass bottle in her hand.

"Still," she continued, "she brought them to me, perhaps thinking this tiny taste of rot would be enough. You always thought you were so kind, and you taught Hortense the same. These tiny, rotting gifts, akin to a drop of water when I was wandering in the desert, lost." Her voice rose, and her tentacles expanded. I cowered in fear, all pretense of being brave gone in the face of her anger.

"The tiniest taste of these decaying plants, a pale imitation of the power I longed to draw from you and your sister, a mockery of what I should have been!" she said, her voice reverberating off the walls of the cellar. I thought she was going to kill me then and there, so great was her rage. She calmed herself, however, and smiled at me, something so unexpected that it chilled my blood, as if I had been submerged in a bath of ice.

"Still, in the end, Hortense gave me what I wanted. It seems I should honor her last gifts to me, as in the end she gave me the ultimate gift, willingly or not. It is Hortense to whom I owe tonight's successes." Cinderella's words caused a wave of revulsion to rise inside me, but there was nothing I could do but sit and watch. I was helpless to leave.

She waved her hand carelessly, and I was forced to scramble out of the way. The pumpkin that lay in the basket began to grow, the wet orange flesh squelching as it expanded. I could see the maggots that had burrowed into the flesh expanding as well, their white, wriggling bodies growing in size along with the pumpkin. The inside of the pumpkin had liquified, and rotting juice sluiced out onto the floor as the pumpkin grew and grew. The foul juice washed over my feet, soaking them, making me gag once more.

The pumpkin continued to change before my eyes. To my left eye, it was as it ever was, a giant, corpulent behemoth, festering and full of extra-large maggots, the stuff of nightmares. To my right eye, however, it took on the appearance of a handsome carriage, round bellied, with wide spaces where glass windows should be. The maggots, I saw to my disgust, took on the shape of footmen, two sitting up near where the driver would be, and another hanging on to the side of the door. The experience of seeing a man superimposed over a gigantic, grotesque maggot is one I would not wish upon any other living soul. I hope no one else on this green earth ever sees the horrors that I saw that night. At the front of the carriage, rats lined up, with horrible strings of pumpkin innards reaching out and attaching to them. I realized with a start that these were the horses, hitching themselves up to pull this monstrous carriage. Cinderella's cell had always been spacious, but with this new addition, it seemed to strain at the edges, the walls growing fuzzy and strange where the carriage and horses butted up against it.

I tore my gaze away from the carriage and turned back to Cinderella, cognizant that she could have been up to all kinds of mischief while I was otherwise occupied. She still held the piece of glass wine bottle that I had thrown at her earlier in her hand. She picked up little shards of glass from the ground and pressed them into the carriage where windows should be. The glass grew and melted and bubbled, and when it was done, both my left eye and my right eye saw green glass, the color of Cinderella's eyes, forming the windows of the carriage. Cinderella then turned her attention to the bottle remnant in her hands and I saw the thick glass heat up and melt, fat globs of glowing glass dripping down the sides of her hands. She squeezed it between her fingers, the heat causing her no visible distress, and she began to work the glass, shaping it and twisting with long pulls of her delicate fingers.

After mere minutes, the glass had taken on the form she desired, although cradled as it was in her hands, I could not see it. She blew into her cupped hands, and the glass cooled, losing the red-orange glow it had taken on while she worked it, and slid back into the green color I was most familiar with. But it was not the olive green of the wine bottle. In her hands lay two beautiful glass slippers, the exact murky green color as Cinderella's eyes.

She slipped the shoes onto her feet. I was sure they would shatter underneath her, but they held. They were two green spots of corruption on her otherwise flawless ensemble, some hint that all was not as it should be. The green did not really match the silver of her gown, but it wasn't that they were merely unfashionable. Looking at them gave me a headache. There was something not quite right about the slippers, with their twisty glass heels and murky green color. I hoped that they would be an obvious enough clue to warn off Prince Credence, but as Cinderella dropped her skirts over the shoes, hiding them from view, I knew that it would not be enough.

Cinderella preened in front of me, twirling once more for good measure, giving me another glimpse of those awful glass slippers, and then held out her hand before her. On the back wall of the cellar, near where her bed sat, the packed earth walls began to churn and spin. The spinning and churning started out small but grew larger and larger as I watched, until a huge circular expanse of the wall was taken up by this nauseating spiral. There should have been just more dirt, set as we were underground, but the spiral hinted at glimpses of a palace, cool night air, and spinning trees. Cinderella clapped her hands, and the spiral solidified. Cool night air spilled in through the hole in the wall, and through it I could see King Reymond's palace, where lines of carriages were arriving, depositing eligible young people for the ball. Our house was nowhere near the palace. She had opened a portal, and she meant to go through it.

Cinderella gave herself one last pat down, checked her hair in the mirror above her dresser, which was unchanged by all of the chaos of the night. She then stepped into the carriage waiting for her. The rotting flesh of the pumpkin parted to let her enter, and the maggot closest to her closed the flesh behind her before jumping up to its seat. The maggot then clicked the reins, causing the rats attached to the front in a mockery of horses to go scurrying forward into the pulsing portal at the back of her cell. Cinderella gave me a wave out the back window of the carriage, which I could see with my left eye was formed by a space where the pumpkin had rotted clean through, leaving a hole with black, jagged edges. Then, with a wink, the portal closed behind her, and I was left alone in the cellar, bleeding, tired, and heartbroken. I fell to my knees and I wept.

CHAPTER

14

The Ball

BY NOW, EVERYONE knows the story of what occurred at the ball. The beautiful, mysterious commoner, showing up fashionably late, dancing the whole night with the prince. Everyone was hearing wedding bells until the mysterious girl left right at the stroke of midnight, to their consternation and surprise. She left behind only one clue to her identity; a green glass slipper. Prince Credence, already maddened with love, declared then and there in front of everyone that he would not rest until he found the owner of that slipper. His father, King Reymond, so moved by his son's change of heart, launched a campaign to have every maiden in the land try on the green glass slipper.

I have my doubts as to the exactitude of this account, but I was not there, so I am unqualified to comment. I also have my doubts that Credence, as unenthused as he was about the prospect of marriage, would be prepared to make a commitment after only a few hours, even with Cinderella and all of her many dubious charms. I find it much more plausible that he latched on to the slipper as an excuse not to entertain more young women and men, and when he made that excuse to his father, King Reymond called his bluff, launching the search. But again, I do not know. I was home, in the cellar, doing my best to repair the wreckage that Cinderella had made of her cell. Even then I had hopes of containing the situation—perhaps the prince wouldn't be interested in her, perhaps she would come home with no one having looked at her twice. Perhaps her strange, off-putting eyes and the carefully matching green of her shoes would have been enough of a warning sign for Prince Credence to stay away, to set his sights on someone else.

I would be lying if I said that there was no spark of jealousy within me when I thought of Prince Credence marrying another, let alone my own sister. However, it is true that it was no more than a spark; jealousy over the prince that I had only met once could not hold a candle to the raging flame of my grief over Hortense. I toiled away, doing my best to fix the ruined doors. Every piece of wood that I nailed with inexpert hands, every rope that I tied with trembling fingers, every handful of salt that I pressed into the dirt walls with stinging palms was an act of grief for Hortense. Despite all my tears that night, I did not have time to truly grieve. I had to work through it, constructing a makeshift barrier that would hold Cinderella once she came back. I did not think of her portal, I did not think of her increased power, I merely worked steadily, glancing at the small brass clock that I had brought down with me.

At ten to midnight, I packed up what I could, made a few last-minute adjustments, and left the cellar, my feet traveling the well-worn wooden steps out of the cellar almost without my permission. Even then, not knowing if she would be back that night, the rules were too strongly ingrained in me. I could not be in her cell after midnight, even if she was not there.

Once out of the cellar, I sat at the top of the stairs, ear pressed against the door intently, struggling to hear any sound, any sign that Cinderella had returned. As I heard the grandfather clock chime midnight, I strained, desperate for a sign of something from downstairs—anything.

I was rewarded.

A fluttering, as of many wings, and a squelching, presumably the pumpkin carriage, reached my ears faintly through the door. Cinderella had returned. The next thing I heard was a vicious, howling shriek. She'd discovered my modifications.

I'd scoured my brain, trying to think of anything that might help keep her contained, now that she'd once broken free of our best attempt at confinement. In the end, I'd struck on a cocktail of old ways and my own ideas. I'd put salt around the entire cell, as if warding off the fae of old, mixed with my own blood. I'd lit torches, studding them into the walls, the pitch burning bright, in the hopes that fire would deter her. I figured that since my blood showed Cinderella for who she really was, it might well have other useful properties. With every bloody handful of salt that I'd pressed into the walls, I'd thought hard of our connection as sisters, and I'd put all my fervent desires to keep her contained into every press of my bleeding palms to the dirt walls.

It was working. She thrashed and howled in the cellar, but I did not hear her at the door, and she did not quiet or give other signs of departure. Eventually, I fell asleep listening to her howls, slumped against the door, the grain of the wood pressing into my cheek as I slept.

15

Trying It On

I AWOKE THE NEXT morning to a loud scream from one of our maids. I sat up, unfolding myself from my ungraceful slump against the door, and looked around. Lilia, one of our newest hires, had dropped a bucket of water in the drawing room in front of me. I didn't blame her; I knew I looked an absolute fright. My hands were bloodied, and my nails were jagged and broken. The ones left intact were full of dirt. My face throbbed where Hortense had scratched me the day before, although when I dabbed gingerly at the aching flesh, my hands came away without fresh blood, so sometime in the night I had stopped bleeding. Sticky trails on my face let me know that the blood from the wound had not left, and when I licked my lips, trying to bring back some moisture to the parched skin, I tasted the metallic and stale flavor of old blood. In short, I was a mess.

I grimaced but pulled myself up to my feet. "There was an accident," I said roughly, hollow with exhaustion. "I'll be retiring to my rooms. The house should keep running as normal, and please remember that the cellar is off limits, as always. If you could please draw me a bath, I would be grateful."

Lilia nodded, her eyes round and huge with fright. I made my slow and painful way to my bedroom. As tired as I was, I needed to be clean more than I needed to sleep, and my scratches wanted seeing to as well. I gingerly pulled off my clothes, dropping them in a pile. I pulled on my softest robe, wincing as the material brushed over my ruined fingers. My joints protested at the act of tying the sash.

Thankfully, Lilia worked quickly and there was a steaming bath ready for me in short order. I submerged myself with a sigh and would have happily spent the next hour there, at least approaching some sort of neutral equilibrium. But no sooner had I fully wet my hair than a knock at my door sounded.

"What?" I snapped.

"Begging your pardon, miss," said Lilia, from the other side of the door. "There's a visitor."

"Tell them I'm indisposed," I said, sinking deeper into the water. Visitors could wait; I had no time for them.

"Begging your pardon once more, miss," said Lilia, her voice timid and weak. "But it's Prince Credence and his entourage. They're here to have you try on the shoe."

"They're *what*?" I yelled, sitting up in the bath with a huge splash of water onto the floor. At that point, I had yet to hear the story of the ball. My sleep-addled mind thought I must be imagining; surely Prince Credence wouldn't be here, to see me. I hadn't even been to the ball!

A slow, dawning horror entered my mind. Cinderella had been to the ball, and now the prince was at our house, wanting some ridiculous thing. It stank of her

machinations. Also, I didn't know how much the exposure had strengthened her. Mr. Father always told me we
had to keep her secret, not just for her sake but to protect
everyone else. We couldn't risk discovery. I heaved myself
out of the tub and wrapped a large towel around me. I
cracked the door open and Lilia was standing there, eyes
as wide as they had been this morning. Mother wasn't
due back for another two days, and Mr. Father three
days after that. It was up to me to deal with this, since
Hortense . . . I pushed that thought down. There wasn't
time to think about Hortense, not with the prince
waiting.

"Tell them I'm dressing and I'll be right down," I
said.

Lilia turned to obey, but hesitated at the door, reluctantly raising her large, terrified eyes to meet mine.
"They're saying there was a girl at the ball last night,"
she said, cautious of my reaction. "Beautiful as anything,
arrived out of nowhere, danced with the prince all night.
But then they say she . . ." Lilia swallowed, so nervous
she could barely speak. "They say she left at midnight,
and no one could find her. She left a glass slipper behind,
and that's why the prince is here. To see if anyone fits the
slipper." With that, she fled.

A yawning dread filled me, starting at my toes and
climbing up to fill my stomach and the cavity of my
chest. A beautiful girl who left at midnight? It could
only be Cinderella. I thanked the stars that Lilia was as
afraid of Cinderella as she was and that our servants
knew about the midnight restriction for the cellar. She'd
put two and two together and found the four as alarm-
ing as I did.

I threw on clothes as fast as I could and tried to
make something presentable out of my hair in absolute

record time. I looked in the mirror and sighed. The scratches across my face had scabbed over, and the skin around them was red and puffy. I looked like I'd been in a fight with a tiger and only barely escaped. But there was nothing for it. I'd just have to meet Credence looking like this.

At that thought, my heart stuttered and my mind went blank. I'd been so worried about the prince showing up and the repercussions from Cinderella's escape that I had forgotten that it was Credence—the sweet, oblivious young man who didn't want to get married that I'd met in the marketplace. How could I face him in this state? But neither could I ignore him—he was still the prince.

I dabbed some ointment around my cuts, hoping to minimize the swelling, although there was nothing I could do in the short term. The prince was waiting for me, and I had no choice but to go and meet him as I was, clean but battered and bruised. I had scrubbed and scrubbed, but there was still stubborn dirt that clung to the undersides of my nail beds and lingered under the torn and ragged edges of my nails. I recalled burying Hortense but shied away from such thoughts. If I was going to meet Credence with any semblance of equanimity, I couldn't think about my sisters. Either of them.

I came downstairs and found Credence and his entourage in the good drawing room, the one farthest away from Cinderella's cellar. It was where I'd had so many talks with Mother and Mr. Father and where I'd learned how to deal with my sister. I had survived the last seven years with Cinderella and these people had not. I couldn't escape thoughts of Cinderella, but somehow this thought was more calming. It gave me courage.

I straightened my back and met Credence with my head held high, despite my injuries.

He looked as handsome as ever, although still a bit lost and sad. My heart, already broken and aching, spared a pang of sorrow for him. His was a position I did not envy, even if I had so recently entertained thoughts of myself as the lucky girl he would marry. I felt ashamed then, for wanting to partake in something that he clearly had no interest in, and felt a brief rush of gladness that I hadn't attended the ball after all. I did not need to be party to the king's efforts to trap his own son into matrimony with someone he barely knew.

Credence's entourage was splayed out around him, the gold and green colors of the palace shining bright on all their clothes. There were so many people that I had no idea what they could possibly all be for. Some held swords and were obviously soldiers there for the protection of the prince, but others carried scrolls of parchment and quills and one had a small wooden box with bright copper bands around it. One of the members of the group, a gnarled woman with graying hair and a large black crow perched upon her shoulder, concealed a magical staff up her sleeve just as I came down the stairs. I blanched. She was certainly a royal mage, and by her dress, a powerful one. I could see my servants peeking around corners and doorways, desperate to keep abreast of the situation and any gossip there was to have. I spotted Lilia with Mrs. Carnelian, both of them listening intently.

A member of the royal entourage carrying a scroll cleared his throat and announced in commanding, regal tones, "His Royal Highness Prince Credence is here on the advice of the royal magicians, who have asserted that this town, and this house in particular, is the source of the girl who so enchanted Prince Credence last night and left behind only this as the record of her presence." He gestured at the man with the box, who opened it to reveal one of Cinderella's green glass slippers.

I swallowed, transfixed by the sight of the slipper, which looked dark and dangerous as it lay inert upon the bed of black velvet inside the box. I looked up and made eye contact with Credence for the first time. The letters we had exchanged were no substitute for the real thing. I saw in his eyes confusion but also a spark of hope. That spark nearly broke me, but it also strengthened my resolve. I could not allow Cinderella to sink her claws into the prince. Not only would it result in the ruin of our kingdom—and from the way she had been talking, quite possibly the world—I could not allow her to corrupt another young life so brutally and so cruelly, the way she had corrupted Hortense for the last seven years. I would keep the prince safe.

The member of his entourage continued: "We ask that if any of the young ladies here in this house attended the ball last night that they be allowed to try on the slipper and prove to the prince that she is the woman who so enchanted him this past evening at the ball. Upon confirmation of this, the prince shall uphold his vow and take her back to the palace to begin preparations to become his bride. Such is the decree of King Reymond, first of his name."

"Eunice—" began the prince, and his court all turned to stare at him, shocked that he knew the name of the young woman before him with the wild eyes and ugly wounds. I myself was shocked—despite the letters we'd exchanged, I'd thought of myself as his secret. I didn't think he'd admit to knowing me in front of witnesses.

"What happened to you?" Credence continued. "Your face—is it all right?"

I nodded, unable to speak. I swallowed the lump in my throat and tried hard not to think about the scratches any more than I had to or I would break down and weep. I had failed, over and over again, and I didn't see a way out of this. But seeing Credence's face, I wanted to try to make things right again, even if I could see no way forward in the moment.

The man who'd been talking earlier shot the prince an annoyed look, clearly upset that his script had been interrupted, and continued as if Credence hadn't spoken. "Is there anyone in this house who would try on this slipper?" he continued.

All at once, everything slotted into place. I could do this. I could atone for my errors, I could stop Cinderella from leaving the cellar, and I could save Credence where I hadn't been able to save Hortense. And they'd just handed me my path to redemption.

"Yes," I said, almost before the words were out of his mouth. "Yes, I will try it on. That's my slipper, I lost it at last night's ball."

Even before I finished speaking, I knew it was foolish. There was no way anyone would mistake me for Cinderella, and I knew firsthand how tiny and dainty Cinderella's feet were, her ridiculous proportions sustained by magic. None of that mattered. If I could somehow get my foot into the shoe, then I could stem the horrible flood of events. And even if it wouldn't bring back Hortense, I could do what I had always done and protect others from Cinderella. I'd failed, but that shoe could be my salvation. I had no idea how I'd jam my foot into the blasted thing, but that was a problem I'd deal with in a moment. For now, I just had to get them to let me try.

A susurration of whispers and murmurs filled the
air, as the people in the room reacted to this outrageous
claim, but I held my head high and ignored it. I could
guess what they were saying. The woman at the ball last
night had been a great beauty, full of grace and charm,
in every way unlike this damaged and ungainly woman
before them now. I ignored it. I would make this work,
somehow. I willed them to just give me the slipper, for
their own sake. If I had the slipper, I could make this
right.

Imperiously, I held out my hand and sank deeper
into my lie, striving to seem unconcerned. I didn't want
anyone to know how desperate I was to keep Cinderella
away from that slipper. They couldn't find out about her.
I didn't want to know the consequences if they did.

"The glass makes it a very delicate, tricky business to
put on. My maid will need to help me, as she did the
night before the ball. Lilia!" I called, knowing she was
nearby, and hoping that her warning from this morning
meant that she would be willing to help me in my deception, praying to any god that would listen that her nervousness wouldn't give me away. "Lilia, I require your
assistance, please." I hoped that she would be able to
cover for me as I stuffed and sweated my foot into that
impossibly delicate shoe.

Lilia emerged from a doorway, looking nervous but
not unduly so. The glance she gave toward the prince
made it seem as though her nervousness were due to the
royalty in the room and not the bald-faced lie I was pulling her into. She came to stand next to me, and to my
great surprise, piped up.

"It wouldn't be proper to try it on here," she said.
"The process of putting on such delicate shoes is involved
and lengthy, and I can't guarantee her modesty, you

understand. Especially in front of the man who may yet become her fiancé! No, I'm afraid I must insist on privacy. Miss Eunice is far too shy and retiring to bring it up herself, but I can see the mortification in her eyes at the thought of needing to expose herself so! So if you will just hand us the shoe, we will go put it on, and pop right back in when we're done." She joined me in holding out an expectant hand, her manner brusque and firm.

I tried not to look utterly surprised by this version of Lilia, and just nodded along and tried to look as shy and retiring as possible. I had seen Mrs. Carnelian's expression at the doorway when Lilia had called me shy and retiring. Her eyebrows had flown up so high I thought they would disappear off her face entirely.

"This is most irregular," sputtered the attendant. "To need to put it on in private! Why, anything could happen! Your Royal Highness, she is clearly trying to deceive us—"

"Let her have it," interrupted Prince Credence. "I trust her. If she's not back in fifteen minutes, we can send someone to go check on her." His entourage exchanged exasperated looks, but he was still the prince, and his word carried an appropriate amount of weight.

I nodded at him gratefully, although once I had the slipper, I still had no idea what I was going to do. Sleeplessness, blood loss, and grief were all taking their toll on my mind. I hope I can be forgiven for thinking this plan ever had a chance of success. The courier handed over the glass slipper to Lilia, she thanked him, and then took my hand and pulled me out of the room.

We ended up in the kitchen, although I had no earthly idea why. I suspect Lilia just found it a comfortable place to be and brought me there without thinking.

"What are you going to do?" she whispered, throwing a nervous glance over her shoulder. I couldn't tell if she was nervous about being overheard by the group in the dining room or by Cinderella. The door to the cellar, large and ominous, stood directly outside the entrance to the kitchen, reminding us of the dangers below. "You know I'd never speak ill of the family, or engage in gossip, but you can't let Cinderella try on that slipper! It won't just be you who regrets it. You've got to make it fit you."

I stared at her, eyes narrowed. Suddenly, Lilia's wide-eyed stares seemed less innocent and more suspicious.

"What do you know of Cinderella?" I asked. "You're new here." New servants were never told anything outright. It's possible Lilia was just sensitive, but it seemed odd that she'd gathered so much information so quickly. I started to panic, worried that I'd have to contain a much larger breach than I'd previously considered.

Lilia blushed, averting her eyes.

"Because," she said softly. "I met her before. When I was much younger. I wanted to bring her a kitten and you got mad at me. And then we had to leave and I never got a chance to apologize."

I stared at her, the pieces slotting into place.

"Leo?" I asked, incredulous, then quickly corrected myself. "Lilia. But—Mr. Calton is your father?" I stared at her, my old childhood friend, changed so much but still the same sensitive and caring individual. Her strange, darting glances and abundant knowledge of the house made sense now.

"Was," she said softly. "He passed away several years ago. I came back here because I knew your father would pay well for discretion. But we don't have time for any of this. We've got to make you fit this shoe."

She lifted the shoe out of the box, and we both looked at it in dismay. It was tiny, much tinier than my feet had been for years.

"Maybe Hortense?" said Lilia tentatively. "She's only twelve, I know, but that has to be better than the prince getting into *her* clutches. Maybe the prince will agree to a long engagement!"

"I know," I said, simultaneously unspeakably grateful for Lilia's presence and her faith in me over my terrible sister, while at the same time cursing that she would bring up Hortense so casually. "But I'm afraid there was an . . . an accident. Hortense is . . . is no longer with us."

Lilia's eyes grew even wider, and she covered her mouth with her hand. She jerked her head in the direction of the cellar door, unable or unwilling to speak Cinderella's name. I nodded. Her eyes filled with tears, and she looked ready to start sobbing. I knew she was thinking of the sweet five-year-old she'd known, the one she'd read to while Hortense had slumbered, the one Lilia had taught to be careful with all manner of bugs and other crawlies. Tears pricked my eyes as well, but I blinked them away.

"I can't think of it right now," I pleaded. My mind was racing. The slipper wasn't something I could have planned for, something that all my years with Cinderella had prepared me for. "I just need to find some way to get my foot into this slipper—" I stopped. There, on the counter in front of me, stuck into a large wooden block, were Mrs. Carnelian's knives.

Lilia followed the direction of my gaze and let out a soft gasp when she realized what I was looking at. I pulled out the largest cleaver. It seemed most suitable for the job.

"Go stand watch," I said. "I can't afford to have anyone see me do this. Let me know if someone comes. Stall them if you can."

Her lip trembled, but she nodded and went to stand at the edge of the room, peering out into the hall. I picked up the cleaver, sat down on the floor, and took off my shoes, peeling off my white stockings and putting them high up on the counter, where they would be untouched by what was to come. I grabbed a few kitchen towels and padded the floor with them, hoping to soak up any mess. I put one between my teeth, gagging myself with the thick cotton. I was as ready as I would ever be. I began. First, I'd take the heel.

The blood wasn't what surprised me. I was expecting the blood, red, hot, and viscous, as it spilled over my knife, streaming down the metal shaft to drip off the tip of my blade into a pool at my feet. What surprised me was the bone, thick and solid in my heel, unmoving under the heavy steel of the purloined cleaver. I'd watched our cook, Mrs. Carnelian, use this same instrument to effortlessly part chickens from their heads, the blade a silver blur as she swung the knife with a confidence born of long practice. The meaty slap of the flesh, the crack of bone, followed by the heavy *thunk* of the knife being placed back in the butcher's block had always made my mouth water with anticipation of the sumptuous chicken feast she was preparing. I'm sure she never anticipated her cleaver being put to a use such as this.

I pulled the cleaver free from my foot with a loud squelch. The blood flowed more freely, staining everything around me, mocking me as it left my veins. The unwavering white bone peeked out of the folds of parted flesh, unyielding and unmoving. I could see a dent in the bone where I'd hit it with the cleaver. My vision swam and danced before my eyes. The pain was excruciating, but I couldn't focus on that. There was work still to be done.

Once more, I lifted the cleaver above my head, and swung, summoning every memory of Mrs. Carnelian I had. My heel was just a stubborn chicken neck that needed another whack to fully separate the bone and sinew. I could do this.

The blade swung down. The bone crunched and cracked. I bit clean through my lip, and the blood gushed into my mouth, hot and metallic, spilling down my chin to join the blood on the floor. But my heel had finally separated from my foot. It lay there, inert, a jagged, pitiful thing. Part flesh, part bone, surrounded by a pool of blood. The glass slipper glinted malevolently next to me, a deep green reminder of why what I was doing was necessary. I took a deep breath and without taking a moment's pause to celebrate my success, I swung again. Cinderella's feet were much smaller than mine. I would also need to take the toes.

A commotion outside the kitchen caught my attention, and I looked up, fear clouding my mind. I hoped Lilia would be a good enough guard to keep whoever it was out. If Credence were to walk in now . . .

Lilia stepped through the doorway and out of my sight, speaking in a low voice to whoever approached. I couldn't hear her very well, both because of the murmuring of all the other voices in the drawing room and also because my head was ringing and reeling from the pain. I felt lightheaded.

Lilia came back in, face pale and drawn, and footsteps followed behind her. I tensed, certain it was Credence, or one of his advisors, or anyone, really, who would uncover the truth of what I was doing and cause it all to come crashing down around me.

Instead, the familiar face of my mother came into sight. She was still wearing her traveling clothes, her graying hair pinned up tightly under a hat she only wore for carriage rides. Her expression, tight and angry when she entered the room, slid into horror as she took in my plight, sitting on the floor with a cleaver in my hand, the gory chunk of heel next to me, blood defiling the well-scrubbed kitchen floor.

"I had a dream that I needed to return—" she said, her gaze trailing over the scene before her. I didn't need further explanation. I was all too familiar with Cinderella-induced dreams. I stared up at her, unable to speak, not with the blood all around me and the cleaver still in my hand.

Mother's hand went to her mouth, her black lace glove stark against her skin, showing how pale she had grown. I looked up at her but couldn't find my voice to say anything.

"Eunice . . ." Mother began, and then stopped, her eyes darting again to the cleaver and the blood, and then flickering to the cellar door, questioning without saying a word.

"She—she took Hortense," I rasped out. "She took Hortense, and—" Tears welled up in my eyes, and Mother sucked in a breath, a sharp, horrified sound that conveyed a wealth of feeling.

"I have . . . I have to fit the slipper. She can't . . . they can't know, that it was her," I said, which I'm sure made no sense to Mother. Thankfully, after seven years of Cinderella, and a lifetime of knowing me, Mother wasn't one to ask unnecessary questions. Or maybe her dream had shown her enough of what had happened the night before to piece together what she was seeing.

She knelt down next to me, careful to keep her skirts out of the pool of blood that still surrounded my foot.

"Then we will fit the slipper," she said, her voice calm. Tears glistened in her eyes, but she kept any sign of it out of her voice. Others might have thought her unfeeling, but I knew it was just her way. She would do what needed to be done.

I lifted the cleaver, ready to take the toes as well, but my hand was trembling with pain, exhaustion, and blood loss. Warm fingers folded over mine, and my mother's hand lifted my own, wrapped firmly around the cleaver. She directed my hand, resting the sharp blade across the line of my toes and slanted the knife to follow the diagonal formed by my foot.

Our eyes locked, and in what I can only describe as an act of pure love, my mother, never breaking eye contact with me, pushed her weight down on the blade, causing it to crunch through the bone of my toes, separating them from the rest of my foot. I let out a soft whimper but remained quiet. The stakes were too high.

Seeing my toes lying there, disconnected from my body, was even more horrible than seeing my heel. The heel was a chunk of flesh with a hint of bone attached; it was not something I generally thought about, and with time I was sure it would heal up nicely. My toes, however . . . Without my toes, my foot looked alien and strange, a square block of flesh attached to my leg that I did not recognize. The toes themselves looked sad and abandoned, no longer serving any purpose. My head swam and spun, but I could not look away from the five little lumps that had until recently been my toes.

I picked up the glass slipper with trembling hands, ready to complete the task and force my mangled flesh into the odious shoe. The wound where my toes had been encountered the glass sides of the shoe, causing me to repress a silent scream, my eyes welling with tears as the glass pressed against the still open flesh. My body shuddered with revulsion as I tried to force the clear glass over the ruined foot. But glass hides nothing, and I realized that this would never work, whimpering as I pulled the shoe off. It had all been for naught. I was overcome with despair. The lumps of my toes mocked me, the slipper mocked me, the blood on the floor mocked me. I had failed, and I would not be able to save Prince Credence from my sister.

My mother stroked my hair, just a brief, soft caress, and then she sprang into efficient motion, leaving me there on the floor. I was bleeding, unfocused, losing my grasp on the world around me, on the edge of unconsciousness, when I felt a sudden searing pain. My mother had grabbed the cast-iron kettle, hot and full of boiling water, from the stove and pressed it against the open wound where my toes had been, cauterizing the wound and staunching the flow of blood.

The pain brought me back to myself somewhat, but before I could say anything Mother heaved the kettle again, pressing my heel against the hot metal, similarly cauterizing the area and keeping me from bleeding to death.

Her face was white, but even then she kept her head. I can only assume years of caring for her unpredictable stepdaughter had led her to this calm efficiency, even in the midst of such chaos.

"Eat this," she said, and shoved a piece of candied ginger into my mouth.

I'd never felt less like eating, but I did as I was bidden and chewed. The bright, spicy flavor of the ginger and the sweetness of the sugar brought me even further back to myself. I realized with dismay that we had only five minutes left and the slipper was still not on my foot.

My eyes met Mother's, then we both looked down at the slipper.

"It will fit now," she said. "But it's going to hurt. Please forgive me."

With that plea the only indication she was bothered by her actions, my mother tore off a strip of her petticoat, from an area where it wouldn't show, and bound my foot tightly. I watched her with gritted teeth, again too grateful for words. My plan had been ill-advised from the start, and without her stalwart actions and presence, I would not only have failed, but I am certain that I would have died, bleeding to death alone on the tile floor.

After binding my foot, Mother slid my discarded white stocking over the makeshift bandages. Without my toes and heel, the stocking was too long, so she had to pull it up my leg as high as it would go, putting pressure on my wounds and causing me to whimper piteously and scrabble at the floor, trying to get away from her gentle but insistent hands. There was a strange deformation of the material behind my ankle, where my heel had previously stretched out the cloth. But she yanked at it and smoothed it until it was almost unnoticeable, the way she'd done when I was a child and was loath to get dressed for a fancy function. Then she picked up my foot and slid it into the odious green glass slipper.

It hurt worse than anything I'd ever felt in my life, but I was able to bear it with the cauterization, the padding of the bandage and the slipper, and my mother's steady hands.

She helped me to my feet, and we managed to walk around the room. I hobbled a little, my foot unsteady and aching, but I hoped it could be explained away by the uneven heels of the shoes I was wearing. The glass slipper was a ridiculous thing, all hard lines without an ounce of comfort to be had, but Cinderella had crafted it well. It did not break under my weight.

I leaned on my mother heavily, and she wrapped my hand in hers, a warm reminder of her presence. We silently made our way back to the drawing room, ready to be judged by the court, the rest of my household, and of course, Prince Credence.

16

Deceptions

WE WALKED INTO the middle of an argument. Prince Credence and a pompous man holding a scroll were facing each other, red-faced and shouting. The woman with the crow stood behind them, her face impassive but eyes sharp and missing nothing from their exchange. We caught the last few words as we entered the room.

"—no one remembers her face!" shouted Credence. "So who's to say it *can't* be her?"

"Your Royal Highness, you must reconsider! While it is true that the details of last night are . . . are hazy, everyone remembers a great beauty! And now you expect us to believe that this woman is the one you danced with all last night? Does nothing ring false about that in your empty, royal head?"

I coughed, and the heads of everyone in the room whipped around. The face of the courtier who'd been arguing with Credence flushed an even darker red, but he gave me a look that told me he did not regret calling into doubt my beauty, and he would do it again if given the chance. Mother was not so forgiving, giving the man a stare that had him shrinking back and muttering apologies where my own presence had not been enough to inspire any such goodwill.

I have no doubt that I looked a mess. Pale from the loss of blood, hair disheveled from tearing at it, clinging tightly to my mother's arm. To be honest, I am surprised anyone believed it for as long as they did, what with the picture I made before them.

"It fits," I said. I did not recognize my own voice. I was a hoarse, rasping creature, my throat dry and my lips sore from having bitten them. I hoped my pain wasn't obvious, but in hindsight, I'm certain it was.

Right then, however, none of that mattered to me. What mattered was the look on Credence's face—an incredulous sort of happiness, as if he couldn't believe his luck. No one ever looked at me like that, much less the crown prince, and so at first I didn't understand. He couldn't possibly be excited that it was me, could he? But then he was striding across the room, and he grabbed me by the shoulders, his hands solid and warm through my dress. I could feel the heat of his palms. Under ordinary circumstances I'm sure it would have been wonderful, an exciting moment for me and my burgeoning womanhood. As it was, I focused on the warmth of his hands as something, anything, to distract me from the overwhelming urge to faint dead away.

"It *is* you," he said, his eyes intent on mine. The crowd behind him began to murmur, shocked and displeased that he knew me. Not even Mother's glare could quell their whispers. I could hear snippets of their conversation—"drab," "plain," "ugly"—nothing I hadn't heard before or thought myself. In other circumstances, I might even have cared.

"I thought . . ." Credence began. "You wouldn't tell me your name last night, and I couldn't remember, exactly, what you looked like, and I thought you were just being shy. Of course, at first I thought you hadn't come, even though I'd invited you specifically, and you said you would, in your last letter. And I was disappointed, because I thought, well, if I must go through with this, at least it will be someone who talks to me like I'm a person, and that maybe if we could both talk to each other like people, then this whole marriage thing wouldn't be too terrible! But then you showed up, looking glorious, and I didn't know what to think! I mean, I hoped it might be you, but I wasn't sure, and then the court magicians told me to come here, and it turned out to be you after all!" His eyes shone, and he smiled at me, delighted with his luck.

My heart sank. Of course he'd responded to Cinderella and her beauty. He thought he was complimenting me, but the whole exchange merely served to drive home how much I could never attract someone like the prince on my own. I smiled back, but I knew it was a weak attempt. His eyes clouded with concern.

"Eunice, you don't look well. Is that why you left early last night? Please, sit down." He gave me a worried look and put a solicitous hand on my elbow, so that he and Mother each had one of my arms. At the invitation to take the pressure off my aching foot, I was so relieved that I almost cried. I felt tears prick at the corners of my eyes, but I managed to contain myself. I took a step forward, and another, still guided by the twin presences of Credence and Mother. I almost made it to the chair he was steering me toward. Almost, but not quite.

I felt a gush of warmth at my toes, and I knew that my foot had started bleeding again. I prayed that the bandages would hold, and that the green glass of the slipper would be dark enough to hide any blood, but in the end, my prayers all came to naught.

I tried not to glance down at my foot, knowing that if I did, it would draw the gaze of everyone else in the room. My foot ached, and the dizziness that I had been fighting since leaving the kitchen threatened to over-whelm me, causing me to sway to the side as I approached the chair, even with my companions' aid. As I swayed, my ankle buckled, just for a moment, and the green glass slipper on my foot briefly dipped down. A hot rush of blood slid along my foot, and I closed my eyes.

I didn't need to look to know that the blood had spilled onto the rug, but I looked anyway, hoping against hope that it was just a spot, something that could be explained away, or that might slip by unnoticed. But that was not the case.

More blood had welled up in the toe of the shoe than I had realized. Without the presence of my toes, the blood had pooled in the pointed slipper, forming a reservoir in the tip that had spilled over when I had lost my balance. The fat drops of blood that had slipped down the side of the slipper formed a pool on the floor, staining the delicate fibers of the gray rug under my feet a deep crimson color. I remember thinking that Mother loved that rug, and she'd be so upset that I'd ruined it. After that, I don't remember much more, as the lack of sleep, blood loss, and pain all caught up with me at once,

and the sight of my own blood, and the failure it repre-
sented, was too much for me. I slipped into unconsciousness to the sounds of shouting, Mother and Credence
and his entourage all mixing together, and I knew
no more.

17

Revealing Cinderella

MY LAPSE INTO unconsciousness was brief—it must have been no longer than five minutes at most. When I came to, the room around me was in chaos. I lay slumped in the chair I'd been trying to reach earlier, but someone had removed my slipper, along with the makeshift bandages Mother had applied, and my mutilated foot was exposed to the world for all to see. My wounds were ugly and raw, and my whole foot throbbed, but it had at least stopped bleeding. The green glass slipper lay next to my foot on the floor, tipped on its side, the interior of that horrid shoe still coated with my blood—although, at that point, much of my blood was on the rug beneath my chair, spilled out like a crimson warning sign, letting everyone know of my deception, and mocking me with my failure. The sight of the blood made me want to close my eyes and fold back up into unconsciousness, but I could not allow myself to do so. If I had failed, and I most comprehensively had, then I was going to need to engage in what was to happen, if I had any hope of keeping

Cinderella from getting involved. In retrospect, I should have just passed out again.

A warm hand still gripped my arm, and with effort, I turned my head to see Mother, crouched by the chair, her face bloodless. I made eye contact with her, letting her know I was awake once more, and her grip on my arm squeezed tighter. It was actually too tight, but the mild discomfort was nothing compared to how the rest of me felt. Mother's eyes bored into me, and I wanted to weep at the sight. Although she stayed near me and spoke not a word, I could read her perfectly well. Her eyes were filled with despair, absent of any sort of hope or encouragement, which I sorely needed. I tore myself away from her terrible gaze and turned my attention to the rest of the room.

Around me was utter chaos. Everyone was shouting at everyone else, without discernible purpose or effect. Mrs. Carnelian was weeping in the corner, having stepped out from behind the counter, and wailing to anyone who would listen that I was a good girl, and they shouldn't hold it against me too much. The man who'd argued with Credence earlier was now shouting at Credence that he knew it was too good to be true. Credence was shouting something at Lilia about her not being qualified to be a proper witness. Lilia was shouting at the old woman with the crow on her shoulder for having taken off my bandages. I had trouble picking out individual words, the hubbub of the room making it hard to focus. The old woman was staring at me with judgmental eyes, and I saw that in her hands she held the bloodied strips of cloth that Mother had used to bind my foot. The sight of the cloths made my stomach heave and my head grow faint, and once more I had to fight to stay conscious.

Seeing that I was awake, the old woman held up her hand, a command for silence. The crowd hushed, all yelling forgotten, and I realized that this was no mere old woman—this must be one of the court mages who had divined that the owner of the shoe was in our home. Of course Prince Credence would bring along one of his famed mages on this journey, when hundreds of young women would be clamoring for his hand and willing to do unscrupulous things to get it. Just like I had done. I should have realized earlier that my lies were doomed from the start, but I cannot undo the past. Back then I only knew that I would have to exercise utmost caution or my heart might betray more of me than I hoped to give.

The mage crouched down in front of me, still holding the bloodied bandages, and took a long, deep sniff of the bloodstained cloth. She then held it up to the crow on her shoulder, and he did the same, turning his large black beak so that the small nostrils on the side would have direct access to the blood. They both reached out and bit the cloth, human teeth and crow beak sinking into the fabric as one, masticating the cloth until it was a wet mess. Still working in unison, they spat it to the floor, then turned and looked at me, human and crow eyes both blown wide, pupils surrounded by the tiniest sliver of matching amber irises.

"Do you know what I am?" the woman asked. I nodded yes. Beside me, Mother made a soft sound of disgust, but the woman ignored it.

"Good. I offer you this truth to begin with: my name is Serena. I offer you a second one, freely: it is important that you answer my questions honestly. I will start simply, and then we shall continue. Please speak everything aloud—it will be recorded by the court scribe."

I nodded, heart in my throat. All my worst fears, everything that Mr. Father had drilled into me, came rushing back. Detection seemed inevitable. I glanced over and saw that the man with the scroll had indeed pulled out a large quill and was recording the conversation.

"To begin with, did you leave that slipper at the ball last night?" Serena asked.

The room was silent and still, waiting for me to answer. Mother's fingers were tight on my arm, cutting off circulation to my hand. Her desolate expression gave me the strength to answer, even though a voice in my head was screaming that the truth would ruin us all. I would reveal only as much truth as was required of me, and nothing more.

"No."

My simple negative broke something loose in the room, and several people began to all speak at once, their voices full of anger, but Serena lifted her hand again, and they fell back into silence. I dared sneak a look at Credence's face, needing to know what he was thinking. The devastated expression I encountered was enough to cause me to look away at once.

"Did you mutilate your foot so as to fit it into the slipper?" Serena asked, drawing me back to her and the crow.

"Yes." I was thankful she wasn't asking more detailed questions, so that I didn't have to implicate Mother for her role. If I could just answer with as little information as possible, maybe I could avoid spilling anything too damning.

"Did you do this to force Prince Credence to marry you instead of someone else?" she asked.

I couldn't look up at him, but I knew I had to speak. "Yes." As soon as I spoke, I heard a sharp gasp that could only have come from Credence. I continued to resolutely ignore him. I refused to see the damage I was inflicting.

Serena's shrewd eyes searched me for a moment more, and then she asked the question that I had been dreading. "Do you know the woman who attended the ball and left this shoe at the palace last night?"

I gritted my teeth, determined not to answer, but the words burbled up inside me, forcing their way over my tongue, past my teeth and lips. Mother trembled beside me, and I knew she was willing me not to answer, to lie, but I was helpless.

"Yes," I said. Although everyone in the room was shocked, they once again heeded Serena's raised hand and said nothing. I couldn't look at anyone, couldn't bear to see Credence or my mother's face. The judgment from everyone in the room was oppressive, despite them remaining silent. Their shifting and their surprised breaths spoke eloquently enough—they were all desperate to be involved in the scandal.

"Tell us." Her tone was final, and although I tried not to speak, once more I was not in control of my own tongue.

"It was my sister, Cinderella. I didn't want her to go, and once I found out she did, I didn't want her to marry Prince Credence so I tried to do it myself, to keep him from her." My words were entirely unemotional, and I'm sure I looked a monster to them, but I was thankful that I was only forced to say the bare minimum. Mr. Father's injunction to tell no one of Cinderella's true nature, lest she grow in power and feed off of their fear, lay heavily in my thoughts. Even then, I could not expose her. It would have meant our doom. Better they think me a callous, wicked girl than that they guess the truth about Cinderella.

I forged ahead, hoping to run with this new idea and make myself monstrous. I hoped that they would see only my own monstrousness and not Cinderella's, which was the more dangerous sort. I don't know what I thought would happen after I painted myself as the villain. At this point I allowed myself to make eye contact with my mother once more, and although her face was heartbroken, she gave me a small nod and I felt relief run through me. I had protected our family.

"Where is she?" burst out Prince Credence.

Without meeting his eyes, I answered, "She's in the cellar."

"You've locked her in the cellar rather than allow her the chance to meet me?" asked Credence. I still couldn't look at him.

"No," said the mage, again turning her discerning eyes upon me. "No, that's not quite right, is it, girl?"

I shook my head and just hoped that they would see my actions as the cruelty of an indifferent girl and not the desperate attempt to keep a monster in our house contained. "No, she lives there. She's always locked in the cellar. I only let her out to do chores. She snuck out to the ball and I couldn't stop her. She wasn't allowed to go."

The sudden uproar drowned me out. Everyone was shouting once more, determined to have their voices heard. Two of the courtiers grabbed Lilia and dragged her out of the room, demanding to be taken to the cellar where Cinderella was kept. The old woman made no move to stop them, just looked at me with her eyes still wide with whatever magic she'd done to compel my truthfulness. I stared back at her, exhausted. If she had pressed me further and tried to get me to speak more about the cause of my actions, I think I would have told her. Why was Cinderella in the cellar? Why was I so intent on keeping Cinderella from Credence? Why, why, why? I had nothing left at that point, wracked as I was with pain, exhaustion, and the unexamined burden of my grief over Hortense. Things might have gone very differently if she had pushed. I will never know. For whatever reason, she did not question me any longer. Our staring contest was interrupted by the arrival of Cinderella.

Gone were the beautiful gown and the pristine clothes that Cinderella always elected to wear. Instead she was in some sort of burlap smock and skirt, playing up the role of the poor victim of the terrible stepsister. Her clothes were old and worn; I had never seen them before. I suspected they were an illusion, but I had no desire to smear blood into my eye to find out for certain. It was also possible she'd borrowed them, or stolen them, or set them aside for just such an occasion. Her skin was still flawless and pale, and her hair in pristine honeyed waves. The contrast between her clothing and her person struck me as hilarious, but I gave a valiant effort to hold in my laughter. I could not laugh without appearing even more villainous than I already did, but the incongruity of her actions was so obvious and heavy-handed.

I knew she was trying to make me look bad, but since I had just been doing the same thing myself, how could I complain? We had accidentally become aligned in our desires to make me seem the monster and not her. I do not know why she chose to hide her true nature in that moment when she had been set free with access to so many humans. Sometimes it seemed like she was exe-cuting a very long plan, with steps that were only known to her. But she was well behaved and committed to her farce as the very human victim of my very human mal-ice. Everything about her appeared fully human in the moment, including her feet. Her tiny, delicate, feminine feet—one of which was bare, as was her custom in the cellar, and the other of which wore the shoe that matched the green glass slipper currently lying on the floor in front of me.

Cinderella let out a soft cry and fell at my feet. She snatched up the slipper from the carpet, and, without pausing to wipe away my blood which still lined the glass, she slid it onto her foot. It fit her perfectly, of course, and then she stood up, managing to make her burlap look as graceful and beautiful as any queen's gown. She gave Credence a smile. I saw him melt before her charms, and I could no longer hold it in. I began to howl with laughter at the absurdity of it all—me trying to trick them, them finding out, and now Cinderella using the same green glass slipper to trick them into thinking she was just a young woman and nothing more. She was more cunning than I'd given her credit for and committed to her plan of becoming queen. I laughed and laughed, unable to do anything other than howl in her presence. It was while in this condition that I was clapped in irons by the prince's soldiers and brought here, to the castle prison where I await royal judgment and the royal wedding with equal trepidation.

Part 3

18

Infection

I SIT ALONE, UNABLE to think beyond the events that led up to my imprisonment. My brain keeps replaying them with unhelpful commentary. What if I'd spoken out sooner and argued with Mother about Hortense? What if I'd had a different reaction to Prince Credence in the marketplace? What if I'd jumped forward and broken Cinderella's neck, all those many years ago, when she first bit Hortense? None of these scenarios were likely, but they swirl within me, over and over and over again in my mind.

I'm also so full of questions that I can hardly sleep at night. For years I was certain that if anyone found out about Cinderella, the world would collapse. The sky would fall and her reign of terror would immediately begin. Instead, she's free, the world knows of her, and yet the sky is still in place, the world keeps spinning, and the only thing full of despair and ruin is me.

The worst is Hortense. I think of her constantly. She was an annoying younger sibling at times, but I went into all of this with her in mind. She didn't deserve this. No one deserved what happened to her.

Although I am lost in my thoughts, time has not stopped around me. The palace's prison is surprisingly active. If I had ever taken the time to imagine what the prison was like, I suppose I would have envisioned a dank, dark hole in the ground, deep under the castle, connected by a series of winding tunnels and stairs, where criminals and traitors to the crown could be locked up underground, away from the decent people above them, who worked hard to pretend they didn't exist.

My own cell isn't actually underground, but level with the gardens, so the scent of various plants wafts in through my window. My cell is reserved for the least important and least threatening prisoners. I know because one of the guards told me so on my first day, when I was dragged from my home and locked in this place. When the guard told me this I didn't know whether to be flattered or insulted. In reality, it's probably an accurate assessment of my abilities. I am not a dangerous prisoner. I am not clever enough to escape. I'm just a girl who failed to contain her sister, and I wait for the kingdom to crumble around me as a result of my actions.

Most of my time in the prison consists of lying on the straw pallet, alternating between tossing and turning and lying flat on my back, allowing my tears to slip down the sides of my face. I don't think I've gone more than about eight hours without crying since I arrived. I want to be strong, but there's just so much. So much anger, so much grief, so much frustration.

There's also the feeling of relief. For the first time in seven years, I am not responsible for what happens with

Cinderella. The sense of liberty this gives me is over-whelming, even if it is accompanied by a sickening guilt so poisonous and rancid that I hurt just thinking about it. How can I possibly be feeling free when I am trapped in a cell, one sister dead, another on the loose and wreak-ing havoc in the land I live in? Yet a sense of relief lin-gers, a sweet sensation of freedom and weightlessness. While I may be worried sick about Cinderella and what she is doing to Credence, there is nothing I can actually do about it, locked away as I am.

These thoughts grow further confused and jumbled by my fever. My foot is not healing properly, and the skin around the wounds is hot and tight to the touch. My whole foot has swollen to twice its size, and I see the pus gathering in the wound, yellowish-white pockets that should not be there, with a horrible smell. I am not well, by any definition, in body and soul.

My thoughts dance and swirl under the fever. I swear that I am not alone, that something haunts my cell with me, be it Cinderella, or Credence, or Mother, or Mr. Father, or even my dear sweet Hortense. At other times I cry for just how alone I am.

Cinderella appears most often, always mocking, always monstrous, often wearing those horrible green glass slippers. Sometimes she appears before me alone, and it is the mutations of her body that frighten: gnash-ing teeth, writhing tentacles, talons like knives. All of which cause me to whimper and try to hide under my thin blanket, cowering in a feverish haze in the corner of my cell. Other times I see her there with Credence, embracing him before she inevitably destroys him in some new, terrible way. In one particularly memorable dream, Cinderella is in front of me with Credence, wrapped around him while they share a passionate kiss.

I watch as her tongue lengthens into a sharp, bladed tentacle, and she stabs it into his mouth, piercing his head straight through, the point of the tentacle sticking out of the back of his skull while his eyes bulge and he struggles before going limp, pinned on her horrible tongue with his blood running hot and red over his body, his eyes glassy and beseeching in death.

I wake from that dream absolutely soaked with sweat and screaming until my throat is hoarse, and my screams draw the guards, who pity me enough to throw me a towel to mop up the worst of my secretions. I have no idea if Cinderella is sending me these dreams, as she did back home, or if my fever, grief, and exhaustion are whipping up these potent cocktails of nightmares that plague me every time I close my eyes. After such dreams I don't think I can ever fall back asleep, but my body is too weak to stay awake for long, and I pass out, not to awaken for many hours.

During my rare moments of lucidity, I listen to the guards, and it is via this habit of eavesdropping that I learn the tale of Cinderella at the ball, how she swept Credence off his feet. It hurts in a distant, far-off sort of way. Here, I am alone in my cell, with the straw-stuffed mattress on the floor and the plain food twice a day, where I am forced to relieve myself in a bucket that I can only heave myself toward half the time. My foot is so painful and swollen that I cannot put any weight on it. My jealousy over Credence is far away and strange, like I'm feeling it with someone else's heart, or seeing it distorted through a broken mirror. It still exists, but I have more pressing concerns.

I am scared for what Mother and Mr. Father have been told, but I cannot focus on that, and my days pass in a haze. I carry on long conversations with Mother, only to be yelled at by the guards to shut up, that there is no one there, but I cannot. In the grips of my fever, my brain is not my own. I have no control over my mouth.

I awaken in the night, covered in sweat, screaming again, but this time I'm not sure why. It is not a nightmare that has awoken me, but pain. Something is wrong, more wrong than usual. I look down at my foot, and the pockets of pus that I've been watching grow during the haze have burst. My foot is leaking brackish, yellowish-white fluid, mixed with blood, all over the straw-covered floor. I feel like I am dying. I do not stop screaming.

Eventually, I attract the attention of a guard, who comes over to yell at me to be quiet, as they always do, but something about my appearance gives him pause. I must finally look as bad as I feel. He speaks to me again, and I try to listen, but it's so hard to hear, so hard to focus on anything other than the sharp pain I'm feeling in my foot, and the fever that clouds my mind.

"Hey!" His shout finally cuts through, and I look up, trying my hardest to focus not just on his words but the shape of his mouth moving. Maybe that's the problem all along—I haven't been focusing on their mouths. I can do better.

"Look, if I come in there, are you going to try anything? You haven't exactly been well-behaved, but you're in a bad way, and I want to check on you." He is not unkind as he says this, even though I think this is one of the guards who expressed his thankfulness that Prince Credence escaped my ugly hag clutches. Or maybe that was another dream. Focusing on the shapes his mouth forms must have helped because I understand his words. I should respond to him. I don't mean to be a bad prisoner. I'd like to think I could be a better prisoner than Cinderella. I would never drain his life force, or kill his sister, or try to take over the kingdom. I try to express that.

"I'd never try to eat you," I say. "The stars don't scream for me. You don't have to worry. I'll be gone soon anyway, one way or another."

The guard swears, and then I hear the sound of the door creaking open. He walks in, holding a sword out at me, as if I'm going to rush him. This strikes me as funny; my whole foot is aflame, I can't even sit up straight, and he thinks I'm going to charge him? I begin to laugh, a wild, hysterical sound that quickly transforms into sobs, and tears are running down the well-worn tracks on my face.

I hear the guard say something, but it's too late. No amount of focus on his mouth can cause his words to pierce my brain, and when I feel the familiar sensation of darkness clouding over my mind, I welcome it and slip ungracefully into unconsciousness.

19

The Dream

MY FEVER RAGES. There is nothing I can do, nothing that penetrates the haze of my illness. Vague shapes come for me, horrible, terrible shapes, and I scream and cry, thrashing, trying my best to get away. They carry mysterious objects that glint with malicious purpose, and they touch my foot, and I shriek and sob, helpless as an infant. Everything hurts, not just my foot, but my whole body, concentrated on my foot and radiating up my leg in dozens of tendrils of sharp, lancing pain that never seem to end.

I do not know night from day. I am soaked in sweat, and as I am no longer capable of crawling, even a little bit. I soil myself repeatedly. The stench of urine, feces, and my own powerful sweat is my constant companion. My throat is raw and hoarse from screaming.

The hallucinations do not stop. Mother is there, entreating me to behave, just for a minute, and pleading with me to hold on. Hortense appears as I last saw her, slit from stem to stern, wrapped in her own intestines. She says nothing, merely watches me beg her for forgiveness before disappearing in a cloud of bloody mist.

I hear Mr. Father's voice, strident and demanding that someone fetch a doctor, but I do not see him. Where he should be is a man I do not recognize, whose face is a stranger to me. The stranger smiles at me with his strange face, and I know, deep in my soul, that this stranger has stolen Mr. Father's voice, and that if I let him touch me, he will steal mine too. So when he reaches out to try and touch my face, I shy back from him, screaming again. The stranger's face is tragic and sorrowful, and Mr. Father's voice emerges from his mouth to entreat me to get well soon. I am somewhat saddened by that, but at least I still have my voice.

Last and most terrible of my hallucinations is Cinderella. I've been seeing her in my dreams for seven years, so it is no surprise to me that she is even here in my little cell, when I have ostensibly escaped her clutches.

She appears before me, looking even more terrible and beautiful than last I saw her. She's gotten a new dress, which is sleek yellow silk, and she's wearing those green glass slippers that match her eyes. Her mouth is red and shows too many perfect, straight white teeth when she smiles. Golden waves of honey hair cascade over her shoulders and glint in the low light of my cell. She smiles at me.

"Eunice, dearest," she says. "It was very rude of you to try and keep me from my dear sweet Credence. But in the end, I suppose you helped us come together. I've told him all about your wicked, terrible ways—keeping me in the cellar, making me do your chores. He's been eager to console me and help me escape from my wicked, wicked stepsister." Cinderella's eyes glow a little, and I cower away from her, somehow managing to find the strength to drag myself and my foot to the edge of the cell, where I plaster myself against the wall, trying to put as much space between us as possible. She smiles at my efforts and continues speaking. She's usually not this chatty in my dreams. I close my eyes tight and put my hands over my ears to block her out, but she goes on. Her voice enters my ears as if she's right there, whispering to me from an inch away.

"So, thank you for that, Eunice. It's given me quite the nice pretext for my ignorance. Whenever I don't know how something works, I just bat my eyelashes at him and say that you never permitted me to try that before, and all is forgiven. Honestly, I couldn't have set up a better path to the throne without you. So I will do this one thing for you, because as you so eloquently reminded me the night after the ball, we are sisters, are we not? Your mother was quite clear on that point as well." Cinderella advances on me as she speaks, until she looms over me, her eyes still glowing.

Her words don't make any sense to me, and I dislike the idea of my hallucinations interacting. Mother hallucination should not speak to Cinderella hallucination; it's rude for them to communicate outside of my mind when I'm the one creating them. I whimper, but I know it's useless to hide from my own mind. The hallucinations will stick with me whether I want them to or not.

"So please hold still, dear Eunice, and remember that this is for your own good." With that ominous pronouncement, she pounces upon me, much as she once pounced upon a mouse at the wedding, many years ago.

Cinderella is on me before I have the chance to even scream. She falls to my feet, and grabs my foot with her delicate, milk-white hands, and squeezes the swollen appendage hard, which causes so much pain that I black out for a moment, my eyes rolling back into my head. I still don't scream. I don't want to give her the satisfaction.

Cinderella yanks my foot up to her mouth and eyes the ruined flesh hungrily, her hot breath an unwelcome breeze against my foot. Her eyes are the green of the pus that has collected under my skin, and her breath smells just like the whiffs I get from my infected foot, whenever the smell is able to pierce the miasma of shit and urine and sweat that clings to me like a cloak. My foot is huge and dark and swollen, my normally pale skin turned purple and red with streaks of white in it. It has tripled in size, and there is no hint of bone in the outline of my foot, or any dip in my ankle. Angry red lines run up my ankle and into my leg, turning my foot into a solid blob attached to the end of another solid blob. Nothing is the right color, everything hurts, and seeing Cinderella's delicate hands on me only exacerbates just how wrong the limb is.

Her mouth opens wider, and her tongue snakes out to lick directly on the open wound, a slimy sensation that burns and sends my pain receptors lighting up. I clamp my hand over my mouth, still determined not to let any version of Cinderella, even a hallucinatory one, have the satisfaction of hearing me scream, but it is a close thing. I gag into my hand at the sensation and sight of her tongue moving over my ruined flesh, licking along the crusted red blood and pus, pressing the flat of her tongue against the pockets of pus.

Cinderella scoops up one such pocket of green-tinted pus into her mouth, the infection leaking out of my body onto her waiting tongue, and her eyes close with relish as she licks it into her waiting mouth. I shudder and gag, repulsed, but there is nothing in my body to come up except the slight taste of some bile. I am wrung dry and empty from my illness, and I must exist here, in this space, with Cinderella treating my foot as her own personal buffet. She licks her lips and her tongue darts out again. I try to close my eyes to block out the sight, but a stabbing sensation sends them flying open.

Cinderella's tongue is no longer the pink, human bit of muscle that everyone has in their mouth. Instead, it has morphed into a long, gray tentacle that is now questing into the wound on my foot. I watch in uncomprehending horror as I see the tip of the tentacle open up, revealing that it is hollow on the inside like a straw. She stabs this hollow tip into the top of my foot, where the skin is tight and swollen like a tick after having feasted on the blood of its host.

Whatever pain I thought I was feeling before is nothing compared to this. Pus and blood and other brackish liquid spurt from my foot where she has pierced it, and the gray tentacle tongue suctions it all up, pulling the fluids into her body. I can see the fluid traveling up the hollowed center of the tentacle, and when I dare glance up at her face, Cinderella's expression is rapturous. Her eyes are open and staring, and I have never seen such a look of bliss on her face.

My resolve not to scream is still in effect, but I am whimpering and crying. As the gush of fluids from my foot slows to a trickle, Cinderella lifts her tongue from my flesh and I heave a sigh of relief. My fevered mind has subjected me to torture before, but it is generally of short duration. I begin to relax, satisfied that the dream will soon end and I will wake up in my cell, perhaps to a guard yelling at me to be quiet.

Instead, Cinderella's tongue rears back like a snake, and she stabs into me again, slightly above where she entered my skin the last time. I scream, all resolve to the contrary forgotten. This time, the pus does not explode outward, although my foot is still swollen, so to get at the fluids, Cinderella wriggles her tongue in deeper. I can see it bulging against my already taut skin, burrowing like a worm into the moist tunnels of my muscle and bone and fat, collecting fluid as it goes, exploring my flesh for pockets of decay and infection, and then dragging them up the hollow tube and down Cinderella's waiting throat.

The wriggling tongue extends past my foot and begins to chase down the red lines of infection that have crawled their way up my leg. Through the tears and whimpering, I watch in disbelief as the lines begin to recede, whatever infection plaguing me sucked up by Cinderella's questing tongue. The pain is indescribable, and I curse myself for this fantasy of the most unlikely of saviors, Cinderella, torturing me even as she rids me of the infection that I am certain will kill me soon. I am not so far gone that I don't realize what is happening to my body, even if my brain is not my own, now or in the recent past. If I could imagine myself being saved from my own demise, I would not have willingly chosen this, and again I curse my fever for subjecting me to this horror.

The tentacle continues to burrow under my skin, chasing down every last drop of fluid, of swelling, of the terrible pus that has built up in my extremities. I see my skin returning to its normal color, losing the red and purple hues that have plagued me. I scream with the pain of having my flesh violated by this tentacle dipping in and out of me and wriggling all the way up my leg as it hunts down its prey.

After an eternity of pain, Cinderella withdraws her tongue and smiles at me. I can see through the beautiful silk of her dress that her stomach, normally trim and willowy, is bloated and swollen with how much she has sucked out of me. She sees me looking and smiles, her hand stroking over the swollen bulge of her stomach, in a faint mockery of a pregnant woman caressing the new life within her. Instead, she caresses what was in me. I keep chanting in my head that it's not real, it's not real; she'll leave soon enough and I won't have to deal with her. There is nothing I want less than to be saved by the very person who killed my wonderful Hortense.

"You're even more delicious than Hortense, my dear Eunice," she says, licking her lips, and speaking as if she has plucked that name out of my head. I freeze. How does she know my thoughts? She smirks at me and continues.

"We're connected now, you realize. I've drunk of your flesh and tasted your very being. Not to mention I've been tasting your mind for years, so we were primed for it. Right now we're still sisters, of course, there's nothing I can do about that. You can still tell me not to harm you and I will not. Now, however, there will be time for some reciprocity." Cinderella gives me another smile and leans over me. "Let's strengthen this little bond of ours, shall we? I never got to finish it with Hortense, and I'm so curious about the effects. Shouldn't take too long now. After all, I wouldn't want my precious prince to worry about his sweet little flower all alone with her wicked stepsister." Her hand shoots out and grabs me under the jaw, forcing my mouth open and my head to tip back. Cinderella leans over me and puts her mouth on mine in a terrible parody of a kiss. Her tongue forces its way into my mouth and pumps a load of foul, rotten paste into my mouth. I struggle to spit it out, to bite her, to fight back in any way, but she pulls back from my lips and clamps her hand over my mouth and nose. I have no choice but to swallow the mouthful.

She smirks at me and wipes her mouth with the back of her hand. I see green sludge marring the whiteness of her skin, and I gag, hoping to spit some of the foul sludge up, but it's too late. Cinderella has tasted me now, and I have tasted her. I can feel the connection between us, like hundreds of tiny webs that connect my essence to hers. I shiver.

"'Til next time, sister Eunice," says Cinderella, and she leaves the cell just as I slip into blackness. My last thought is that I would rather die than undergo another hallucination like this one again. I hope I have the chance.

20

Mother

I AWAKE STILL IN my cell to a beam of sunlight shining directly into my eyes. I raise my hand to cover my eyes and brush against my hair. It is clean and dry, as opposed to wet and greasy, the way it has been every single day since I arrived in the cell. I don't recall washing it, but I have more pressing concerns than trying to figure out this mystery. For once, I am not covered in sweat or screaming upon waking, and I marvel at my good fortune. But I do not entirely trust it. I am thirsty, and as my brain seems to be cooperating for the moment, I take a risk and prop myself up on my elbows. I look around to see if a guard has left the water close enough that I might be able to get to it without too much pain.

"Oh, darling, you're awake."

I sigh, and flop back down on the straw mat. Apparently my brain isn't as cooperative as I thought. A hallucination of Mother sits across from me, on a spindly wooden chair that I know isn't in my cell, drinking a cup of tea from a cup and saucer that is equally improbable here in my austere abode. She sets the saucer and cup on the floor and walks over to me. She kneels down by my bed, placing her hand on my forehead. I jerk back. Her hand feels so real, much heavier than I would anticipate, and despite my hesitance as to Mother's realness, I can't help but lean into her hand. I've been so alone; I just want to be comforted by my mother, even if she is a product of my fevered imagination.

Mother strokes my hair, her hands soft, and I can smell her perfume, the one she started wearing when she and Mr. Fitzwilliam were courting. As a child I'd hated it, because it signified a change from how things used to be. But now it's just another part of her scent, familiar and comforting.

"It's odd," I say, my eyes closed against the vision, even though I can still feel its weight against my hand.

"What's odd, dearest?" says the hallucination of my mother.

"I can feel you," I respond. "I couldn't feel you any of the other times I dreamt you were here. Or hallucinated you. It's been hard to tell the difference between sleeping and waking. You also smell perfect. It adds to the whole illusion. I like it. Feel free to continue."

"Oh, darling," says Mother, and I can hear her voice choked with tears. She does not let up the gentle stroking of my hair. "I'm really here. It's not a dream or a hallucination. Ever since they took you, I've been begging anyone who would listen to let me in to see you. They finally did, and here I am."

My eyes snap open, and I take in my surroundings more fully. I'm lying in the cell, just as I was before, with the rounded outer wall made of stern gray stone, the itchy straw-stuffed pallet, and the large wooden door, strapped with iron fittings. It is all as I remember. What's different, besides the presence of my mother, is my own condition. While I have trouble remembering in detail, the last time I was cognizant of my own state of hygiene, I was well disgusted with myself. I had been soaked with fever sweat, unable to get up from my pallet to reach the latrine in the corner, and thus had soiled myself in a variety of ways. All of that has been washed away. My skin is clean and free of grease, and my hair, as I'd already noted, has also been washed. I am wearing a new shift of plain linen, but it feels like heaven. I have never soiled myself in this garment, and that in and of itself is a novel prospect at this point.

Much as I long to luxuriate in this feeling of cleanliness, I am too confused to spend much time lingering on the mystery of my clean body and the absence of the acrid stench of sweat, urine, and feces that has been my constant companion almost since I entered confinement. I have no recollection of how I could have gotten to this state. The last thing I remember . . . but I refuse to dwell on that fever dream.

In a slight daze, I look down at the source of my fever and accompanying hallucinations—my mutilated foot. I am shocked.

Where before there was a weeping, oozing stump, with pieces of straw and dirt stuck to the open edge, and a crust of dried blood and fluids, there is now a neat white bandage. Nothing hurts, but I realize with growing alarm that there are round white scars all along my foot and up into my ankle—scars that match the events of my most recent nightmare starring Cinderella. The rough texture of my bed cover, the tightness of the bandages—they are all just normal sensations, albeit slightly more sensitive on the round scars. Am I still dreaming? I hope that I am still dreaming, for if I am not, these scars mean that the other incident was not a dream either. I look up at Mother, too panicked for words, and she misreads the question in my eyes, attempting to fill me in on less important matters than whether or not I am now permanently tethered to the bane of my existence.

"You've been in this cell for ten days now. After you left, there was some talk of taking me along as well, but ultimately they decided you alone were responsible for the horrors of the evening. They didn't want to let anyone in to see you; they said you were a threat to the crown. But then your fever took a turn for the worse, and the guards allowed a doctor to treat you. With some begging, I was also allowed in. I'm already on rather thin ice with the crown at the moment, but I pointed out that I was much cheaper than having the doctor care for you all the time." She looks me over, paying special attention to my foot, and nods in satisfaction at what she sees before returning to her chair and picking up her teacup and saucer, taking a long sip. Her trembling hands cause the pieces of plain white china to clatter against one another, and I can tell she's trying to calm herself. I must have been worse off than I thought.

"Was it—was it so bad as all that?" I ask tentatively.

Mother looks at me and her eyes well with tears. "You almost died," she says, her voice as trembly as her hands. "The doctor wasn't sure you'd make it, even as recently as yesterday. Your father and I were begging them to seek other treatments, but they said that they'd already done what they could for you. The infection in your foot . . ." Her breath catches again, and I can see her force herself to go on. "It was out of control, spreading up your leg. The doctor told me to expect the worst, and that I shouldn't—shouldn't hope for a better outcome. I didn't know what to do. I couldn't . . . I couldn't bear to lose you too, Eunice. After Hortense—" she cuts off.

I close my eyes. I don't want to think about Hortense, but she is present in every breath I take, every waking moment as well as my dreaming ones. There is no escaping my lost, idiotic, wonderful little sister. I look back up at Mother and see a mirror of my own sadness.

Mother's hands are shaking so badly that tea is sloshing over the sides of the cup, and her mouth is a twisted, unhappy line. But her eyes are dry. I imagine the tears have already come and gone for her. I'm not sure I will ever run out of tears. She continues, avoiding my gaze, focusing on the spilled tea on her hands and dress.

"I didn't know what else to do." Mother's eyes are bright and intent, and I want to hide from her gaze. She gets up from her chair and walks over to me, kneeling down once more next to my sorry mattress, her long fingers cupping my cheeks. I do not want to hear what she has to say. I lift my gaze to the ceiling, refusing to meet her eyes, tears welling and running down my upturned face. This does not stop her from continuing to speak, her voice low and quiet, too low for any of the guards who may be stationed outside my cell to hear.

"So I went to Cinderella," she says, and I'm so startled that at last I meet her eyes, horrified. I open my mouth to protest, but she shushes me and continues, offering incontrovertible proof that my worst fear is a reality.

"Hush, Eunice. Yes, I went to Cinderella last night. I begged her, out of all the familial affection in the world, to help her sister. To eat the rot out of you and to save you from certain death. She did not want to at first, but eventually she gave in and she came here last night, under cover of darkness."

My tears are flowing freely now. I shake my head rapidly and begin to mutter denials.

"No, no no no, no no, it can't be, nonononononono." I'm rocking and holding my arms around myself tightly. Mother wraps her arms around me and holds me as I shake to pieces. I wail and cry, denials spouting from my lips, but she just holds me tighter.

"Why did you do it?" I finally ask through the tears. "Why did you let her touch me? I would rather have died!"

Mother doesn't let go, just strokes my head and presses a kiss to my hair. "Darling, if you died, how could I possibly go on? If I lost you to that monstrous girl, what was it all for?"

I shake my head again and let out another sob.

"She killed Hortense!" I wail. "She killed Hortense because she always hated her and wanted to complete what she started when she was twelve! And now you've let her sink her hooks into me as well! You haven't saved me at all, you've just delayed my execution!"

I can feel Mother's tears in my hair, and we sit and rock together on the mattress in my cell. The sunlight filters in through the tiny window set high in the wall and I can see the dust motes lingering and floating in the stagnant air. Mother tightens her arms around me and speaks at last, her voice low and urgent in the stillness of my confinement.

"I have to believe that isn't true. There must be something we can do to keep you safe. I'll consult with Adrian—"

She's cut off by the door creaking open. One of the guards stands just inside the doorway and motions impatiently at Mother. "Time's up. You were permitted to be here until she woke up, and it's already past that. Time to go."

Mother looks at me, her eyes sad and wide. All the anger I felt with her a moment ago evaporates.

"Don't go," I plead, clutching her arm. She disentangles herself and kisses the top of my head.

"You heard the man. I must leave. I will—I will visit again, if permitted. Be strong, my love. You are still alive, and there are people who love you. That is always cause for hope." With a last lingering touch to my hand, she is gone, leaving only the scent of her perfume behind. The heavy door thuds shut behind her and the metal bars that keep me imprisoned slot into place. I shudder, not at the unpleasant sound but at a sudden realization. This is what Cinderella must have felt like every time we closed the door and left her alone in the cellar. I am not sure I like this rush of empathy for her that fills me, thinking of her alone and lonely in our cellar, much like I am now.

CHAPTER

21

A Surprise

AFTER MOTHER LEAVES I don't move for a while. I am distraught over the revelation of how my health has been bought, and I can feel the tiny webs that connect me to Cinderella. If I concentrate, I get the sense that she is to the east of me, although I have no way of knowing if that sense is true. I also get brief flashes of things that cannot be unseen—a bloody handprint wiped up from a palace wall, a dark corner filled with the scent of rot, and a pair of green, decaying eyes staring back at me from a mirror. These images are often accompanied by the sound of distant stars screaming, but at this point I'm able to block that out. The images are new, but they're in the same vein as all my other dreams. When she's not actively in the same room as me, working her dark powers, I am capable of being blasé about Cinderella. It's a defense mechanism without which I would not have survived the last seven years.

Now that I am no longer wracked with fever, lying still on my straw mattress grows boring very quickly. I decide to investigate the gift for which I have paid such a terrible price. Hunching over like some sort of goblin, I inspect my foot. The white bandage remains clean and pristine, although I have not tried to walk on it since I awakened from my fever. That will soon need to change or I will be back in the position of soiling myself on my straw mat in my new clothes, and I have no intention of going down that road again if I can at all help it.

Round, circular white scars dot my leg, and I remember from my dream that Cinderella used her tongue to pierce into my flesh. I touch one of the scars with a curious hand and I discover that they are icy cold, although the skin around them is my normal body temperature.

I take a deep breath, and peel back the bandage, nervous for what I will find underneath. The white bandage takes an age to unwind from my foot. I spool it out onto my hand with my eyes closed, not peeking until my foot is completely bare.

It looks . . . strange. There are still no toes, and my heel is severely diminished. My foot does not look like a foot. It's an odd block at the end of my leg, some strange appendage that has taken the place of the foot. I flex it, and it does not hurt, so I am encouraged to actually look at the space where my toes used to be.

I expect carnage and horror, even if it doesn't hurt. It has not even been two weeks since my mother and I inexpertly chopped off my toes, and then she subjected me to cauterization with a kettle and walking on the bleeding stump. I expect it to be awful. Instead there is a smooth, healed plane of skin, with a thick white rope of scar tissue running along the front of my foot like a seam. It looks like an injury that has healed over the course of years, not days. My heel is the same. There is a mess of white scar tissue but when I prod it, although it does ache, it is a distant ache, that of a wound long healed, not that of a recent trauma. I had no idea Cinderella was capable of anything like this.

Curious, I reach a hand up to my face, where previously I'd had deep scratches caused by Hortense in her dying moments. In the agony and trauma of my foot, I'd forgotten all about them. When I prod my eyebrow, I can feel the shiny skin of another scar bisecting my brow, but there is no open wound, no blood, and no scratch. Cinderella has healed my body from top to bottom, and I do not know what to make of it.

I sit contemplating my foot, staring at it, cautiously flexing the muscles to make it bob up and down. Where before I would have curled my toes, now I am waggling the tip of the foot. I decide that I may as well put it to the ultimate test, and I heave myself up from the floor. My balance is different, and I must adjust my stride to make up for the missing toes, but walking does not hurt. I don't know how that makes me feel.

I hear a tinkling laugh float in through my window, and I freeze midstep. Cinderella is outside.

Slowly, I make my way over to the tiny window set into the wall of my cell. If I stretch very tall, with perfect posture, I can just see out through the narrow bars. Water trickles down sometimes, and I realize it is because my window is actually flush with the ground, the grass of the palace gardens growing right up next to the bars. Looking past the plants, I catch a glimpse of honey blonde hair and I know it's her. Standing next to a marble fountain filled with lily pads is Cinderella, my stepsister, and the last person I want to see.

She's smiling at something I cannot see, given my limited viewpoint, half sitting on the edge of the fountain and trailing her fingers in the water. Her skin glows in the sunlight, and she's wearing a soft blue gown that drapes over her legs and shows off the beautiful curves and proportions of her body. Cinderella beckons with a delicate hand, and Credence steps into my view, joining her at the edge of the fountain.

I don't want to keep watching, but I can't bring myself to look away. As recently as two weeks ago I envisioned myself in her position, enjoying a stroll around the palace gardens with Credence. His back is to me, so I can't see his expression, but his legs are long and lean, and his curls are a beautiful riot atop his head. He inclines his head toward Cinderella but doesn't say anything. I strain to catch what she's saying, and I am surprised to find that her conversation comes easily to my ears.

"The water's so lovely!" says Cinderella, still trailing her hands in the fountain. "All these growing things inside it. You must teach me their names! Eunice . . . Eunice didn't let me out much."

I jerk back from the window. I was not expecting to hear my own name. Credence responds, but I can't hear him. The acoustics must be wrong for it, because Cinderella's voice comes in clear as day.

"A lily pad—how wonderful! And that's a frog! How delightful. I must get better acquainted!" With those words, Cinderella shoots out her hand into the water, faster than a human ought to be able, and pulls a fat, wriggling frog out of the fountain. I stare at its limbs, transfixed.

Credence says something that must please Cinderella, because she beams at him, showing off her even white teeth, the frog still wriggling in her grasp. She looks up at Credence from under her eyelashes, and then brings the frog up to her mouth. With a savage jerk of her teeth, she rips the frog's head off.

Credence jerks back from her, and I can hear his high-pitched yelp. Cinderella's expression is smug and pleased while she chews the frog but grows sorrowful in response to whatever Credence is saying. Tears prick her eyes like luminous drops of dew, and she is the picture of beautiful dejection.

"I'm so sorry!" she says through her tears. "I just thought—well, I wasn't ever allowed out of the house, and this looked like it might be a treat! I can't believe I've embarrassed myself like this in front of you yet again!" Her performance is impressive, and I wouldn't fault Credence for believing her. Cinderella reaches out to touch Credence's hand and I suck in a sharp breath. Touching Cinderella is always a bad idea, and Credence has none of the protections against her that my family does.

Credence allows the touch for a moment but then pulls his hand away. I heave a huge sigh of relief. He's wearing gloves. I hope this means he's figured something out about Cinderella, but it is a bit chilly in the garden right now. Maybe he's just cold.

Cinderella wipes her tears away and smiles up at Credence.

"You're so good to me," she says. "I feel like I've been given a fresh start after Eunice . . . well, after Eunice." Credence responds, but I don't even try to hear his words, because as she says my name, Cinderella looks directly at me across the lawn, making eye contact with me through the bars of my cell.

I throw myself away from the window, panting. I'm not used to moving on my foot without its toes yet and I misjudge one of my steps, collapsing to the floor in an ungainly heap. I berate myself. How could I have been so foolish? I know that Cinderella and I have some sort of connection and she was close enough that I could see and hear her. Of course she knew that I was there. I tremble on the floor for a little while longer, too afraid to move in case Cinderella should show up at my window, her hands lengthening and reaching in to grab at me through the bars. But no one is there. I am once more alone with my thoughts in my cell.

22

Connections

T HE REMINDER THAT Cinderella is in the palace influencing people stirs something within me. I cannot sit idle while she works to ensnare Prince Credence. My own feelings aside, the thought of Cinderella with unfettered access to the throne and all the powers that come with it makes my stomach churn. Our kingdom may not be perfect, but it absolutely does not deserve to have Cinderella in power.

I lie in wait by my window, straining my leg muscles until they burn keeping myself propped up so I can see through the little bars. If Credence was in the garden one day, he may show up again, hopefully without Cinderella.

After three days of impatiently waiting, I am rewarded. Prince Credence is in the garden, wandering aimlessly through the well-manicured stretches of lawn, occasionally pausing to inspect equally well-maintained flowers. I seize my chance.

"Credence!" I hiss through the bars. He looks up, startled. I can see that the bags under his eyes mirror those under my own. Living with Cinderella is no easy feat. Despite this, he still cuts a handsome figure as he walks through the lush gardens.

"Credence, over here!" I repeat. I don't want to draw anyone else's attention, but it's a risk I am willing to take. This time he spots me, and his eyes widen. He rushes over to me and drops to his knees next to my window so that his head is level with mine.

"Eunice!" he says too loudly. I shush him. I don't want anyone to know we're speaking. He gives me a reproachful look but continues in a softer voice. "Eunice, what are you doing here? I asked after you and everyone told me that you were sick, but that you deserved it, and even if you did get better you were still sick, to keep poor Cinderella locked up like that. And I must say, I'm not sure I should even be here talking to you! How could you, Eunice? Keeping your own sister locked up like that!"

I snort. I'm not so far gone into my melancholy that I can't derive humor from the words "poor Cinderella." It occurs to me that perhaps I should not laugh when the future ruler of the kingdom accuses me of something monstrous. I try to compose my expression into something more neutral, but Credence is already giving me a hurt look.

"How could I? Credence, I know she's been filling your head with lots of stories about me, but I want you to think, for just a moment, about what motivations I could possibly have had for keeping Cinderella locked up."

I can tell I've struck a nerve. Credence jumps and then looks over his shoulder, as if to check that we aren't being watched. He has some sort of instinctive fear of Cinderella that I want to encourage.

"Think of any time she's done something strange, or something you can't explain. Maybe even something that horrified you. Remember the frog? Do you really think that if you were trapped in a cellar for years, you'd go around eating live frogs' heads the first chance you got?" I prod further, and Credence is visibly startled.

"How do you know about—ah. The fountain's just right there, isn't it? I will admit, the frog thing was strange. And the way some of the servants assigned to her chambers act now—" Credence breaks off and shudders. My heart sinks.

"Let me guess," I say. "They're suddenly obsessed with her and will do anything she asks, no matter how bizarre. Their personal grooming suffers. Maybe you've found them doing something odd, something you couldn't explain, and their only answer as to why they did it was because Cinderella told them so."

Credence is looking at me with dawning horror. "I thought it was my imagination," he says. "I'm always being told I'm too imaginative. And that I trust people too easily. It's why—" He breaks off again, looking embarrassed. Everything slots into place in my mind.

"It's why you believed that I was a monster," I finish for him. "You thought you'd been taken in by my letters, that I'd been deceiving you in some way. I suppose it didn't help my case that I never wrote about Cinderella beyond acknowledging that she existed. Or rather, you didn't think I was such a horrible person based on my letters, but you don't trust yourself when it comes to trusting others."

Credence nods, looking sheepish. I grasp the bars of my cell window and speak with urgency.

"Credence, I am telling you now—you *must* trust yourself when it comes to Cinderella. All of those little inconsistencies, all of those moments of unreality—do not ignore them. You've been having nightmares about Cinderella, yes? Listen to the nightmares! She is not like you and me. She's not safe. I know it's probably hard to believe that, coming from me, but I'm begging you—trust your instincts. Trust that I'm not a monster and that maybe, just maybe, there's more to Cinderella than her pretty face." I'm unable to keep the bitterness out of my tone when I mention Cinderella's beauty. I can only hope it doesn't hurt my cause.

Credence is looking thoughtful, but I can tell he doesn't quite believe me. Maybe I shouldn't have told him to listen to his nightmares. Even as I think on those words, I realize that it may have made me sound like I'm losing touch with reality. He begins to get up from his knees, ready to leave the crazy girl in the cell to her craziness. Against my will, I think of Cinderella again. Did she ever feel as I do now, desperate for someone to stay and talk, but unable to do anything about it? I try one more time to get Credence to listen to me, pushing away my empathy for Cinderella. I am not ready to forgive her.

"Ask her about . . . about Hortense," I say. It hurts to say her name. Credence's brow furrows. "Make sure you're not alone when you do. I'm not sure . . . I'm not sure how she'll react." I feel tears beginning to prick at my eyes, but I will them not to come. Credence nods solemnly and then gets to his feet. I return to my straw mat on the floor, unable to watch him walk away once more, and let the tears come as I allow myself to grieve for my little sister.

The next day Prince Credence shows up at the bars of my window almost as soon as the sun is up, kneeling on the grass still wet with dew. He looks as sleep-deprived and lovely as he did the day before. Actually, he looks more sleep-deprived than the day before, which makes sense, if he's had another night of nightmares and no time to rest.

"I asked her about Hortense," he says, not even giving me time to say hello. "I asked her about Hortense with some people I trusted around, like you said, and I'm glad I did. Eunice, she hissed at me and her eyes went murky green. I was legitimately afraid. She didn't sound like a young woman then. She sounded like some sort of creature, and I thought she might strike me. After I stepped back she tried to play it off and laugh, and just said that Hortense was her younger stepsister and they'd never gotten along. But it was like a layer of her had been peeled back and I could see that she was really angry about the question. I know she wasn't telling me the whole truth. So I'll ask you—Eunice, who is Hortense and why did Cinderella react that way?" Credence's face is serious and drawn in the early morning light.

Something inside me snaps. I don't want to be alone anymore. I close my eyes, and I tell him everything. I start with Cinderella's arrival at our home and I end with her coming into my cell to save me. I leave nothing out; I sugarcoat nothing to save my pride. I speak in a dull, flat voice, giving no emotional weight to different details, but at the end, both Credence and I have tears glistening in our eyes.

We sit like that for a minute or two, allowing ourselves to feel. Eventually, I break the silence. "I don't know if there's anything we can do with all this knowledge, but I think it's better you know. Cinderella is not to be taken lightly."

Credence nods and looks down at me. His face is still solemn and he hasn't brushed away his tears, so they've carved long wet tracks down his face.

"I'm sorry about Hortense," he says, and that simple acknowledgement feels like a balm. It doesn't heal the hurt inside me but does soothe it.

"Thank you," I say. No one has actually said that to me since she died.

Credence continues, "You can't stay here. I can't bear to have you locked up while Cinderella goes free. Eunice, what are we going to do? My father expects me to *marry* that creature, and the thought of even looking at her again . . ." Credence trails off and shoots me a beseeching look.

The thought of being out of my cell is so beautiful that words fail me momentarily, as I imagine my freedom. But then I deflate. I can only nod, my heart going out to him.

"I'm honestly not sure if that's possible. They've only let my mother in once to see me since Cinderella healed me."

Credence smiles.

"Now that is something I think I can help you with. Being a prince does have some benefits, you know. It's not all terrible arranged marriages and watching people you care about get locked up for crimes they didn't commit."

23

Reckonings

CREDENCE LEAVES MY window, brushing the dew off the knees of his trousers. I spend hours waiting, wracked with sick anticipation. Each second that passes is one where I am sure he will never return. But my faith is not misplaced and freeing me from imprisonment proves remarkably easy. The heavy door to my cell creaks open, and Credence stands before me, dressed more formally than I have ever seen him. He tells the guards he needs me for questioning of a sensitive nature and that no one else is to know. I'm having a hard time paying attention, because I cannot believe that I am about to be liberated. The guards permit me out of the cell, and we emerge from the dungeon into the crisp air of twilight. Credence's hand is tight on my arm, and I can tell he's nervous.

"This only buys us a little time," he says, once we're out of earshot of the guards. "People will talk, and eventually everyone, Cinderella included, will know that something's amiss. We need to figure out what to do with you."

"Where are we going now?" I ask. I have to lean on him heavily, my balance thrown off by the lack of a heel and toes on my foot and my muscles atrophied from my long illness.

"My chambers," says Credence grimly, as he looks around the corner carefully before drawing us down a long, luxurious corridor.

For once, luck is on my side, and we make it to his room without anyone seeing us. I heave a huge sigh of relief when the door to his room creaks closed. Collapsing into an overstuffed chair next to a roaring fire, I close my eyes and allow myself to savor the freedom of being outside of my cell, and the comfort that comes with someone believing me. I open my eyes and smile at Credence, who gives me a tentative smile back. I know that this peace is temporary, but it is the best thing I have felt in weeks.

A knock at his door shatters my tranquility.

Our eyes lock, both of us wild and panicked. Credence grabs me and shoves me into a wardrobe, where I stumble and struggle, but manage to wedge myself into the corner of the dark, cramped space, trying not to breathe.

I hear the creak of the heavy hinged door and Credence's voice says, "Ah, hello." I can't see who it is, but I can hear that he's not happy about his surprise visitor.

"Hello, Credence dear," says the mystery visitor, and my blood turns to ice in my veins. Cinderella is at Credence's door, at night, right when I have arrived. This cannot be good.

I listen again to their conversation, my fear having momentarily distracted me from paying attention to their words. I don't seem to have missed much, as they're still exchanging pleasantries.

"Might I come in?" says Cinderella. I hear a rustle, and then the door closes. I hear the sound of skirts brushing across the stone floor, and then a creaking that means they must both have sat down in chairs.

"This is not quite proper," says Credence, "for you to be alone in my rooms, although of course I can deny you nothing. What do you need from me this evening, my dear?"

Cinderella laughs, and the sound is as tinkling and lovely as ever. I try my hardest not to breathe at all, lest she discover my presence.

"Oh, you!" she says. "Always so worried about propriety. That's funny, in its own kind of way. You see, my dear Credence, I was in my room, preparing for bed, when I realized something quite extraordinary!" I wince at the endearment but manage to make no sound, "My beloved, my fiancé, the man who has pledged to make me his wife, has brought someone else into the castle!"

Silence meets her proclamation, and she speaks again, her voice losing some of its careful politeness.

"What makes this even more distressing, as I'm sure you'll understand, beloved, is that the other person in question appears to be none other than my own sister, Eunice! Eunice, dear," she says, her voice dripping insincerity, "why don't you come out of that wardrobe and we'll all talk about this together?"

My heart goes into my throat. I knew she'd figure out that I was out of my cell eventually, but I thought we had more time. I have no idea what I'm going to do when faced with her again, but I cannot just ignore her. The tendrils that connect us are as strong as ever, and I curse myself for having underestimated their power.

On unsteady feet, I stand up in the wardrobe and open the door. Cinderella sits in the chair I had collapsed into earlier, with Credence seated across from her. Her gown is pristine, but her face is curled into a cruel expression that saps most of the beauty from her features.

"Hello, sister," I say.

"Hello, Eunice," she says back. "Planning on catching the prince for yourself, I see."

I shrug. "Among other things," I say, and I studiously ignore Credence's expression as I stretch out my hand, grabbing a sconce off the wall and hurl the lit torch into her hateful face. I don't know what I'm thinking, but I do know that Cinderella does not like fire, and this is the only chance I have to make her feel as scared and helpless and hurting as she's made me feel over the past weeks, months, years.

My aim is true, and the fire connects with her face, smacking her between the eyes. At first, nothing happens, and I deflate, feeling foolish for ever assuming something as banal as fire could affect my horrible sister. But then something about her skin changes, where the flame beats against it. It makes an awful hissing noise, like a piece of meat going into a hot pan, and Cinderella begins to scream. Her very being bubbles and re-forms, as if she can no longer control her shape, and where before a mostly human young woman sat, now there sits an abomination from beyond the stars, a truly monstrous spectacle.

Her face is warped and twisted. It still has eyes, a nose and mouth, but her eyes have mostly taken over the space, filling it with a huge green expanse of decay, with no pupils left in them. They have multiplied and cover her face unevenly, so that I am staring into a dozen or so eyes that all blink in unison. Her mouth is a churning maw of teeth, concentric circles of gnashing fangs that I am certain will do more than just bite me if they come close enough. Her body remains fairly humanoid, but tentacles spring forth from every nook and crevice in her, so that the shape of her form is obscured by the waving masses. Her hair, that honey blonde curtain, still remains, lifting and taking on the appearance of so many worms writhing in the air. She is more transformed than I have ever seen her, and when she opens her mouth wider and lets out an inhuman scream, I feel a pop in my ears. When I clap my hands over them to try and block out the noise, I encounter warm, sticky blood. The distant stars are so loud, and there is nothing I can do. I cannot escape her gaze.

My eyes catch on the spot where the flaming torch initially connected with her head. I can see now that there is a small wound. Not enough to stop her but extant. Her skin still smolders around the edges, open and raw, an oozing sore that does not match the rest of her gray and mottled flesh.

I grope for another sconce on the wall, removing the blazing torch from within, and throw it at her. The fire makes its mark, sizzling into her skin with that horrible cooking meat sound and again she screams. I hear the tinkle of broken glass, and Cinderella rears up, screaming louder. My nose begins to bleed as well as my ears, and I grow lightheaded. Credence has thrown a lit lamp at her, and it burns her skin.

We raid the walls, trying to push this newfound advantage, and the fire makes contact each time, and each time it is followed by another scream from Cinderella. With each scream I can feel the blood from my ears and nose increase its flow, and at some point I start bleeding from my eyes as well. Everything is a blood-red haze, and I am reminded of my night of terror, first seeing her as she truly is. As it did then, the blood adds to my vision, enhancing it, allowing me to see the true Cinderella. This time, I do not see the dissonance between the human and the monster, because Cinderella is done hiding. What I do see is the extent to which our fire is wounding her. It's not enough. She cannot remove the wounds from her body, but it is not inhibiting her to the necessary degree. The room is dark and cold now, with the torches gone from the walls. The hearth is burning low and of no use to us. Cinderella sees that we are out of ammunition and lets out another scream that sends a fresh wave of blood out of my facial orifices. But this scream is different; I can hear the triumph in it. She knows we have lost.

Credence grabs my arm and I turn to look at him. His dark eyes are also red with blood, and I can see trails of blood seeping from his nose and ears as well. I grab his face and kiss him, hard, more of a smashing of lips and teeth than anything else. He tastes like blood and sweat, but I don't care. If this is how it's going to end, I want to kiss him just once, to have a moment of selfishness in a life I have spent sacrificing myself for others.

He surprises me by kissing me back, although at another scream from Cinderella we break apart, slapping our hands over our ears to block the sound as much as possible. The blood that has run from our noses and mouths is now smeared around our faces. We look like we've been feasting on fresh meat. Credence says something to me, but I can't hear him. I point at my ears, and, even now, at the end, he laughs and shakes his head. I want to smile at him, but I am out of smiles. All I do is grip his hand in mine and steel myself for Cinderella's advance. I look to the side, away from her, the only source of light in his dark, dim room. We spent the rest of the flames fighting her. I may be about to face my own death, but that doesn't mean I have to literally see it coming.

Now that Cinderella has us where she wants us, there is no urgency to her movements. One of her tentacles brushes my face, and I close my eyes, a single tear trickling down my cheek. I wish she would end it now, rather than drawing things out, but as I feel the slick flesh of the tentacle on my face, the raised suckers catching at my skin, I know this will not be the case. Cinderella will toy with me before she ends it and I will somehow have to endure it.

A loud crack fills the room, startling me enough that I open my eyes. The door to the room flies open, smashing against the wall, and in the doorway I see the most welcome sight of my life—a member of the royal guard, decked out in green and gold livery, complete with sword in one hand, torch in the other. At the sight of the guard, Cinderella shrieks and pulls back her tentacle from my face, drawing herself up to face the new threat. I cover my ears, trying not to let the shrieks affect me, but I can feel more blood pouring from my ears, nose, and eyes.

More guards rush into the room, bringing all manner of weapons with them. Cinderella shrieks and wails, and the guards flinch at her cries. But blood does not pour from their ears and they do not stop advancing on her, more and more of them pouring into the room. I marvel at this, until I see that every one of the guards has tufts of cotton wool sticking from their ears, held in place with thick, sticky pitch, blocking out the sound of her terrible cries. I don't know how they knew to protect themselves from her screeching, but I am too grateful to care.

The incoming guards and soldiers herd Cinderella into a corner. There are so many of them that she can't find a good way to fight back. Every time she waves and snatches at one of them with a tentacle, another is there to keep her pinned. I can't understand why she is so afraid of them, until she gets too close to one of the guards on her left. She makes a break for it, trying to barrel through their lines, shrieking the whole time, and a guard brandishes his torch at her, using it as a prod to keep her contained. It catches on her sleeve, a flammable, flimsy thing that goes up with a whoosh.

She wails again, as the flame on her body rages, and she cannot escape it. I curse myself for not aiming for her clothing earlier. I see real panic in those murky, rotting eyes, and she flails and tries to get away, but at this point it is too late. The soldiers have her right where they want her.

The quality of her noises shifts. Before, they were the angry cries of a predator intent on doing harm to her prey. Now the sound of a wounded animal fills the room. I feel a pang of something for Cinderella, some last vestige of empathy that her call manages to evoke in me. I also know what it is like to be trapped, feeling like there is no escape after freedom was finally within my grasp. This vague instant of fellow feeling vanishes when Cinderella's wounded animal cry causes a fresh wave of blood to emerge from my eyes, sending my world red again, causing my head to spin. I don't know how much blood I've lost, but I recognize the signs that point toward too much.

Cinderella continues her shrieking as the guards advance on her. She tests the boundaries and is met by more flame. Another part of her dress is set alight, causing her to shriek. But the plugs in the soldiers' ears stay firm, and they are able to confine her to the corner of Prince Credence's room.

The door to the room swings open again, revealing more guards, this time carrying a large, metal box. It is of a similar style to the one that Cinderella arrived at my house in seven years ago. There are no windows, only a large door yawning open toward Cinderella. Instead of being fitted to be drawn behind horses, this one has metal poles so that it can be balanced atop four sets of shoulders, a giant metal palanquin.

Before I fully comprehend what is happening, the guards bring the metal box fully into the room and use long metal poles, swords, and more burning torches to herd Cinderella inside. I can see the box shaking and vibrating, but her screams are muffled enough that I no longer bleed from every facial orifice when she voices her displeasure at being confined.

Credence and I watch, dumbfounded, as our unanticipated rescue plays out. If she had been allowed to fight us even a moment longer, I am certain we would have been killed. Cinderella is quickly and efficiently corralled. The highly trained palace guards then carry the box out of the room. They leave as suddenly as they arrived, Cinderella shrieking impotently from within her new prison. I am at a loss to explain how this has happened. I turn to Credence in search of an explanation, but his eyes are fixed on the doorway into his chambers, through which Cinderella has just departed. I follow his gaze and my breath leaves me. There in the doorway stands King Reymond and behind him by two paces is Mr. Father.

24

An Unlikely Savior

KING REYMOND LOOKS like Credence. Or rather, I suppose it's more correct to say that Credence looks like King Reymond. The king is fair and pale, with light blond hair, while Credence has his late mother's dark skin and hair. Their eyes, though, are the same deep brown, with little flecks of yellow in them. Their noses could be shaped from the same mold, so similar are they. This is perhaps why I am so startled by King Reymond's expression. Credence looks at the world in an open, honest manner, and I've seen his eyes crinkle into a smile with regularity. King Reymond's eyes are cold, and if they have ever crinkled with a smile, I see no sign of it now.

Beside me, Credence is stiff, holding himself differently than I have observed before. He inclines his head toward the king, his manner formal.

"Father," he says, and then hesitates. I don't blame him. Where can he go from here? I have no idea how much King Reymond knows, or rather, how much Mr. Father has told him. I know I should be feeling relieved and grateful that the king sent guards to save us, but looking into King Reymond's cold eyes, a shiver runs up my back.

King Reymond does not share my hesitation. "Credence," he says, and his tone is glacial, nothing at all like the way either of my parents speak to me. "I see you are once again in the habit of believing things people tell you. Are you so easily fooled that you did not notice your bride-to-be was a monster?"

Credence attempts a smile but it's pained. "Well, I figured it out eventually," he tries. "Surely that has to count for something. And we trapped her before the wedding, so she won't be able to take over the throne. Never fear, Father, you won't have a monster for a daughter-in-law."

"On the contrary," says King Reymond. "I have no intention of calling off the wedding. Make no mistake, you were a fool not to notice this young woman's differences, but in this case, your foolishness may have helped us. I will admit, I was angry at you when Mr. Fitzwilliam first came to me with his outlandish tale of his daughter, but I have seen my way through that, and it is now clear to me that this is what is best for the crown, to have that sort of power at our disposal. No one will dare encroach on our kingdom if we have that creature as queen. This man here," he says, waving unconcernedly at Mr. Fitzwilliam, "tells me that she will not listen to us unless we make her our family, officially and legally. I have every intention of following through on our offer of marriage to the young lady."

I can't believe what I'm hearing. King Reymond must not understand. I shoot a look at Mr. Fitzwilliam, but he's nodding along. None of this is new to him. I can't keep to myself any longer.

"Your Majesty, you don't understand! Cinderella is not just a young lady with monstrous qualities—my sister is an actual monster! She's already wrecked my family's lives. Don't give her the opportunity to do the same to yours!" I am near to tears and I'm sure everyone can hear it in my voice. I hope that calling Cinderella my sister and a monster in the same sentence will cancel each other out and that our bond will not be affected.

King Reymond turns his attention on me briefly, frowning, and then turns back to Mr. Fitzwilliam.

"She shares your concerns, I see. Well, then perhaps this is for the best, after all. We need to test to see if the young lady is as monstrous as you say. Family is supposed to constrain her, no? If she's going to marry into my own, then I want to know the limitations that family can have upon her. Guards!" He snaps his fingers, and the guards still in the room with us jerk into action.

I don't know what I'm expecting, but the guards' strong hands closing around my upper arms is not it. I look at King Reymond, uncomprehending, while beside me Credence stiffens further and Mr. Father pales visibly from his spot next to the king.

"Get her cleaned up and then have her placed with Cinderella for the evening. Make sure you don't let Cinderella out in the process. We need her to stay put. It won't do to have her roaming loose in the palace again. We've already lost too many good servants."

King Reymond sweeps out, and his guards follow. I look behind me, still hoping for some explanation, but another look at Mr. Father's drawn face puts to bed any last hope I might have had. I am to be locked in with Cinderella, and there is nothing I can do about it. Credence calls my name, but softly, so softly that I think I might have imagined it, except for the look of pity on the guards' faces as they march me to my doom.

True to the king's command, the guards take me to a small wash chamber, where I am given a bucket and some flannel. I dither over the water, but they grow impatient and threaten to do it themselves if I do not hurry. I have no desire to be forcefully bathed, but neither do I wish to be hurried to my destination, so I take as long as I reasonably can washing up and then allow myself to be marched away.

The long, slitted windows let in no light as we make our slow, ungraceful way deeper into the castle. The guards have procured a torch from somewhere, and we must rely on its light amid the strange shadows to guide us. I close my eyes, despite the risk of stumbling, trying to block out what the darkness is telling me. Sunset comes later and later during these summer days, so I know it's only a matter of hours until midnight. We enter an area that is familiar to me, the corridor to the cells where I was kept before. Our pace is slow, due entirely to me. I haven't yet mastered walking the way I used to, with most of one of my feet gone. There is no pain, no lingering soreness, but my balance is completely different and my gait is lopsided.

In a way it seems fitting that I will meet the same end as Hortense. I think of her, not as I last saw her, driven mad and hurting, but as she was in life, stubborn and smart and refusing to be anyone other than herself, no matter the consequences. I think of that as the guards lead me deeper and deeper into the castle, far below where I was kept in my garden-level cell.

It can now be called nothing else but a dungeon, given how deep and dank it is, carved into the foundational rock of the palace, with heavy iron bars and thick locks. I try not to look at the inhabitants within the cells, but their wails and cries reach out to me. I know that I will soon join their wailing, but I'm almost numb to it. It's like my brain can't process that, after so many years of following the rules perfectly, I'm going to be forced to break the same rule that Hortense broke, the one that I couldn't break on my own even to save my sister.

A polished steel door looms out of the gloom ahead of us, and the guards' fingers tighten around my arms. The heat of their palms radiates through to my skin, and the contrast with the chilly air makes me shiver.

Unlike everything else down here, which is old and decrepit, the metal at the entrance to the cell is bright and new, gleaming even in the low light. Although Reymond clearly does not believe Mr. Father about the rules and the necessity of keeping away from Cinderella between twelve and three, he has at least made sure that the cell can contain her. Or at least, it can contain her when she's in her normal state. Once she's fully powered, I have no idea if anything will be enough to keep her in these dungeons. The door is cranked open using a heavy locking mechanism, a third guard, who is stationed outside, and a special key. The door yawns open, revealing only darkness within.

Before I can process what I'm seeing, I'm shoved inside by eager hands and the door is quickly closed behind me. The guards are no more eager to be near Cinderella than I am. I turn back to the door, but I'm met only with an implacable wall of steel.

Some of the feeling that I've been shoving down begins to rise in me, and I panic. I pound against the cold metal with clenched fists, the thuds oddly muffled by the heavy stone around me.

"Let me out!" I yell, a note of desperation entering my voice. "I can't—I can't be in here! I'll stay, I won't run away, just—just let me stay on the other side! Please."

I'm met with silence. I have no idea if they can even hear me. If they can, it doesn't matter. I pound against the door a few more times, hard enough that my hands hurt. I'm sure that if I make it to the morning I'll have some lovely bruises, but it makes no difference. The door is shut and I cannot get out.

I breathe heavily and my emotions return full force in a way they hadn't when I'd still been safely separated from Cinderella. I turn slowly to look into the rest of the room. The blackness is so thick and dark as to be almost impenetrable. Almost, but not quite.

Out of the darkness comes a rattling sound, and Cinderella emerges, not as I last saw her, a monstrous creature weakened by fire, but as I am used to seeing her, a beautiful young woman with long, honey-gold hair that hangs just so and rows of perfect evenly white teeth filling her mouth. Her clothes are now filthy rags, something she would never have allowed normally at home. Her face is dirty, with long wet tear tracks streaking through the grime to create stark white lines under her eyes. The rags and the tears only serve to make her more beautiful. Her expression is sorrowful until she sees that it's me. Then it twists into something I don't recognize.

"Eunice?" she says, and her voice is not full of harmonics or layers or the screaming of stars—it's just a voice, albeit one that is slow and speaking very carefully. Words don't always come easily to Cinderella; this must be one of those times. "What . . . you're here?"

She's glowing faintly, which is the reason I can see her at all. She was rattling earlier because iron shackles attached to heavy chains are wrapped around her wrists, although they are attached to nothing I can see.

"Just don't come any closer, please," I say. My voice is weak and pathetic to my own ears, but I cling to the knowledge that I still have some power here. It's not midnight yet and Cinderella should still have to listen to my commands.

She cocks her head at me, and a frown creases her beautiful face. She walks sideways, circling me, and I curse myself for not being more specific. Technically, by maintaining a circle around me, she's not coming any closer, just changing her position. Still, I'd rather she wasn't moving at all. My panic is interfering with my ability to give good commands.

"You're in the cellar too," she observes, and I can only nod, not willing to get into the semantics of dungeons versus our cellar at home. Her eyes flash putrid green and that is enough to make me shudder. Even at home I almost never went into her room to be alone with her like this. We are in uncharted waters.

Cinderella continues to circle me, and I turn to keep pace with her, not wanting my back to her at any time. Her eyes continue to flash between a more normal green and a menacing color that I associate with danger. It's enough to have me trembling. My whole body is screaming at me to run, but there's nowhere to run to. We're trapped in here together, until they deign to let us out.

Cinderella returns to her starting position and her lips curl up over her teeth, like a snarling dog. But it's an odd expression; I can't actually tell if she's menacing me or not. She has much more creative ways to frighten me than just showing her teeth.

No sooner have I had this thought than I see her stiffen, and the shadows, faint in the dim light she's casting in the room, begin to lengthen and grow. Her eyes flicker into the green of rot and decay and stay there. She swells in height and size before my eyes, and the stench of rotting leaves hits my nostrils.

"You shouldn't be here," she says, continuing her circle. The temperature around me drops, a chill breeze blowing from her direction causing the skin on my arms to prickle and the hairs to stand straight up. "It's almost midnight."

I stare at her. I didn't know that Cinderella was that aware of her own rules, but she always likes to surprise me.

I say nothing, uncertain of how to respond to her, unable to think of a single thing to say to the being I've lived with for the past seven years.

"You shouldn't be here," she repeats, her gaze intent on me, as if she expects me to just leave.

I clear my throat and manage to croak out a few words. "I can't leave," I say. "I'm trapped here too."

Cinderella shakes her head in apparent rejection of my statement. "No. You shouldn't be here. Leave!"

The last word contains the screaming of stars, and I wish so much that I could follow her command, that I could obey her like she has to obey me. But I'm as stuck as she is. It must be hard for her to accept that I can't come and go freely, after all her years of watching me do exactly that.

"I can't," I repeat, my voice soft. "There's . . . there's nowhere for me to go. I can't leave."

She shrieks at this and recoils into a corner of the room, the one farthest from the door. Her shadows sway and don't retract with her, staying near to me and hovering overhead.

"Eunice," she says from her position in the corner. "If you won't leave, then I suggest you *hide*."

At this last word, her teeth lengthen and her arms elongate into the tentacles that I know she favors. The shadows that were dancing on the wall lunge toward me. I can't help it; I turn and run toward the door, pounding on it again, screaming at someone to let me out. There is no response, and the thick door doesn't so much as shudder under my pounding. Finding no escape there, I fling myself into the corner of the room furthest from Cinderella, putting my arms over my head and cowering, trying to squeeze myself into the smallest ball possible. I can no longer see Cinderella, but I can hear her.

Her screams echo in the chamber, interspersed with every evil sound I've ever heard. It's Hortense's dying wails, and the last breaths of my cats, and the stars screaming in my ears all at once, a cacophony that I can't hope to shut out. My ears protest once more, leaking blood, and I dimly wonder if I've already sustained permanent damage by hearing her scream so many times in such quick succession.

The room gets colder and something wet falls onto my hand. Against my better judgment, I pull my hand away from my face and peer at it. Another droplet hits me from above, and I look up, careful to avoid casting my gaze too closely on the corner where I last saw Cinderella. Her shadows have followed me and are roiling on the walls around me and the ceiling above me. As I look up, another fat droplet of *something* falls from them, this time connecting squarely with my face. The substance is dark and thick, and when it hits my skin it sticks to it.

I scrub at my face, but the droplets will not move. The shadows grow thicker and the patter of droplets increases. Each one burns slightly where it hits my skin, but in a mild way, like the scrape of a fingernail over flesh that pushes just slightly too hard. The smell is strange, almost metallic with the characteristic scent of decay. I can't help but chase the thought that I've smelled it before.

All at once it hits me—this is the smell of Cinderella's blood. This same smell filled the room when Credence and I attacked her. I shudder and consider leaving my corner, but Cinderella is still thrashing and screaming opposite me. As much as I don't want her shadows to bleed on me, I want to get closer to her even less.

The patter of drops is more of a deluge now, as her thick, tar-like blood continues to rain down on me, covering my face, my hands, my dress. Some pours into my mouth, and the taste of rotting leaves and hot iron repulses me. I gag, spitting onto the floor, but the blood coats my tongue and my mouth and does not leave, not even when I scrub at my tongue with my hands, which are also covered in the stuff.

The heavy downpour continues and in short order I am covered from head to toe. The blood drips into my ears. As soon as her blood enters into my ears, forming a seal, the sounds of her shrieking, while still present, are muffled. Although I cannot be certain, I think that my ears have stopped bleeding. I dare to open my eyes to see if maybe Cinderella is just shrieking at a reduced volume. But before I can catch a glimpse of her the blood drips into my eyes, and they are covered with a dark film through which I cannot see.

If the sensation of fingernails dragging over me was unpleasant on my skin, it's almost unbearable on my eyes, but there is nothing I can do. I'm afraid to even scream, fearful that it will allow her blood into my throat and then I will be unable to breathe, drowning in her fluids. I just have to sit and endure, sightless and in pain, feeling the too-hard press of nails against my delicate corneas.

At this point every inch of me is covered in her blood and although I know she must be out there, at her most monstrous, I am shielded from it by a layer of her own making. I think of Hortense's caterpillars and the way they'd hide in their chrysalises, waiting to emerge as beautiful butterflies. Is Cinderella protecting me from herself, by turning me into a chrysalis?

The layer of blood is cold and smells horrible, but as time creeps forward, despite being in the same room as Cinderella, despite the knowledge that it must be midnight, then one AM, two AM, three AM, I pass the night unharmed, if uncomfortable, with nothing more than some shivering for my trouble.

For some reason that I do not fully understand, after an indeterminate amount of time has passed, the blood that has coated me the whole night shudders and, instead of sticking to me, slides into a more viscous form and drips off of me. It drains from my eyes, leaving behind no trace of itself. I watch in horror as it coalesces into a black pool at my feet and then slithers across the room, where it flows over the huddled form of Cinderella. The blood flows over her, obscuring her features, and then all at once sinks into her, disappearing back into her body as if it had never left. She sits up and glares at me from across the room.

Before I can even think about a response, or process that what has saved me from Cinderella this night was nothing other than Cinderella herself, the huge steel door to the cell clanks and shudders, opening and admitting a squad of heavily armed guards carrying torches.

They look around the room only briefly before grabbing me by the arms and marching me out in the same manner that I'd been marched in, ushering me out the door quickly, clearly not wanting to be in the same room as Cinderella for longer than necessary. My uneven gait slows the guards and they almost carry me out, so desperate are they to be gone from Cinderella's presence.

I glance over my shoulder and see Cinderella still crumpled on the floor, her intense green eyes still burning into mine until the heavy door swings shut between us.

25

Misunderstandings

KING REYMOND'S FACE breaks into a smile as we enter his little study. It's sumptuously appointed, with rich furnishings and a merry fire crackling in the hearth. It seems almost too warm for this man in front of me, for even when he smiles his eyes remain like chips of ice.

"Ah, good. She survived. Yes, this will make going through with the wedding much easier. You see, Fitzwilliam, your superstitions are all well and good, and I understand that you were working with what you had, but it's clear to me now that you've been overly cautious."

Mr. Father hovers anxiously to the side of the king, his eyes on me and his mouth open in shock. He mouths something at me, I think asking if I'm all right, and I give him a weak smile. I'm exhausted and confused after my night with Cinderella, but it's clear to us both that I've somehow survived without becoming her thrall. I wish I could talk to him, but there's no way I'm going to speak frankly in front of the king. Still, I have to try and convince Reymond of the foolishness of his assumptions. Cinderella is dangerous, and while I'm still grappling with the implications of how or why she could have saved me, I know that this isn't usual. Hortense didn't die so the king could assume Cinderella is safe to spend the night with. Especially not when I know it's poor Credence he's planning on throwing into her clutches.

It galls me to say this, but I'm hoping it will appease the king. "Sire, begging your pardon, but you're wrong. Cinderella is *not* safe to be around between the hours of midnight and three. I know that we may have gotten some of the other rules wrong, and maybe we have been overcautious in some respects, but—"

Before I can finish speaking, King Reymond's smile has slid from his face, leaving only the ice chip eyes staring at me, his expression cold and forbidding. He turns to Mr. Father but doesn't take his eyes off of me.

"See to it that your daughter learns her place. You convinced me that she could be of use, but if she doesn't learn to control her tongue I'll find other arrangements for controlling Cinderella. For now, I think it's best that Cinderella remain confined until we can be assured of her cooperation. You may leave us now."

Mr. Father grabs my arm, steering me from the little study into the hallway. Part of the royal guard from King Reymond's entourage comes with us. I eye them warily, but they keep their hands to themselves this time so apparently I'm no longer going to be imprisoned.

I yank my arm out of Mr. Father's grasp and glare at him. He turns his hands up at me, his expression pleading.

"Eunice, please stay calm," he says. "King Reymond was quite serious when he said that you are expendable. I'd rather it didn't come to that."

"What have you done?" I hiss. "Cinderella is going to marry Prince Credence, the king thinks she's safe to be around at night, and you're telling me I should stay calm?" My voice is rising louder and louder. Mr. Father shushes me and grabs my arm again.

"Let's get somewhere we can talk," he says, hurrying us along the corridor of the palace. I look up, taking in my surroundings for the first time. The palace is large and grand, made of stone like the hallways to the dungeons but much nicer and with more creature comforts. Huge tapestries in rich colors adorn the walls and the wide corridors are a bustle of activity. Servants and nobles alike make their way through the palace. All of them shoot us curious looks but give the royal guard that lurks nearby a wide berth. Under normal circumstances, I think I would be very impressed and curious to see more of the palace. As it is, I don't care about the finery around me or about making a scene in front of others. I just want to talk to my stepfather. But the habit of being circumspect about Cinderella is not one easily broken. I allow myself to be hurried along the corridor, down a flight of stairs and into a small, drab room, with nothing more than a cot and a chair in it. I am forcibly reminded of my cell and I freeze up, but it is too late. Mr. Fitzwilliam pulls me inside and closes the door in the guards' faces.

"We'll be just a moment!" he calls out to them. Now that we are out of sight of the guards he sags, becoming smaller before my eyes. The bags under his eyes are purple and pronounced, and red veins are spread across the whites of his eyes. I feel my anger drain out of me.

"How's Mother?" I ask.

Mr. Father shakes his head and doesn't answer. He doesn't need to. I don't know why I asked that question when I know all too well that Mother is not doing well. One daughter dead, the other locked up for treason, her eldritch stepdaughter about to marry the crown prince— her life as she knows it is over. I wait for him to speak, deciding that he should be the one to drive this conversation. My patience pays off.

"I know you must be upset," he begins. I snort and he gives me a look that I recognize very well, a look that tells me not to sass him, to listen. It's as effective now as it always has been, which is to say, not very. Mr. Father is not exactly a disciplinarian. I just spent the night convinced that at any moment I would become Cinderella's thrall. His harsh glance cannot touch me now.

"Let me finish, Eunice. I know you must be upset, and I don't blame you. I too am upset. Your mother is upset. Upset is not really the word for all the feelings and torment that we've endured over the past two weeks. I cannot speak as to how glad I am to see you as *you* after spending the night with—well, after being gone last night. If I could have spared you . . ." He trails off and looks into the distance. I'm horrified to see tears welling in his eyes. He takes a deep breath and dashes them away with the back of his hand before he continues.

"Eunice, you must understand that we had no choice. Hortense was dead, you were hovering on the brink of death, and she was poised to marry the prince! I had to do *something*," he says.

I glare at him. "You're trying to defend your actions to me, but I don't even know what you've done! Why does the king want to marry Credence off to Cinderella, having some proof of what she is? Or does he not realize? I have no clue what's going on and you're not making things clearer!" I'm shouting and I'm sure the guards beyond the door must be able to hear me, but I am beyond caring.

Mr. Father wrings his hands in front of me and makes a shushing noise. Despite myself, I calm. The need for secrecy involving Cinderella is still strong.

"Let me explain! From the moment I returned and found your mother frantic at home, with Hortense . . . gone and you locked up and Cinderella at the palace, I have been working on this. I didn't know where else to turn, so I went to the king. At first he wouldn't see me. But I was persistent, spent every waking moment pestering people, and I guess they'd been having issues with the household staff who attended to Cinderella—doing things they'd never done before, ending up in strange places. The day King Reymond finally agreed to see me was after a young servant girl had gone missing. They found her spiked on the tallest ramparts, and several witnesses reported Cinderella as having gone there earlier that morning. The king was more willing to listen after that. So I told him everything—no, don't make that face at me, I told him everything. He needed to know! If Credence marries Cinderella, the same rules apply to him as do to us. He would be family. We need to get her under control again, and if she marries Credence—yes, I know it's distasteful—if she marries Credence, then King Reymond will be her father-in-law."

This long diatribe takes all the energy out of Mr. Father, and he sits down on the floor of the drab room, face pale and sweaty.

"How am I involved?" I ask, my voice flat and unemotional. "The king said I could be cut out of the plan. That I'm expendable. I don't understand how this involves me. I think I've done enough, don't you?"

The specter of my night with Cinderella hangs heavy in the air around us, and I can tell he's thinking not only of Hortense but his own father. He reaches out and clasps my hands between his, as if needing to reassure himself that I am alive and well. I grip him back, taking comfort in the simple touch of another human being.

Mr. Father speaks to the floor this time, not meeting my eyes.

"No one wanted to let you out of the cell," he says. "Even after finding out she was a monster, even after knowing that what you did you did in some sort of reckless attempt to save Credence from Cinderella, they wanted to keep you there and let you rot next to her. I couldn't bear it. I didn't know what else to do. I told King Reymond that you were invaluable, that you knew Cinderella better than anyone else. That you'd be able to keep her safe and make sure everyone else is safe. I told him no one was more dedicated than my daughter Eunice and, after some convincing, he agreed on the condition that you work with him to make sure Cinderella obeys his commands." Tears are sliding down his cheeks, dripping onto the dusty floor. "It was this or have you locked up in that cell with Cinderella until the wedding. And while I have no idea how you survived the night, I know my daughter and I'm certain you could not have done so for a week more." His words are genuine, even if he won't meet my eyes while he speaks.

I'm no longer certain I agree with him about Cinderella, but I don't have it in me to argue. For all I know, last night was a fluke and if she saw me again, instead of protecting me she'd just swallow me up whole, reduce me to her thrall in moments. Maybe letting her victim stew for a night makes them better behaved when she finally twists them to her dark bidding. What did I know? I sit down next to Mr. Father, let my shoulder brush against his and my tears drip down onto the stone floor to mingle with his.

"I don't want this," I whisper. It's important to me to say it out loud, even if it doesn't change anything. I'll be tied to King Reymond and there will be no escaping my duties.

"I know," he whispers back. "But this is the only way to keep you safe. Darling, he's the king. If he decides fewer people need to know about Cinderella, he's not going to settle for just locking you up. Don't force your mother and me to live through the loss of another child."

We sit in silence for another few minutes, shoulders brushing in silence. Eventually, Mr. Fitzwilliam gets up. I move to follow him, but he shakes his head.

"You'll be staying here," he says. "Just until the wedding. It was part of the deal I made with King Reymond. He's worried you'll—well, let's just say he's worried. If you work hard and keep your head down you can be out of here very soon."

He slips out the door before I can respond. I am left alone in another cell. I recall my moment of hesitation when Mr. Father first brought me here and I feel an odd sense of remorse mixed with sadness. I should have trusted my instincts that told me this room was just another prison. After all, if Mr. Father was willing to lock up his own daughter for years, why would he have any qualms about locking me up when it was most convenient for him? I sink down onto the cot against the wall and lean back against the cool stone. Nothing has changed.

26

Wedding Preparations

THE DIFFERENCES BETWEEN my old cell and my new one are apparent at once. Down in the castle dungeon, delirious with fever, isolated from the world, I had been cut off from any news. Now, in my small bedroom in the palace proper, that's not the case. It turns out that my cell is not actually a cell at all, but part of the extensive servants' quarters. As such, it's nestled among the other servants' chambers, and all the best gossip passes by my door. I almost feel like my old self, a little, as I collect the gossip floating by, spending hours lying on my bed, catching snippets of what's going on outside the walls of my dingy little room. Unsurprisingly, the vast majority of the conversation is about the upcoming nuptials of Prince Credence and Cinderella. The gossip ranges from the mundane to the scandalous, but I drink it all in, desperate to be kept in the loop.

"A thousand white roses and a thousand red! To be delivered by Friday! Beatrice was almost in tears when she told me, but I think we'll manage to get the whole lot in time."

"The king wants the whole royal guard at the wedding, which is most unusual. We're going to have to work overtime to get dress uniforms made for them, and I hate to think of the quality. There are long nights in our future!"

"No one has seen the future princess since last week! Kenneth thinks she's pregnant and they're hiding it."

That comment made me snort, although no one heard it. They're certainly hiding something, keeping Cinderella locked away, but it's not a secret pregnancy.

None of the palace staff knows where the princess is being kept. They assume she's in her rooms, and that she's been assigned special staff to care for her. This has been the subject of much speculation and bitterness. The conversations have been hard to piece together, but from what I can gather, the staff is split into two factions. One group thinks she's too needy and spoiled, thereby requiring a special staff who can be on call night and day. The other group thinks she must be scared and alone in the palace and that she's brought servants from home to attend to her. The truth is of course quite different.

After Mr. Father had left me, a palace doctor came to my little room to clean my wounds. He made me drink several foul-smelling tonics. Then a woman with kind eyes dropped off a bucket of water and a bar of soap. I'd never been so happy to see something as simple as a bar of soap. I almost didn't wait for her to shut the door before stripping off my dress and plunging my arms into the water, splashing it up onto my face and allowing it to run down my neck and chest. Dried blood is itchy and I was desperate to be rid of it.

The simple act of bathing exhausted me, and although I was certain there was still blood caught in some of the crevices of my face and body, I was too tired to do anything other than collapse into bed, where I fell asleep at once. The sheets were plain and simple but clean. That was all it took to lure me to sleep.

I awoke at three AM, gasping for air and sweating through my nightclothes. I'd had another Cinderella-induced nightmare, one in which we'd fought her with pitch, but this time no guards had shown up and I'd watched as she feasted upon Credence, knowing my turn was next.

The nightmare was disturbing, as Cinderella's nightmares always are, but more disturbing was the implication. The whole time I'd been in prison, I'd had no nightmares unless Cinderella was near. For me to be having another nightmare now meant . . .

A cold presence slipped into my mind, pressing itself into the crevices of my brain like a long, wet tongue. Cinderella was near. I shivered, both from fear and cold. I closed my eyes, trying to use the tenuous connection that I'd formed with Cinderella to pinpoint where that cold presence was coming from. It took a few tries, but eventually I was able to follow the long, cold tongue back to its source. When I realized where Cinderella was, I almost laughed. Cinderella's cell was directly underneath my own, much as my room had been directly above hers when we both lived in the manor house. Nothing had changed. I might have thought I was free back at our old house, in our previous arrangement, but really I had been bound tightly by Cinderella and my duty to her, as surely as I was bound by the confines of my room now.

I now have nightmares every night. It is almost comforting, in a way, to have something that had been a part of my life for the past seven years make a return. The nightmares leave me gasping and shaking, but since there is nothing I can do about them, I'm able to go back to sleep fairly quickly afterward. Cinderella is still trapped, and I am trapped, and there is nothing either of us can do to one another in our current state.

The days pass in the little room and I develop my own routine. I am brought food three times a day. My chamber pot is emptied at precisely five in the morning, and every other day the kind-faced woman leaves me soap and a bucket of hot water to bathe with. The cooks pass by my room in the morning and at night, and they reliably talk about wedding preparations. The cleaning staff walk by at all hours. Seamstresses keep unusual evening hours, and the decorators come and go with increasing frequency, as more and more of them enter the palace to prepare for the wedding. I do not see Credence, or Mr. Father, or my mother. I do, however, see King Reymond.

I am lying awake in my room early on the morning of the fifth day of my confinement. My chamber pot has already been emptied and I am not expecting anyone else until eight, when a scullery maid brings my breakfast. I want to go back to sleep, but the nightmare I woke from two hours earlier still lingers with me. Every time I close my eyes, I see Hortense, dying on the platform of my tree house. Better to keep my eyes open.

I am not in the most charitable of moods, so when the door opens unscheduled I do not respond graciously.

"What do you want?" I snap, without looking over from my contemplation of the ceiling.

"Many things," says a deep voice, and I startle, flailing a little as I right myself on the bed to face King Reymond.

"Your Majesty," I say. I'm uncertain how to recover from being rude to the king so early in the morning. Thankfully, he chooses to ignore my blunder and continues on.

"I am sure your father told you that I have use for you. He was correct. In three days' time, Cinderella is going to wed my son, Prince Credence. Your father has explained to me all her rules, about family and such, and it is my understanding that she will not consider us, the royal family, her true family until after the ceremony has taken place. Interesting, that a monster should care so much about our legalities, but I suppose we must take it as a boon and question it no further."

Internally I wince when he refers to Cinderella as a monster, but I do not correct him. Really, he should already be referring to her as his daughter-in-law, even now before the wedding, but if Mr. Father didn't tell him, or if he chose to ignore that, then it's none of my business. He's the one who wants to bring that monster into his family. My sister. I correct myself, mentally, out of habit. Safer to keep her as family than to reject her, even in my own mind.

"I have my doubts as to the advantages of your help long term, but it does seem we will need you in the short term. Consider this a chance to prove yourself valuable to your king and country." I hear the implicit threat in his words just fine. Make myself useful or face the executioner's ax. Got it.

King Reymond does not pause before continuing on, after indirectly threatening my life. As king, I suppose he does a lot of that.

"The wedding is this Friday. Your task at the wedding will be to keep Cinderella under control. Your mother is going to help her get ready before the ceremony, your father will walk her down the aisle, and then you will be in charge of her for the exchange of vows. No one will question that Cinderella would want her sister to stand up with her, and your father tells me you performed a similar task when he and your mother married. Is this within your capabilities?"

I nod. Controlling Cinderella at a wedding doesn't sound like a problem. I'm certainly better now at all things related to Cinderella than I was when I was eleven. I'm somewhat worried about the large crowd of people that comes with a royal wedding, but I'm sure I can do it. Also, after another four days of staring at the walls, I'm desperate to do anything, as long as it's outside the confines of my bedchamber.

King Reymond smiles. In general, I think people look much nicer when they smile. Credence, for example, has a smile that lights up his whole face, turning him from a very handsome young man into someone I can't look away from. When King Reymond smiles, it doesn't reach his eyes. His similarities to his son vanish. There is no light, no dawning handsomeness. It's just a gesture, one he has learned how to make through mimicry of others rather than genuine feeling. The fake smile sends a shiver down my spine. It reminds me of Cinderella, and the way she can carefully copy human behavior, without actually knowing any of the meaning behind it.

"I'm glad we're in agreement," he says and sweeps out of the room, closing the door behind him. It's too late for the cooks to be about and too early for anyone else, but I still hold my breath, hoping no one sees him. Nothing good can come from a king leaving a bedchamber in the servant's quarters, and even if it's not for the reasons people think, I don't want his visit broadcast among the palace staff.

He leaves without incident, and I don't hear any later gossip about his visit, although I listen even more intently than usual. A small mercy.

The next morning, preparations for the wedding begin for me as well. A seamstress visits me and takes all of my measurements, clucking her tongue the whole while. I can only assume she's disapproving, but I don't know of what. It's just my body. After the seamstress comes the florist, who tells me about the flowers I'll be holding and makes sure I know to take Cinderella's bouquet from her hand, so she can clasp hands with Credence during the ceremony. I will have a single white rose and Cinderella will have a huge bouquet of red roses. I wonder if the flowers will stay fresh until Friday, or if they will rot and decay faster than expected. Cinderella often has that effect on cut flowers. We gave up on keeping them around the house.

After the florist comes one of several wedding planners, who goes over the schedule with me. I've heard his voice before, in the hallway, but this is the first time we've met. He talks about the timing and how important it is to make sure everything goes right. He also complains about the lack of a rehearsal.

"I don't know how we're supposed to do this, when that poor girl won't have done any of it before," he says. "And King Reymond says we mustn't overwhelm her with the details of the schedule, so it's up to you to help guide her through what happens. Nonsense, if you ask me! I mean, I'm sure your sister is rather overwhelmed by the prospect of being a princess, but don't you think she'd want to hear these things for herself?"

I smile blandly at him. "Whatever Cinderella needs to know, you can say to me," I respond. The planner rolls his eyes, but he does a good job of making sure I know where everyone is going to be and when, then leaves me a little roll of parchment with the schedule so I can study it further once he leaves.

The rest of the following days pass in a similar manner. I am fitted for my dress, I study the scroll, I make sure I know what to do with the flowers. I get a new pair of shoes, one of which is stuffed at the toe and heel with cotton fibers. It helps me move a little more comfortably and will hopefully keep me standing and prevent me from falling over during the ceremony. My hair gets washed and braided by a young woman, and I'm told to keep it nice until the wedding when someone will be by to arrange my hair again. During all this I do not see Cinderella, although every night her nightmares come to me. I know that she is still in the castle, somewhere deep below me. I vacillate between being desperate to escape my room and hoping that the wedding will never come. Despite my wishes, time advances on and finally, after what seems an eternity in my small room, Friday morning is upon us and it is time for the wedding.

27

The Wedding

I AM WEARING THE nicest dress I have ever owned. My hair is piled atop my head in a braid with red and white roses woven through it. Someone has applied a shiny red cream to my lips and powder to my face. It is not enough. The toll of Cinderella's nightmares is a harsh one. I catch a glimpse of myself reflected in a pane of glass and, despite the best efforts of many of the talented staff, I look much the same as I always do. My eyes are sunken and tired. The bags under them are dark and purple. My skin is pale and sallow. The blush sits on top of my cheeks like it doesn't belong there, and my hair droops within its elaborate braid.

I stand at the front of the long throne room of the palace. The dais upon which the thrones usually sit has been cleared to make way for the wedding party. Ornate arched ceilings soar above me, and the galleries on the first and second levels of the room are packed with spectators who have come from far and wide to witness the happy occasion of the royal wedding. Mother sits in the front row, looking much like I feel, with dark bags under her eyes and a general lack of energy. I try to muster up a smile for her, but the effort is poor. She just looks more concerned after I make the attempt, so I ignore her and try to focus on my surroundings once more.

Everything is huge and grand and covered in beautiful white and red roses. The roses are barely rotting at all, despite prolonged exposure to Cinderella. The florists have outdone themselves.

Looking at this splendid room, I can almost believe that it's my wedding day. Credence stands across from me on the dais, decked out all in white. His wedding clothes emphasize his broad shoulders, but he looks almost as terrible as I do. I'm sure to the spectators here to witness the wedding he looks fine, but up close I can see that his eyes are sunken and puffy and his hair is lank and greasy, much as mine has been.

Our eyes make contact briefly, but I look away after the merest of moments. I do not want to see whatever emotions are in Credence's eyes and I do not want him to see whatever is in mine.

We have only been on the dais for a minute or two when the blast of trumpets announce the arrival of King Reymond. The gathered crowd shifts, getting to their feet as one to honor his entrance. I am already standing so I do nothing. This feels like a small, secret defiance, even if no one else would see it that way. I do not care to recognize the king.

King Reymond arrives at the dais and addresses the assembled crowd. He says things about love and fortune and matrimony, but I am not listening. All of my attention is focused on the back of the hall, where any minute now Cinderella will arrive.

Another round of trumpets and she is there, clinging to the arm of Mr. Father, who looks as tired and worn out as Mother. Despite myself, my breath catches in my throat when I see her. Cinderella has never looked more luminous. She is impeccably dressed, as always, but the seamstresses have gone wild for this occasion, the first royal wedding in more than thirty years. Her dress is made of stiff gold fabric just a shade darker than her hair. The gown catches the light pouring in from the tall arched windows. Her hair is caught up in a net of fine golden threads set with tiny diamonds. The whole ensemble sparkles and glistens. Her skirts swell out, emphasizing her trim waist, and a fitted bodice swoops up to reveal just a hint of pale, creamy flesh at her throat. The crowd sighs as one, so deeply moved by her beauty are they. I want to roll my eyes at their reaction, but I can't risk someone seeing so I just keep my gaze fixed on Cinderella. I hope that to the casual observer I look just as entranced by her beauty as anyone else when really I'm just trying to keep myself focused on the task at hand.

Cinderella's skirts swirl up for a moment, revealing her delicate feet under the mountains of fabric. I swallow to keep from gagging. On her feet are those horrible green glass slippers. The green is again just the wrong shade to compliment her dress, exactly as it was when she dressed for the ball. Every flash of the green glinting glass on her feet causes bile to rise up in my throat. My memories of the day I mutilated myself keep flashing through my mind, threatening to overwhelm me. I can't think of it. I have a job to do, and throwing up or panicking or running off the dais is not going to accomplish my task of keeping Cinderella in line.

Cinderella and Mr. Father arrive at the dais, walking up the single low step to join Credence. Mr. Father hands her off to Credence with a grimace that I think is supposed to be a smile, then falls back, standing a few feet away from me. I can't think about Mr. Father right now; all I can do is look at Cinderella and Credence, a vision of wedding perfection. She smiles at him, sweet and pretty and with just a hint of too many teeth. I'm surprised, since she doesn't usually show that many teeth among strangers. She's done hiding, it seems. Cinderella extends her pale hands toward Credence, waiting for him to take them.

Credence stands frozen, staring at her hands. His fingers twitch against his sides, but he doesn't move to take her proffered hands. King Reymond clears his throat, and Credence reluctantly moves to put his hands in hers.

I can tell the exact moment he makes skin-to-skin contact with Cinderella because his pupils flood his eyes, all but obscuring his irises and a deep, full-body shudder runs through him. Cinderella's lips curl up even further, and I can tell she's draining him even now. I glare at King Reymond. This could have been avoided by Credence wearing gloves, but apparently it's up to me to make sure Credence makes it through the wedding without becoming a shell. I want to glare at Mr. Father too, since he could have warned against this, but I have more important things to do.

"Cinderella," I say, keeping my voice low so that no one besides those of us on the dais will be able to hear. "Do not harm Credence. He's your fiancé and that means he's about to become part of our family."

Cinderella cocks her head but does not take her eyes off of Credence nor does she drop his hands. Something in my words must still get through to her, though, because Credence takes a huge, shuddering gasp and his pupils contract, allowing some of his brown irises to peek through once more. He sags a little, but whether in relief or exhaustion I cannot say. King Reymond continues droning on about matrimony, but I cannot hear him. I'm too busy keeping an eye on Cinderella. I know she will try something again; it's not in her nature to just stand quietly and allow someone else to dictate her day. She licks her lips, just a little, and I have a moment of perfect clarity.

I don't know if it's enhanced by the way Cinderella bound me to her when she healed me, or from when she protected me in the dungeons. Or maybe prolonged exposure to her has just twisted my mind to resemble hers more closely. But I swear I am suddenly in her head, seeing what she sees. I see her picturing kissing Credence and using her sharp teeth to bite his face, much as she did to Hortense's finger all those years ago. She's planning on having the bite be deep but using some of her own spit to clot the blood before it spills out over his chin. She's thinking how good his blood will feel running down her throat and how later, after the wedding, when she's finally alone with him, she will sink her teeth into his neck and thighs and penis, drinking from the large veins there and allowing the blood to flow freely.

"Cinderella," I say, forcing myself out of the mental image, trying desperately not to linger on the images in her mind. "Do not bite Credence. Not now, and not later, and especially not with your teeth." I know it's a little repetitive, but with Cinderella it pays to build in redundancies.

Again, she doesn't look at me, but her shoulders shift a little and I can tell she's irritated. I'm hoping that her frustration with me won't cause me problems later, but I still don't regret giving the command. It's a small price to pay for thwarting her machinations.

I glance over at Credence, and he's looking at me wide-eyed and fearful. He understands the implications of my having given such a command to Cinderella, as I do not give idle commands. I smile at him, very slightly, trying to reassure him. Better that I've warned her off and alerted him to her plans. He should go into this marriage with a clear head and then maybe he'll survive for a bit. Or maybe he won't. There's only so much I can do.

My warning was just in time. I pay attention to King Reymond just long enough to hear him say, "I now pronounce you husband and wife. You may kiss."

The crowd erupts into cheers at King Reymond's words. Tension I've been carrying the whole ceremony drains out of me. I want to cry or laugh, I'm not sure which. Cinderella leans in toward Credence, attempting to plant a big kiss right on his lips, but he manages to dodge her and gives her a chaste peck on the cheek instead. I'm sure that from a distance everything looks normal, but I am close enough to see his evasion. I don't know that it matters one way or the other, but I approve of his caution. I can feel Cinderella's contentment like a living thing between us. It's a sick feeling, one that I would gladly scrub myself of, but I remind myself that our link is helpful and allows me to get a closer glimpse of what she's really feeling.

King Reymond steps down from his place as officiant and moves closer to Credence and Cinderella, looking for all the world like a doting father welcoming his new daughter to his family. Again, I am close enough to hear what is actually said.

"Well done, both of you. Cinderella, you'll go with Eunice after this. Credence, you'll come with me. We need to have a little meeting, just for family."

His words freeze the blood in my veins. Cinderella lifts her head up slowly and fixes her unsettling green eyes on King Reymond's face.

"A meeting for family?" she asks. "And I am not invited?"

Mr. Father immediately starts babbling, but no one is listening to him. He's panicking, not even forming real words, and when he steps forward to try and intervene with the king, a nearby guard grabs him, keeping him from interfering with the moment.

I think about saying something. Credence is legally wed to Cinderella now. She hasn't ripped King Reymond apart or rejected Credence. There's still time for King Reymond to take it back, to rephrase, to say the meeting is only for male family members or just that he needs a moment with his son. If I intercede, I'm sure he would change his wording enough to meet his purposes and not repudiate Cinderella. But I say nothing.

"Yes, just for family—me and Credence," he repeats, annoyed. Even now he could still save the conversation, but he seals his fate with his next words. "I'm not about to take a monster in as my daughter."

Such arrogance! I step back hastily from the king, no longer caring how it looks to the crowd, knowing only that I want to be far away from my sister when she explodes.

And explode she does.

28

Cinderella Unleashed

THE TALL, ARCHED windows that I admired earlier shatter, sending a rain of broken glass down over the assembled crowd. Shrieking and wailing fill the air, and there is a mad panic as everyone tries to leave. I close my eyes and turn my head away from the crowd, just for a moment. I hope they all make it out, but I fear they won't be fast enough. Especially Mother and Mr. Father. I turn back to Cinderella, squinting, hoping that she isn't already so monstrous that merely looking at her will cause me to bleed or scream or panic. With Cinderella, it's best to be prepared.

I'm shocked to see her still looking like a normal human woman. Her shoes have shattered along with the rest of the glass in the room, and she is standing there in her wedding dress atop a bed of green glass shards. Credence whimpers and a quick glance over at him shows that one of the shards had embedded itself into his palm. Blood is trickling out of his hand and down onto the cuff of his once pristine-white wedding ensemble, but he seems otherwise all right. I do a quick self-check; none of the shards have hit me.

Mother rushes from her seat and runs to me, skirting around Cinderella, intent on seeing if I am safe.

"I'm all right," I murmur, as she runs her hands frantically over me, checking for shards of glass. "It didn't hit me."

That's more than Mother can say for herself. A small gash above her brow leaks blood down onto the contours of her face, and the red is stark against her pale skin. She turns away from me, determination in her eyes, and seeks out Cinderella.

"Cinderella!" she cries. "Put all of this to rights!"

As far as commands go, it's a good one. We've often given Cinderella commands to fix things that she intentionally ruined when she was feeling fractious, and this has the feel of routine to me. I almost relax, knowing that Mother's going to take care of things and that Cinderella will soon fall back into line.

Cinderella turns from where she's standing and spits at my mother, a delicate arc of green sludge that catches the light coming in from the newly bare windows. It hits my mother in the face and she drops to the ground. Frantic that Cinderella has killed her, I fall to my knees next to Mother. She's breathing, strong and steady. She's just fainted. I scrape the sludge off of her face as best I can, but I do not have time to focus on my mother for long.

A deep groan from behind me draws my attention, and I look over at King Reymond. A large shard of green glass is sticking out of his shoulder. I think it's the heel of one of Cinderella's shoes, given its size and shape. He must be bleeding, but his formal robes for the wedding ceremony are red in color and thick across his shoulders so I cannot tell for certain. King Reymond's eyes are alight with anger, and he wastes no time in turning that anger on Cinderella. "Stop this at once!" he roars.

She smiles at him and walks toward him through the sparkling field of broken glass. The glass cuts her feet and causes tiny streams of brackish green fluid to pour from the cuts, but she ignores them, intent on her target.

Mr. Father finally breaks free of the fleeing crowd, escaping from the press of bodies running in the opposite direction. He adds his voice to the fray, stepping in front of Cinderella, blocking her access to the king with his body.

"Cinderella, sweetheart, remember, the king is family now, so that means—"

Without even breaking her gaze from King Reymond, Cinderella bats Mr. Father away with a wave of her hand. He goes tumbling backward, off of the dais. With another wave of Cinderella's hand a swarm of rats, drunkenly swaying the way that they do when under her thrall, come rushing out of the cracks and crannies of the throne room to pin him down. They do not harm him, but neither do they allow him to come closer to the action, keeping him still while he struggles and cries out at Cinderella to listen to him, to please stop.

Cinderella does stop, directly in front of King Reymond. She tilts her head at him, and, for a moment, I think she's just going to talk to him. This pause is another opportunity where I could step in, could coach King Reymond on what to say and do, but instead I remain silent, watching her stalk her prey. I climb to my feet at Mother's side, hoping to get a better vantage. No one pays me any attention, too fixated on the sight of Cinderella before us.

With an almighty shriek, Cinderella abandons her human form. Huge, leathery wings burst out of her back, unfurling into the air above her. Her skin becomes mottled gray and green and a powerful scent of decay enters the room along with her transformation. Her face splits in two, her human features distorting and falling away to reveal a new visage that is totally monstrous. I watch with a strange detachment. I wonder if her face has always been that way, something not quite reptilian, not quite piscine, not quite avian, but a blend of all three, lurking just below the surface of her human skin.

Cinderella's skin continues to split. Her human face falls fully away, leaving two disparate halves of flesh, as if she was wearing a suit made of human skin that she finally sheds. Cinderella lifts a hand and rips away the excess flesh, casting away her old face with hands that are now tipped with long, curving claws. Tentacles, always a favorite of hers to manifest, erupt from all over her entire body, concentrated at her neck but with more sprouting from her torso and legs. Her legs shift and lengthen, turning from the straight lines of a human to a bizarre, broken angle that I can't look at for too long without it hurting my head. Her feet also sprout long, dark claws. Muscles ripple under her skin, seemingly growing from nothing.

With every new addition to her body, Cinderella's wedding dress is ripped to shreds. When she is done transforming, she stands in front of King Reymond and Prince Credence with scraps of torn golden fabric hanging from her. The green patches of her skin are the same color as the shards of the glass slippers that still litter the area around her.

It becomes clear to me that I have never before seen Cinderella in anything approaching her true form, not even during our ill-advised confrontation in Credence's chambers.

Predictably, her true appearance has an effect on those around her. I feel the telltale hot blood trickle from my eyes. At this point, it's hardly a concern. I should probably worry more about bleeding from my eyes and ears, but life with Cinderella has inured me to certain horrors.

King Reymond and Credence have no such advantage. King Reymond is trembling like a leaf, and blood flows freely from his eyes to his dark-gold beard, turning it a deep rusty color. The blood from his ears trickles down his neck onto his red robes where it disappears. I cannot see the blood on his clothes, but it shows up starkly where his pale skin is exposed.

Credence whimpers again, but just as Cinderella is fixated on King Reymond, so am I. I cannot look away to see what is happening with Credence even though I fear what I will see when Cinderella finally ends the strange cat-and-mouse game she is playing.

Cinderella strikes. She darts forward, neck elongating as she runs at King Reymond. Her hands, wings, and tentacles all bear down on him, wrapping him until he is completely covered by Cinderella and her many appendages.

Soldiers finally arrive on the dais, but she unwraps her wings from King Reymond and uses them to beat the soldiers away. Soldiers go flying with each leathery sweep. Some of them get up from where they land on the floor, but others hit stone corners or land in an awkward way and they stay still.

The whole time she is knocking soldiers away, Cinderella is undulating around King Reymond. It is impossible to see what is actually happening, but Cinderella pulses and shudders while entangled around the king, until all at once she releases him and steps back. King Reymond falls to the floor, pitching over so that his face smacks against the stones. His skin is putrid and rotten, and, close as I am to him, I can see the maggots wriggling under his skin, helping along the decay of his flesh. The scent washes over me and it is truly foul. At this point in my relationship with Cinderella, I can handle a bit of rot. Still, I shudder, thinking about what a horrible way to die that must be.

As that thought enters my head, King Reymond lifts his head and gasps. I can see his face is the same ruinous wreck as the rest of him, with decaying skin turned green and gray, his cheeks sunken into his face, the meat underneath rotted away. He opens his mouth to say something, but his tongue is a shriveled husk in his mouth and he makes only another gasping sound. His teeth are loose in his skull, and even the act of raising his head causes teeth to fall from his mouth in a brown cascade. His bones are as rotten as everything else in his body.

I have no love for King Reymond, and yet this is beyond what I could have imagined wishing upon my worst enemy. I rush to his side, dropping to my knees, desperate to see if there is anything that can be done for him. He turns his face toward me and makes that horrible gasping sound once more. Then his head falls to the floor and the light goes out of his eyes. My own eyes brim with tears, but I do not have time to shed them.

In my haste to go to King Reymond's side, I have turned my back on Cinderella and on Credence. I remember this when I hear a loud scream. I turn slowly to look at Credence, not wanting to view any more carnage but knowing there must be more behind me.

Cinderella has not wrapped Credence up like she did his father. She stands in front of him, legs spread wide, wings unfurled behind her. Her tentacles wave and undulate in the air, smashing into any soldiers still brave or stupid enough to come toward the dais. Her mouth is curved into a cruel smile and one hand is outstretched toward Credence's face. I understand now why he screamed.

Stuck through on one of Cinderella's long, black claws is an eyeball. Her claw has gone through the brown iris, piercing it all the way through to the back of his eye. Various trailing strings dangle from the back of the eye, and I realize that they are not strings but the vital bits and pieces connecting Credence's eye to his head. And there is no doubt that it is indeed Credence's eye. A quick glance at his face is all that I need to see that he is missing his right eye. Blood trails from the empty socket, and the area where the eye once was is already beginning to swell.

Credence is crying softly, and Cinderella has her entire attention fixed on him. It occurs to me that I could leave, right now, and Cinderella would not stop me. No one would stop me. I could leave this palace, escape into the night, and return home. Those who know that I am supposed to be locked up or who knew of my deal with the king are either dead or dying. It would be so easy.

Unbidden, Hortense's face flashes into my mind. I think of that horrible night when I left her. I knew Cinderella was loose in the house and still I locked myself in my room instead of trying to help her. I cannot live through that again.

I pick myself up from the ground and spit out a mouthful of blood. I clear my throat, and despite the fact that Mother and Mr. Father already tried to stop her, I cannot help myself. I speak.

"Cinderella," I say. As soon as the word leaves my mouth, I know I'm on to something. I can feel the connection thrumming between us, stronger than it ever was before. I could not have done this as a child. Even a few months ago, this would have been beyond me. But we are truly bound to each other now, having sheltered each other, not just me caring for her. I speak again.

"Cinderella."

At first, she ignores me, stalking closer to Credence, lifting her other hand toward his remaining intact eye. I am certain she is choosing to ignore me rather than not hearing me. I am no stranger to Cinderella's tricks—and it's about time she started remembering that.

"Cinderella," I repeat, my voice stronger, full of certainty that she will listen. "Stop that at once. Turn and look at me while I'm talking to you."

Cinderella lets out an almighty shriek, but she does not turn. She continues to menace Credence, who has stopped crying and is staring at me with his one remaining eye. Emotions that I can't parse cross his face. I reach deeper, squashing any feelings of despair, and press on.

"Right now, Cinderella," I say, in the tone I used when she was being willful at home. I focus on the connection that I feel to her now at all times. It's still growing and new but very present. I give it a mental tug to emphasize my words.

With another shriek that sends fresh blood trickling from my eyes and ears, Cinderella finally turns and looks at me. Immediately I wish she hadn't, but I hold firm. Right now, all that matters is keeping Credence from going the way of his father.

"Cinderella," I say, putting every ounce of authority and confidence I have left in me into that single word, "You are going to leave this palace. You will leave me alone, you will leave my parents alone, and you will leave Credence alone. You will not harm any of us. You will leave this kingdom and find someplace else where you can be." I try not to just say these words but to *feel* them, to pull on the invisible threads that bind us, both the ones from our childhood and the newer, more unfamiliar ones.

Cinderella lifts her wings, and her tentacles writhe in the air around her. She forms words, her long tongue slipping out from between her pointed fangs. It is not easy for her to speak, but she manages it.

"I don't—listen—to—YOU!" she screams. Every muscle in her body is corded and taut under her mottled green and gray skin, and I am certain she means to pounce upon me and make me her next meal. Nevertheless, I hold firm. I take strength from the fact that Credence is still alive though she most certainly wants him dead.

"You *do* listen to me," I say. "We've been over this before. I am your sister, and that means you listen to me."

Cinderella shrieks again, her rage sounding in the air. I hear it echoing off the stone chamber, now empty of guests. It's just family now, me, Cinderella, our parents, and her new husband. I think it still counts, even if she did mutilate him as soon as the ceremony ended. This emboldens me. There's no need for secrecy, not when everyone else still living is gone. I stand taller and look Cinderella directly in the eye. She's fuming.

"I do not have *a sister*," she hisses.

I am shaking my head before she even finishes. "You *do* have a sister. Actually, you have two, but one

of them is dead now. Just because King Reymond
didn't treat you as family doesn't mean you get to aban-
don me. I've called you sister since I was eleven. You'll
have to do more than behave badly at a wedding to get
rid of *me*," I say, maintaining firm eye contact with her.
I focus on the bond between us, trying to pour all my
commands, frustration, and firmness of spirit into the
link, even though it feels like something is wrenching
in the pit of my stomach. I don't know exactly how this
works, but I am used to utilizing every tool at my disposal to control Cinderella, and I'm not about to let
this one fall by the wayside just because I don't understand it.

She lets out another shriek, but this one is softer. I
feel her wondering at the bond, but she doesn't seem to
know how to use it, beyond testing that it exists between
us. I feel a surge of triumph. I can tell she's giving in.
Cinderella speaks one last time.

"Yes, sisters we are, bound by law and word. And
you owe me, sister. So I shall leave but remember—you
are still in my debt. Being sisters doesn't mean that you
are unscathed by our connection. This thing," she
strokes the bond somehow, sending prickles of adrena-
line racing up my feet, "is an open path. *We are entwined.*"
With that parting line, she flaps her enormous wings
and lifts herself into the air. I feel an answering tug on
the bond between us, a sickening lurch of my heart that
brings up the taste of mold in my mouth, but I don't
care. She is leaving. Cinderella uses her powerful wings
to carry her out of one of the smashed windows of the
hall, and I watch her fly away until she is no more than
a distant speck in the sky.

Credence groans nearby, and I tear my gaze away
from the window to rush to his side. He's collapsed, one

hand covering the open wound of his missing eye, but he is alive. For right now, that is enough.

"Is she gone?" he asks, leaning into my hands. I pat him down, trying to see if she's damaged him in some other way. To my relief, it seems to be only his eye that she has taken.

"She's gone," I reply, and Credence's face breaks into a beautiful smile, despite the blood in his mouth. I am helpless but to smile back. It turns out I am still capable of some positive emotion after all.

Credence's hand creeps into mine. Mr. Father struggles up from where he'd been knocked clean to the ground and comes over to us. Together we wake Mother, who rouses easily now that Cinderella is gone, the noxious substance slipping away from her face. We sit in the ruin of the great hall, laughing and crying together, clinging to one another as we contemplate a life without Cinderella. Although I put on a good show for Credence and my family, her last words ring in my mind:

"We are entwined."

I push the words aside and work with Mother and Mr. Father to lift Credence from the floor. He sways and clutches at his eye, but we manage between the three of us to haul him to his feet. We take a wide berth around the corpse of King Reymond. I'm not sure it's safe to bury him—I'll have to make sure his body is burned, even if it means doing it myself.

Slowly, we hobble out of the hall. Mother and Mr. Father take turns supporting Credence on the left and I support his right, the side now missing an eye. I try not to look at the gaping hole where it once was, but it's hard.

We make our way to the edge of the hall and finally encounter another living being. A man in sumptuous, official-looking robes greets us. He looks about ready to clap all of us in irons, but a word from Credence stops him.

"See that they're taken care of," Credence commands and then promptly passes out. The official gives him a startled look, but then nods at us before hurrying off, seemingly following orders.

We continue to usher Credence along the hall until we're met with a flight of physicians, who must have been summoned by some forward-thinking servant. We pass Credence off to them. Mother and Mr. Father and I are then left alone in the hallway of the palace. The empty spaces where Hortense and Cinderella should be are huge and painful. I stare at my parents, wondering how on earth we are ever going to fill them.

29

Epilogue

I AWAKE IN A cold sweat, my dreams haunted with swirling tentacles and grotesque gray-green wings. I swing my legs out of bed, ready to run downstairs and intervene with whatever Cinderella is doing but stop as soon as my eyes fully open. I am not at home. Cinderella is not in the cellar. I'm in my new bedroom in the palace, which is on the third floor, with large open windows on three sides that let the light spill in. There is a fire stoked high in the hearth, making the room warm and cheerful.

I flop back onto the bed, staring up at the canopy. Soon, someone will be in with my breakfast and to replace the flowers on the bedside table. No matter how often they are replenished they always seem to smell of rot. The servants in the palace are either used to replacing things frequently or they are well trained enough not to notice that the flowers in my room always seem a bit off, no matter the weather.

It's been two months since Cinderella's wedding day. I've spent almost all of that time at the palace. Mother and Mr. Father have moved back into my childhood home, but I couldn't bear to do it myself. The memories—of Hortense, of Cinderella, of everything—are too strong. After the wedding, Credence was out of his mind with pain and infection, unable to give directions of any kind, but the captain of the guard, a shrewd man who knew which way the wind was blowing, offered me rooms in the palace in exchange for information on Cinderella. I gladly accepted.

The palace physicians were able to get Credence's blood loss and infection under control, although there was no saving his eye. He wears an eyepatch now, and it makes him look much more severe and brooding than he really is. I can't help but think it's a good thing, now that he's king. It might make other heads of state take him more seriously. He's adjusting to being king and grieving his father. Their relationship was a difficult one, but Credence only had one father and now he's gone.

My feelings toward Credence are complicated. There's been no time to muse on our little connection, but for now, I am content to wait. Once he's had time to grieve his father, and I've more fully grieved Hortense, perhaps we can explore something between us. Or perhaps not. I've met very few people my own age and I might like to see a bit more of the world. I'm not sure I want to be queen. Or that I should be.

Breakfast arrives, interrupting my musings. It's brought by a young girl I don't know and she reminds me of Lilia. I haven't told Mr. Father of Lilia's connection to our family for fear he'll want to fire her as he did Mr. Calton. She just needed a job and knew that our family would pay handsomely for discretion. I will not betray her secret, not after she protected me as best she could.

Today's breakfast is eggs, fluffy and hot, and fine white toast with butter and jam, alongside a fragrant pot of tea with cream and honey. I take a little bit of everything, moving the food around on my plate to make it seem like I've eaten more than I have. I know that the food is delicious, of finer quality even than Mr. Father provided in our house growing up, but it doesn't satisfy. I'm still hungry.

I get dressed quickly, glancing at the tall grandfather clock that I had brought from home. I still have forty minutes before my meeting with the captain of the guard. I update him on any Cinderella news I have, so that the kingdom can be prepared. If I close my eyes and focus, I get the impression of forests and cold winds. I think she's near the base of some mountains, with a stream running nearby. The royal cartographers and soldiers take my impressions and try to plot them onto a map. Cinderella is probably near our eastern border at the moment, in an uninhabited stretch of land. I have no idea what she's doing there.

I pad through the castle with a hood up, hiding my face as best I can. Most people are polite enough not to ask what I'm doing, and while many people know of me as the girl with the monstrous sister, few of them recognize my face. The deep hood still gives me comfort, however, and makes me feel less exposed.

I make it out of the palace easily enough and continue on to the back of the gardens. No one comes here if they can avoid it. It's where the waste water and kitchen scraps get tossed, left to rot and turn into compost.

The smell is horrific, putrid and with hints of rot. I breathe deep and feel myself relax. Moving quickly, aware that I do not want to be caught here, I sink down to the ground, heedless of the wetness seeping through my clothes. I reach into the pile of scraps and I pull a big handful up to my face: a rotting orange, half a dozen slippery onion skins, and two chicken bones.

I pluck out the orange first, examining it. The rot is spreading out from a single point, a large green circle rimmed with white. I close my eyes and then take a big bite, directly from the center of the mold. It squishes in my mouth, foul juices filling my throat. I swallow and then take another bite, and another, devouring the rest of the orange before moving on to the onion skins, which I allow to slide down my throat with relish. Then it's the chicken bones. I suck off any remaining rotted meat, then crush the bones between my teeth, slurping marrow from the centers.

I hear a movement nearby and I startle, getting to my feet quickly. My skirt is wet, and I hide it with my cloak. But it's just a bird, flitting from one tree to another, doing the same thing I am, hoping to find some food scraps. I smile and slip away. The bird can have its fill. My hunger is sated. For now. I know that first thing tomorrow morning I'll be back.

Cinderella was serious when she said that our connection ran both ways—the price I pay for being healed, for her protection that night, is that she shared some of her nature with me. So far, the only ways it manifests is this hunger, this desire in the pit of my stomach that can only be satisfied by that which is dead and dying. And of course the flowers that begin to wilt and die as soon as they enter my room.

I'm monitoring myself closely, to see if any other signs of Cinderella make themselves known. For now, there's nothing that makes me think that I am a danger to others. But if that changes, I have a plan. I'm relatively certain I can use my connection to Cinderella to track her down and follow her to her hiding place. If my symptoms worsen, and I feel myself slipping, I'll chase that connection to its end. And then we'll see how Cinderella likes a re-do. This time with one of her own kind.

ACKNOWLEDGMENTS

I WANT TO START by thanking the team at Crooked Lane for seeing Cinderella, for helping her realize her full potential, and for helping me to realize it. Thank you to Dulce Botello, Mikaela Bender, Mia Bertrand, Stephanie Manova, Megan Matti, Rebecca Nelson, Thaisheemarie Fantauzzi Pérez, Doug White, and Matt Martz. Thank you to my wonderful agent, Emily Keyes, for championing this book, and supporting me the whole way. I know this would not be possible without her. Thank you to Matt Burgess for being a wonderful professor at Macalester, and not only teaching me how to improve my craft but how to take writing seriously. Thank you to Electric Boogaloo for celebrating my successes, and to Writer's Inc, who were sure of my success before I was, and who provided amazing feedback (and a plethora of foot emojis) as I went through my drafts, editing, and more drafts, and more editing. Thank you in particular to my readers: Darlene, for 2 AM reads to get this manuscript ready; to Venom and Kathy, for being crucial early voices who loved Cinderella; and to Sam and Nicole, who volunteered to read their junior-high friend's work of unknown quality. Thank you to

Kelley and Kevin for being the best writing retreat buddies a girl could ask for, and for talking me through Cinderella while I drank one million cans of sparkling water. Thank you to my mother for supporting me and being my number one fan, to my father for instilling my love of reading and writing, and to my partner, Tom, who has done so much in our daily lives to make sure that my writing habit could flourish. And thank you, dear reader, for getting this far and reading through my acknowledgements.